THE ASCENSION MACHINE

ISBN: 978-1-951122-08-9 (paperback)
ISBN: 978-1-951122-13-3 (ebook)
LCCN: 2020933061

Cover Design: Ian Bristow

Printed in the United States of America.

Shadow Dragon Press
9 Mockingbird Hill Rd
Tijeras, New Mexico 87059
www.shadowdragonpress.com
info@shadowdragonpress.com

THE ASCENSION MACHINE

BY

ROB EDWARDS

CHAPTER 1
MEANWHILE

It began with a lie.

"That's nothing," I said, "I once convinced an auto-teller I was a Brontom clone."

"Ha! No, you didn't." I don't remember the guy's name, but I remember the smell: beer and travelled-in clothes. He took another swig of his drink. "How? Look at you! How does a twelve-year-old—"

"I'm seventeen."

"—human kid convince an auto-teller that he's seven feet tall, green, with, like, four arms?"

We sat in a bar on Meanwhile Station. The kind of bland, soulless, no-questions-asked sort of place you'll find on any large transport hub. Not technically humans-only, but the décor, the music and the sports on the screens were all Terran-themed. By station time it was early, there were only a handful of patrons in, and my ripe-smelling friend was the only one drinking in earnest. I was hustling for breakfast, so I was wide awake and drinking coffee.

"Well I didn't, of course," I admitted. "But I didn't have to. Brontom may be big—"

"Very big."

"—green—"

"Very green."

"Sure, yes, and they do have four arms like you say."

He slapped his thigh. "Ha! Yes! I knew it!"

"But get this, they are clones, right? Identical.

Fingerprints, retina prints, bone structure, even DNA matching can't tell one Brontom from another. They all, literally, look alike.

"So, while I couldn't convince the auto-teller that I was a Brontom, I could convince it I was a *particular* Brontom. After all, it can't look at your retina, or fingerprints, your height, weight, none of that. It doesn't even count your arms. Do you know how they tell themselves apart?"

"Names?"

I fought the urge to roll my eyes. All I needed to do was get to the end of the story. Just keep his attention a little longer. "By scent," I corrected, "each Brontom has a unique chemical signature. So, to convince an auto-teller that you are a *particular* Brontom all you do is to spray it with some specially made Brontom perfume. Simple."

He ran a hand through his hair, shaking his head. "That's unbelievably amazing," he said.

"Yes," I said. "It is."

The thing on the table that I'd told him was my minipad beeped. My Ripper, all done. I got up to leave.

"Hey, kid, what's your name?"

"Mark," I lied.

"Nice to meet you, Mark." He raised his empty glass in a toast. "What happens when they find out? Do you get some angry green dude chasing you around the station?"

I paused. "Not usually. I never take much, enough for my next meal maybe, and never enough to be worth coming back for. If you wake up tomorrow and realise your credit stick is light by twenty credits, would you fly all the way from Brontom Prime just to get it back?"

He shrugged. "Guess not."

"Good to know," I flashed him a grin. "Oh, hey buddy, I think they're calling your flight."

I may have gone too far. Something I said — and we may never know what — made him check the levels on his credit stick. As he struggled with basic arithmetic, I made for the door.

"Hey! That kid robbed me!"

I ducked through and cut left, accelerating between a few surprised passersby. Cut left again, and hard right. If he was as drunk as he seemed, that should be enough to lose him.

I cast a glance backwards. He was still with me, face red, but arms and legs pumping. *Huh. Okay, Plan B.*

The next turn put me on a balcony overlooking a shopping arcade. It would be quiet this time of day I knew: perfumes and triangular chocolates are afternoon purchases, even on station time. I ran the length of the balcony, counting off railing posts. At the seventh, I planted one hand on the railing and vaulted over. I dropped a metre and caught myself on the top rung of a safety ladder, shifted my grip to the outside, and slid down to the ground.

That should do it, only a drunk idiot would try and follow that stunt without knowing the ladder was—

Oh, right. Plan C. Plan C will work.

I sprinted across the arcade and ducked through a Staff Only door.

When I'd passed this way earlier... yes! A little further along the corridor than I expected, but still there, and still well-stocked: a cleaner's cart. I swiped a bottle of cleaning spray as I ran by.

Bouncing off the wall, I turned right at the end of the corridor and spared another glance back. Considering he was middle-aged, drunk and jet-lagged, he was keeping pace disappointingly well. Maybe he ran half-marathons at the weekend back home. He hadn't seemed the type when I tagged him but live and learn.

Foot traffic was busier now that we were off the tourist lanes, there's always work to be done, and people were setting up for the day. I threw some apologies to those

I clipped in passing, managed to avoid a full-on collision with a last-minute body-swerve, and missed sprawling flat on my face only because of a clumsy hop over somebody's toolkit.

And still, he followed. A massive over-reaction for the price of breakfast, but people can be strange, sometimes.

Time for a calculated risk. Three pressure doors, each with a gut-squeezing two-second delay between hitting the open button and the hatch whooshing upwards. Each pause gave the drunk guy a few more paces on me. As I slapped the third hatch open, I heard him, no, now there were two sets of feet beating the corridor right behind me.

I dived under the third hatch as it opened, grasping fingers grazing across my shoulders. I tucked my head in and pelted into Hydroponics. Rows of… green stuff blurred by. I'm not sure what it is they keep in Hydroponics, but I know they're super careful with it.

While it's called a Hydroponics Bay, it's more a series of smaller compartments, each one designed to be sealed separately in an emergency. The idea being that no crisis should be able to wipe out the entire supply. I'd been careless on a cleaning job a few jumps back and the chem sensors had reacted spectacularly to a trivial spill. At the time I was mortified, but I'd filed it away as useful.

I slowed at the far hatch, slapped it open. Enough of a lead. Just.

I pointed the cleaning spray at the chem sensor and pulled the trigger, hurling myself back as I did.

It took half a second for the chemical fumes to hit the sensor, then the protective hatches slammed shut.

"Attention please," an automated voice intoned, "anomaly detected in Hydroponics A. Please stand by. Maintenance crew to Hydroponics A, please."

It would take at least five minutes to clear the area as safe, plenty of time to make myself scarce.

There was a window in the hatch. On the other side, the drunk guy and someone that I vaguely recognised from the bar earlier, were red-faced and breathing hard. The drunk guy was holding his side in some pain. I waved the cleaning spray at them and was disappointed I couldn't hear their shouted replies through the hatch.

I twirled the spray bottle around on its trigger and made to slide into a holster. Not that I had a holster, but they couldn't see that through the hatch window.

I turned to find a Hydroponics engineer and a Cholbren from station Security staring at me.

We sort of considered each other for a moment.

The Cholbren recovered first, her shoulder fur rippled. "What—"

And off I went again!

CHAPTER 2
BARGAIN

When I tell people I live my life flitting from one planet to the next, getting by on my wits and charm, no job to speak of, no ties, no connections... when I tell them all that, some people get it into their heads that it's romantic, exciting, somehow. "All the places you must see!" they coo.

Truth is, of course, you see one station, you've pretty much seen them all. Stations are all about encouraging travellers to travel, and if you want to invite the galaxy to your door, you need to make sure that your doors are big enough. And the food is edible. And there's appropriate plumbing. There aren't many space stations with any personality. Their doors are all big enough for a Germile to get through, because not only are they the biggest sentient species in the galaxy, they are amongst the wealthiest. You want Germile shillings? Make sure they can get into your shop. Though you will also need to provide a ramp for the Bright to use. You don't want to turn away Brightish dollars either.

And that's just the ways in. The walls all tend to be the same shade of yellowy-brown. A maintenance tech on Beacon station once told me it was the least offensive colour to the most diverse possible array of visual sensors. Who knew? Yellowy-brown.

But that's the point. Stations are bland. Samey. Inoffensive. So, this idea that my life is romantic or exciting, it's a little naïve.

Also, true, of course. I have an awesome life.

# # #

I waited out the chase wedged in a gap above an air processing unit. I'd reached it by a circuitous route that avoided cameras and pesky facial recognition. It gave a good view of the corridor below, and the two people from security working their way along. One was the Cholbren from earlier, the other her partner, a man I didn't recognise. The trick with Hydroponics must have riled someone up, I'd never been chased like this before. Not for a twenty-credit scam, anyway. My hidey-hole was good; I'd used its equivalent many times, and if nobody looked up, I was fine.

Still. I pressed further back into the shadows as they drew closer.

I used the time well, transferring the cash my Ripper had taken from the drunk's credit stick onto my own. Money. I tried not to rely on it too much. When on station, I'd take odd jobs here or there to earn enough to eat, drink and breathe. I didn't need more. I've no real vices to speak of, my Ripper was my only extravagant possession, and I hadn't entirely paid for that.

When it came time to move on, I usually worked passage aboard ships to get from place to place. I'm an experienced crewman, but if I ended up cleaning toilets for a few weeks to get to somewhere new, that's what I'd do. I never stayed in one place long, always looking for the next journey, going further out, further away. Because I love seeing new places, even if they are all yellowy-brown with huge doors.

Just me, my Ripper, and the infinite depths of space. Unnoticed and unmissed.

The two security goons were right below me. The human one showed a holo of me to a station cleaner, while the Cholbren looked around. She was a potential danger,

I didn't know much about their spatial awareness; we humans don't think very three-dimensionally as a rule, but the Cholbren...

She looked up.

I squeezed back, pressed against the processor, its heat warming my back uncomfortably.

She took a step forward, head tilted to the left, squinting. Her shoulder fur twitched and rippled.

Her partner tapped her on the elbow. "He's not here. Come on, let's try down on West Twelve."

She waited a long, long moment before following her partner.

I sagged. A little too close. Cholbren looked up. I'd remember that for next time.

# # #

I gave them half an hour before I moved, unfolding myself from my niche, hanging from the air processor, then dropping down to deck level.

I probably needed to leave. Sure, I could keep ahead of security, might even be fun for a while, but with a dozen other stations just one jump away, why bother? Find some place new. I always moved on eventually. Sometimes, if I felt like staying in one place for a while, I'd find something legitimate to do. It never lasted. Sooner or later the stars called out to me.

I'd see about getting a ship out as soon as I could, but breakfast came first; seemed a shame to earn the heat without getting the reward. Meanwhile is a big old station, if they were still looking for me, I was better off where they were unlikely to look.

Most people don't realise that station security is pretty limited. I mean, sure, there's a load of inspectors working dockside checking arrivals and departures for contraband, but the day-to-day policing of people on the visitor side?

Not so many. They couldn't flood the station looking for me. Wouldn't, even if they could. They would have to search by sector, and they'd start where I was last seen. Places where I looked like I fit in.

Fortunately, looks are easy to change. I dumped my jacket in a recycler, my t-shirt would do, and looked smart enough for where I was headed. I wandered across the station and caught a lift to the nicer levels. Security wouldn't get around to searching there for a couple of hours, if I was lucky. I kept an eye on my blind spots all the same, tried to keep my back towards any cameras. It's part of the game, even if they didn't know they were losing.

Besides, top of the station has the best views. Because forget what I said earlier about all stations looking the same. They do. But right at the top, in the nice part of town, you will always, but always, find the most expensive restaurant, with a massive viewing window looking out at the planet below.

And looking at planets, that never gets old.

This one was a beautiful swirl of orange and red, the winds on the surface, assuming it had one, must be fierce, because the skin of the world was an ever-changing tumble of clouds. I saw shapes form and vanish before I could name them. Flashes of light that might be storms or signs of gas mining. I wasn't sure what planet this was, or if it was used for anything more than a transport hub. I'd try to find out its name before I left, a sight like this was worth remembering properly.

I sat on a bench outside the expensive restaurant and ate a sandwich that I'd bought with my hustled credits. A ship left the station and passed in front of the window, I decided it was the drunk guy's and gave it a wave b'bye. It probably wasn't though. The one thing I did know about Meanwhile Station was that it was quite the interstellar interchange. Ships came and went every few minutes.

Another reason to remember the place, I'd be back this way again, no doubt.

I treated myself to a tube of fresh water too, not much more than a mouthful, but it was supposedly imported and hadn't passed through the kidneys (and functional equivalents) of the station crew and visitors fifteen times before reaching me. It was probably a con, but it wasn't my money, and I swear it did taste different. The one thing that groundsiders don't appreciate enough, it's water. Never make that mistake. I sipped and savoured.

Someone sat down on the bench next to me. Another thing groundsiders don't appreciate enough, I reckon, solitude. But it's a free station.

"Nice view," said the newcomer.

I nodded, not wanting to engage.

"That story about the Brontom? Is it true?"

I almost spat out my water. But I wasn't wasting it. I swallowed. "I think you have me mistaken," I said.

"I don't think so. What's your name?"

"Warren," I lied. I drank the rest of my water. If I needed to run again, I wasn't leaving it for him.

He didn't look like Security. He was human, about my age, not much more than twenty anyway. Extremely well dressed, and the wrist pad in his sleeve was top of the range. He smelled of money. Not Security, then, but the kind of guy who Security would listen to.

"Sorry, I was in the bar earlier, I couldn't help overhearing your conversation. Don't worry, I'm not here to get you into trouble." He stopped; laughed. "Well, that may not be entirely true."

"Okay," I said and stood up. "Nice meeting you."

"Wait, no, look, I need your help. I've been looking for you since the bar. I'm kind of desperate, and the way you ducked Security, I'm even more sure you're the man for the job."

"You put Security on me? I take it back; it was not nice meeting you."

He put a hand out to stop me leaving, I'd have shaken it off, but there was a credit stick in it.

"Sorry about that, Warren. They won't bother you again, I promise. I've sorted it. Look, take the credit stick. There's 200 credits on it. Think of it as an apology and an introduction. I just need five minutes of your time."

"No thanks. Keep your money." I'd run enough cons to know a hook when I saw one.

"No hang on... I want to employ you, an hour's work, nothing illegal, or dangerous, or, y'know, weird. I just need an hour of your time, and I'll pay you five thousand credits."

That was way more than a hook; he'd over-played it. Every sense of self-preservation I had told me to get gone. But, dammit, now I was curious. *How far was he going to go*? "Give me the 200. I'm listening."

"Okay," he said, handing me the credit stick.

I sat back down.

"You should know we, or at any rate, I, am being watched. My personal security. He's not here for you, but his job is to see me safely onto the next leg of my journey. I mention him only because I don't want you getting spooked if you notice or recognise him."

I looked over my shoulder. The second guy who I'd trapped in Hydroponics, stepped out of the restaurant entrance and leaned against the doorway, arms folded, giving me the stink eye. At least he didn't look like he intended getting closer. "I'm not spooked."

"Good. I sent him after you, sorry about that."

Yeah, I was spooked. I checked all three exits again. The guy's bodyguard was covering one, but the other two looked clear. But what if he had more than one hired goon? Tell me about one so I wouldn't go looking for the others? I planted my feet, leaned forward a little, shifting my centre of balance. If I needed to run, I wanted a sprint start.

He carried on regardless. "I need your help. I thought I'd missed my chance, but then I saw you just now. I came for breakfast before my flight. Next time you come through this way, make sure you try the continental breakfast, it's great."

"If you think the casual chat will put me at my ease, I'd like you to know it's not working."

"Okay." He paused, seeming to be lost for words.

"And if that's all?"

"No. No. Look. You steal people's identities sometimes, right? Do you think you could be me?"

"What?"

He sighed. "Okay, right, yes. Look, the short version is that my parents are funding this expedition, they have a very particular destination in mind. One I have no intention of reaching. But I cannot simply abandon it, they are bound to be monitoring me. I need them to believe I am complying, let them see 'me' leaving, long enough that I can... make alternative arrangements."

"That's the short version?"

"As short as I can make it, yes."

"Okay well I need a longer version then," I said. "Who am I trying to fool? Because if it's your bodyguard, sending him after me seems unhelpful."

"No, not him, he's mostly on my side. And besides, he's off the clock as soon as I check-in, he's being redeployed, I won't need him where they are sending me. But there is no question, my parents will have other agents on the station, ones I won't recognise. I don't know who or where, but they will certainly monitor the departure gate. If they see someone who looks enough like me, who checks in using my name, that should assuage their suspicions a little. And the longer you can keep up the pretence, the more of a head start I can get. Do you think you can do it?"

There were half a dozen ways this could go badly for me. More if the guy was actively trying to trap me. Time to rabbit. “No. No, I don’t think I can. Have a nice trip.”

He slammed his hand against the bench. “You have to help me. I’m out of options. It’s not like my parents actually care. They only have people watching me because they can’t be bothered to watch me themselves. Too busy to see me off on a trip I didn’t ask for!”

That struck a nerve. Despite myself, I felt a pang of sympathy.

He leaned forward, hands stabbing the air to emphasise his points. “I have an hour to find a way out of this. If I don’t check-in, they’ll hunt me down. Not because they have any interest in me, oh no. Only because of how it would appear. But if I do go, I’m not getting out for years. You, on the other hand, eluded security with ease. I don’t need you to get on the flight. Just tease it out as long as you can, then leave. A man of your skills should have no problems. You can get out of this. I can’t.”

To sum up, he’d tried me on greed, sympathy and now my pride. I was impressed. I was not convinced. Still. Curiosity got the better of me.

“This isn’t a prison ship? I’m not checking in as you, only to discover I’m being sent to prison ‘for a crime I did not commit’? I’m too busy staying out of the brig for misdemeanours I *did* commit.”

“You’ll do it?”

“I didn’t say that I asked if it was a prison ship, or military school, or…?”

He clapped me on the shoulder. “No, it’s not a prison ship. Honestly, nobody is going to force you aboard. But if you find yourself on the flight, the worst you’ll have to fear is a pleasant journey on a first-class ticket, a conversation about the misunderstanding, and then a flight back out again. I promise.”

I drummed my fingers on the bench. There was no way this wasn't a trap. True, I couldn't see what he gained from it that summoning Security on me then and there wouldn't achieve. But it was so suspicious it must be a trap. Somehow.

But I really wanted to see how it played out.

"It's not impossible, I suppose," I drawled. "We're both shortish, lean, same mud-brown hair... I'm a little paler, but bronzer can fix that. We don't look so very similar, but from a distance, if the people don't know you too well. Stand up and walk for me. We can't fool face scans, but yeah, if I can get your walk, maybe from a distance."

He bounced up and began to walk nervously back and forth.

"No, not like that, as normally as possible."

"Right, yes, of course," he said, controlled his breathing and took a few more measured steps. "This isn't easy, now I feel too self-conscious."

"Yeah, I see that. Well... tell me about yourself. Hopefully, it'll distract you, and it won't hurt for me to know more about you. Your name would be a good start."

"Oh, sure. Yes, sorry. My name is Mirabor Gravane," he said, continuing to pace for me.

"'Mirabor' your parents must hate you."

"You cannot conceive how much. I'm the embarrassing sixth child. First takes over the business, second into politics, third into the military, fourth into medicine, fifth into research... and then there's me. Even my sister the research chemist feels like a bit of a, well, a fifth wheel. But they had no idea what to do with me. For a while they just ignored me. That was bad enough."

I caught myself nodding. I don't think he noticed.

Gravane just kept right on talking. "I came to terms with that. Fine. They can ignore me. I was all for being the useless black sheep of the family, but apparently, that wasn't an option. So, they finally notice me, and suddenly

I'm being shipped off, to the back end of nowhere, away from friends and... friends. And I'm not going." His step was accelerating again, but I let it go.

"So, your family is super-rich, and you're the embarrassing son they didn't want. Right. Well, life is tough all over."

He shook his head. "I know how it sounds, but this isn't just me being a spoiled rich kid. I just want to find a life of my own. Forge my own path. It's not like the family business falls apart without me, I'm already surplus, so why can't I choose my own life?"

"Right," he still sounded like a spoiled rich kid to me, but one who wanted to make me a comfortably well-off kid, so I wasn't going to argue too much.

Instead, I jumped up, and walked beside him, approximated his pace and posture. It wasn't perfect, but from a distance, for a brief period, in front of people who didn't know him well. It might work. Except... "The hair is a problem." I wore mine short but scruffy, his was down to his shoulders.

"Oh, I thought of that," he said. "I have a wig for you."

"Definitely not. Props make a disguise too fussy; wigs are too easily dropped. No, we need to get you a haircut down to my length."

He didn't look impressed.

"Oh, and the final thing. I need you to record a message for me. If I get into trouble over this, I need something with you saying this was your idea."

"I told you, you won't have any trouble over this."

"All the same. I'm going to need that recording."

He shrugged. "Fine."

"Five thousand credits?" I asked.

He began to look hopeful. "That's right."

"And if I get spotted immediately?"

"I'll still pay. I'm paying for the chance at freedom, I

know it may not work, but as long as you give it your best, keep it going as long as you can... I can get a better head start."

"What the hell, let's do this."

It was a trap. Just not the way I thought.

CHAPTER 3
FLIGHT

The fruit juice was cold, sharp, sweet and best of all free. I'd never conned my way into the first-class lounge before, but I saw the appeal. Oh, yes.

The chair moulded itself to my body shape, firm enough for support, but soft enough for indulgence. The air scrubbers and conditioners were keeping me cool, but not cold, with no smell of grease or ozone. The drinks were free, server bots passed out snacks, and even the walls were a particularly pleasing shade of yellowy-brown. This was the life.

There was some grit in the grease. There was an itch between my shoulder blades which didn't come from the excellent chair, or even from the shirt of Gravane's I wore. That was of even finer material than the chair and guaranteed allergy-free. No, this itch was a familiar feeling, one that saved my skin more than once. Someone somewhere was watching me.

Of course, it might be my imagination. But, after all, someone was *supposed* to be watching, that was the point. I fought the urge to scratch the itch. *Cool, calm and collected, don't draw the wrong type of attention. I want them looking, just not looking too closely.*

I flicked my gaze across my fellow travellers. *One of them, surely*? The girl at reception I dismissed immediately. If she was the spy, the game was already lost. *Let's be at least a little optimistic.*

The family pod of Welatak that sat near the toilets weren't looking at me at all. The prime of the pod was playing a game that made the podlings clack with laughter, while the other adult in the group fiddled with one of the podling's saline suits. They needed their suits to keep saltwater on their skin; Welatak dried out quickly in oxygen. A paired couple of Frantium sat as far from the rest of the passengers as possible. I thought they were arguing, but their expressions were hard to read, hidden in shadow behind their manes. Whatever, they were so wrapped up in each other, I dismissed them too.

Perhaps one of the humans? There were five of them scattered about the lounge, all well-to-do types, which I guess was only to be expected in first class. One was on his comm, pacing back and forth, one hand stabbing his point home. He had a silence field on, so I couldn't hear what he was saying, but I saw enough. Loud, rich and obnoxious. On another day, I'd enjoy tapping him for lunch funds. But the spy would be one of the quiet ones, I was sure.

Movement by the door caught my eye, and I glanced over to see the girl at reception greeting a new customer, a wall of green, four arms. A Brontom.

Where did he spring from? I'd not seen a Brontom in months, not, in fact, since I'd scammed one. Had my story summoned him up? *Wait, is he looking at me*? *Does he look like I owe him money*?

I slouched down into my seat and tucked my chin in. The odds of it being that particular Brontom were tiny but better safe than sorry. I kept watch on him out of the corner of my eye; he was chatting with the receptionist, but he was looking over her shoulder into the lounge. *Towards me*?

The problem with a species that all look the same, they evolved ways other than looks to tell each other apart. So if it was the same Brontom, it wouldn't matter if I was wearing the best disguise in the galaxy, he might still recognise me.

And I wasn't wearing the best disguise in the galaxy.

I deliberately looked away. Nothing telegraphs guilt in quite the same way as staring at your accusers. Although conspicuously not looking their way was as bad. I forced myself to relax, let my mind and gaze wander, and so happened to be looking at the departures screen when a few flights, including "mine", lit up as ready for boarding. A couple of my fellow loungers started gathering their belongings to head to the gate.

As casually as possible, I stood up to join them. *Might as well keep my Gravane act going, plus it would get me out of the lounge*. I engineered my move such that my gaze naturally passed by the Brontom, and to my dismay, he passed the reception desk and was stomping his way across the lounge in my general direction.

Logic told me, this Brontom was not after me. But the morning chase, the paranoia about the spy: if I'd been more on edge, I'd have cut myself. Logic wasn't playing. I made my way in the opposite general direction, towards the departure gate.

I quickened my pace, trying not to look guilty, and was first out of the door. A series of hatchways on my right would let me into the other bays, but the first two were closed and secured; the third hatch, the one for my flight, was open. An animation of a cheery fellow in a flight attendant's uniform appeared on the screen by the hatch and asked to see my boarding card, and I waved Gravane's ticket at him.

He beamed at me. "Welcome aboard Mr. Gravane, we really hope you enjoy your flight. First-class seating is—" he glitched for a moment as the system dropped in information outside of his normal patter. In a slightly mismatched tone, he continued "not available on your flight to—"

I was already past him. I was sure I heard the heavy tread of a Brontom just entering the corridor, and I wanted to be in the bay, free and away amongst the cargo pallets before he caught up.

Which was not going to be as easy as I thought. First-class on this flight got their own private boarding tube, from gate to ship without having to mix with the riff-raff in standard. Which didn't make sense when there was no first-class seating and meant there was nowhere to go but aboard the ship.

Well, I hadn't planned to leave, but Gravane could hardly complain if I boarded. After all, I was supposed to be as convincing as possible, for as long as possible.

I slowed and looked back. Nobody was following me. The others must all have been heading for other flights; I saw the shouty human from the lounge cross the end of the tube and carry on.

Still, that was all to the good, if the Brontom was still behind me and following, he might be unsure which flight I'd boarded. Better not make it easy for him, time to get out of sight.

I stepped into the ship.

# # #

Going from the luxury of the first-class lounge to the accommodation on the ship was quite a comedown.

This ship was tiny, run-down and seemed to be held together by the liberal application of yellow and black hazard tape. The bulkheads were bare metal. The twenty acceleration couches, arranged in five rows, were covered in old cracked plastic. Everything looked functional, kind of, but was in such a state that a great deal of effort must have gone into passing inspection by the barest possible margin.

There were only four other passengers aboard. They and the lone cabin crew looked surprised that someone had come in through the first-class entrance.

The steward fixed a smile on his face and scurried

forward. He had to travel the length of the compartment to reach me. "Welcome aboard the *Metropolitan*," he said. "Sorry dude. Guess I should have been by the door to say hi, but I thought the two first-class passengers on the manifest were a mistake."

Not, I suspected, the standard greeting he was supposed to deliver for his high-profile passengers.

"No," I said with a smile. "Not a problem."

"Can I show you to your seat? No carry-on luggage?"

"Just me. And by all means, show away." 'By all means' sounded like something Gravane would say. "Are we expecting a full flight today?"

He checked my ticket, took three steps, gestured to my seat. "Nope, this is the last pick-up on our circuit. We're just waiting for the last passenger and then we can be off."

"Another first-class passenger? That's unusual I take it?" I sat and began fastening the safety harness, purely from habit.

"Yeah, but here on the *Metropolitan*, we take all sorts, as you'd imagine."

"Right, yes," I said, none the wiser. I wished I'd asked Gravane more about where this flight was taking him, but I'd never planned to be aboard it. As the strangely unprofessional steward wandered away again, I checked my ticket, but the destination was only listed by its designation, C23580, not by its name. Once we were underway, I'd check the stellarnet for any clues.

The steward behind me greeted the last arrival. "Hey, welcome aboard. Can I show you to your seat?"

And then the unmistakable rumble of a Brontom's voice. "Yes, please, extra wide."

My hand went back to the buckle of my harness. The Brontom was at the first-class hatch, the hatch to the cockpit would be sealed, but maybe the hatch to standard was open. *Where is...? There.* But it was sealed too. There wasn't enough time to get to it and unseal it before they reached me. *Wait. The Brontom has a seat*?

The steward shambled back, gestured the Brontom to the seat across from mine. The Brontom lowered himself into the chair, fussing with the armrests. He nodded at me, and I returned a skewed smile. So, he hadn't been chasing me. I'd known it all along, of course, the odds would have been ridiculous.

The hatch whirred shut and sealed with a loud clunk. It turned out, I'd never needed to board, but now it was too late to leave. Bad enough to walk into Gravane's trap, I'd well and truly trapped myself. *Looks like I'm going for a ride. I really hope this isn't a prison ship.*

CHAPTER 4
ADVERTISING

The steward had already taken up station over by the intercom. He switched it on, though I'm not sure why as his voice would have carried anyway. He said in a loud, over-enthusiastic tone, "Welcome to the last leg of the journey guys, stow your stuff because we'll be on our way any second. Kick back and relax, and we'll have you rescuing old ladies from trees and helping kittens across the road in no time!"

This was not the normal safety talk I'd expected. I cast a confused look around but everyone else seemed to be taking it in their stride. The Brontom looked across at me and his face split into the broadest grin I had ever seen. "Can you believe it," he said in an excited rumble. "We're going to be superheroes!"

"Superheroes?" I must have misheard, but I couldn't think what else he might have said.

"I know, you know! I've dreamed of this moment since before they completed my forced maturation cycle! I love the advert. What's your favourite part of the advert? Mine is when they fly away at the end, but the classes look so interesting too." He leaned towards me as he spoke, bracing on his armrests with one pair of hands, gesturing wildly with the other pair. Being chased by a Brontom was scary but having a wall of green enthusiasm loom over me was just as intimidating.

"I've not seen it... in a while," I said. When blagging

your way through a subject you know nothing about, try not to be trapped into details too quickly.

The Brontom's face lit up. "We should totally watch it again! They must have it on the in-flight entertainment." He reached over one meaty hand and switched on my seat pad.

The familiar angular 'G' logo appeared on the screen. *Wait, that stood for 'Gravane' didn't it? Was I... was Mirabor part of that family? He would be beyond rich if so.* I was still pondering that question when the advert started.

"So, you want to be a space alien superhero?" the man on screen asked. Okay, no question, I'd definitely heard 'superhero' that time too.

He was handsome in a classic square-jawed, clean-cut, kind of way. He was dressed in a tight-fitted black leather uniform with the image of a bird of some sort outlined in gold across his chest. A yellow cloak clasped to the shoulders of his jacket fluttered artfully in the breeze. A caption on screen proclaimed him to be Captain Hawk. *They were really going all in. Were superheroes a thing? Why hadn't I heard?*

He grinned. "Well, here at the Justice Academy we can help you reach that dream!" The picture cut to an impressive ultra-modern monolith of a building, people of dozens of species were congregated around the entrance, all happy-looking youths, positively brimming with enthusiasm as they went about their day. *That was clearly fake; I'd never seen that many people in one place looking happy.*

The scene changed again showing, presumably, a series of classes; groups of wildly excited students watching classmates swinging between buildings, or throwing each other around, or putting out fires. The voice-over continued. "At the Justice Academy, we will equip you with the skills to be the hero the galaxy needs. Self-defence! Clue Analysis! Parkour! Rocket-Grapnel Maintenance! Rescueology!" *Rescueology?*

"But we will also teach the other side of being a superhero." And now there was a flurry of more studious, earnest learning scenes. "We have award-winning classes in marketing and public relations, costume design, and even philosophy, morals and ethics." This at least I recognised as a school. Or what school was supposedly like, anyway. Most of my education came from online classes with a healthy dose of practical experience.

Captain Hawk appeared again, this time with a reassuring smile. He hovered mid-air, bright sunny skies around him. "We are proud of our ethics courses here at the Justice Academy and of our 100% record: none of our graduates have ever gone on to become super-villains." Tiny text flashed up on screen as he said this. I paused the video and read, "Statistics quoted do not include graduates being possessed or brainwashed." *Was that a thing*? I set the video playing again.

My stomach turned with vertigo as the camera followed him as he swooped downwards, landing amongst a crowd of students from a multitude of species.

"But maybe you're worried that you're not 'special' enough to become a superhero?" Hawk said, looking serious. "Maybe your parents weren't murdered in an alley? Perhaps you've never been bitten by a radioactive anything? Perhaps when you tried to build yourself power armour you found you couldn't move in it, let alone fly?

"Well, we say 'phooey' to that. It's a big galaxy. Somewhere in it, whatever you can do, whatever you are, *is* special, and here at the Justice Academy, we will help you find that place. And you don't have to be rocketed there as a baby, or even have your home planet explode.

"So... you want to be a space alien superhero? Join me, Captain Hawk, at the Justice Academy, and before you know it... you will be!"

The final shot saw three students, two humans and

a Welatak, in graduation gowns and mortarboards. They threw off their gowns to reveal brightly coloured uniforms underneath before launching into flight, zooming out of shot, and on to implied heroic destinies.

The screen faded to black.

"Wow," I said.

"I know, right?" the Brontom said. "I had to delete it from my pad, or I would have been watching it non-stop still. So exciting."

"That's certainly one word."

"Hi," he said. "I'm 4,923,016,734, but my friends call me Seventhirtyfour."

"Nice to meet you Seventhirtyfour. I'm... Mirabor Gravane," I lied. "I saw you in the first-class lounge, didn't I?"

Seventhirtyfour looked embarrassed. "Yeah, but I'm trying not to call attention, you know? I mean, sure there are plenty of billionaire superheroes, but that's not the backstory I'm trying to build, you know?"

I guess money was embarrassing if you had too much of it? "Sure thing, I'll pretend you have no money, if you pretend the same about me, deal?"

"Deal," he beamed and extended his lower-right hand to shake on it. Returning his grin, I obliged.

"So, what made you want to be a... superhero?" I asked.

"Oh, the usual. I read comic books while maturing, saw the holos, they really spoke to me, you see..." he lowered his voice to a conspiratorial rumble, so low and deep I could feel it in my bones. "I'm a mutant."

He looked around to see if anyone else had heard. I was sure they had, but nobody paid us any attention and that satisfied Seventhirtyfour. He continued "I don't know if you know, but we Brontom are clones."

"I'd heard... something about that."

"The cloning process isn't totally perfect. Every now

and then, there are divergences, differences. I am one." He took a deep breath, one of his right hands over his heart, then confessed: "I am almost two centimetres too tall."

"Gosh."

"You mustn't tell anyone. It's a terrible, shameful thing. I try to stoop to hide it, but I know everyone notices anyway."

If it was that deep and dark a secret, why tell me? "Mum's the word."

He brightened. "But it's not just that. I always suspected it, but in the entrance exams, I actually tested positive for latent psychic abilities!" He looked wistful. "I'm hoping I'm telekinetic, that would be cool, you know?"

"Definitely." Entrance exams? What... what was I supposed to be able to do? Was someone going to suddenly expect me to bend a steel bar because Gravane could? He didn't look the sort, but the guy in the video could *fly* so, who knew?

"I wish I'd seen my entrance exam results," I began in a low voice. "My... parents didn't want me coming to Justice Academy and were furious when they found out I applied. I managed to get to the exams without them knowing, but they intercepted the results. If I hadn't used a secondary contact for the application, I might never know I'd been accepted."

Seventhirtyfour nodded along. "Oh, that's good backstory, that is. Every hero should start with conflict. But... we can look up your results now if you like?"

"We can? Sure, sounds great... um... how?"

"Log in to the Justice Server from the seat pad. Your student ID should be on your ticket, there..."

"Oh, sure."

"And just type your password, there."

"Right." Password. Okay. At least it wasn't asking for biometrics, but I was still out of luck. Gravane had never given me any of his passwords.

Not on purpose.

I closed my eyes to think. I'd seen him type his bank passcode in when he paid for his haircut; I hadn't been deliberately shoulder-surfing, but habits are habits. *H-d-7-B*. I watched his hand move across the pad in my mind's eye. *Y-8 or U-9*? Even if I could remember, it might not be the same password for this system. *Y-8*. I typed on the seat pad, my finger followed the memory of Gravane's.

"There we go," Seventhirtyfour rumbled. "Now just go to Student, and press Results."

Wow, it worked. "Got it."

"No problem. I won't be nosey while you look but tell me if you scored high in Psychic or Self Defence, we might have classes together."

In my brief interaction with him, Gravane came across as well-educated and canny, an impression contradicted by the scores on the screen. But then, how hard did he try on these exams? Gravane didn't want to be at the Academy, he could just have failed the exam to spoil his parents' plan. Instead, he'd passed everything, mostly by the barest possible margin, with spikes on maths and problem-solving. Passive-aggressive test-taking. They had a weird family.

At least there was nothing in these scores to live up to.

# # #

"Thank you for flying the *Metropolitan*, we will shortly be arriving at our destination," the steward announced, and gave a whoop. "Awesome time here we go. Freshers, stay in the quad just outside the Arrivals Hall, the rest of you get to your hall allocations. Anyone taking Introduction to Parkour, or Grapnel Gun Basics, I'll see you in class."

A couple of people cheered, and Seventhirtyfour turned to me and gave me a massive thumbs-up, all four hands.

I forced a smile onto my face, didn't want to stand out. Everybody else was exactly where they wanted to be, keen to get on with their studies. I was too distracted to think about any of that though because there outside the window, I could see clouds.

My plan had been simple; when the *Metropolitan* docked at the station, I'd lose myself in a service corridor or storage locker, hop the first ship out, and be away and free, unnoticed and unmissed. What I now realised, what in hindsight should have been obvious, was that we weren't going to dock with a station. We were going to land. On the actual ground. Like some sort of... ground... walking... animal. Even my similes were suffering.

Drop me in any station, anywhere in the galaxy, I'd find my way in and out of trouble, as required. But ground-side? Did they even *have* storage lockers?

As I looked at all the blue out of the window, I was also beginning to appreciate that it had been a long time since I'd been under a sky, rather than a roof. I mean, intellectually, I knew that my ancestors had navigated life without a roof for millennia, and with planetary gravity being less susceptible to power glitches, the chances of me floating up into the sky were small. Still. It felt unnatural.

The *Metropolitan* hit ground, and there I was, at the very bottom of a steep gravity well. There was no way out, but to go with the flow.

I dragged my heels following Seventhirtyfour through Arrivals, down the hall to the doors out into the quad, I found myself creating reasons to stop. I checked my shoe fastenings. Checked that I had my fake id and meagre belongings properly stowed in the correct pockets. I licked my suddenly dry lips and fought to control a slight shake of my hand. I turned and looked back at Arrivals, concentrated on the corridor, contemplated the ceiling, tried not to notice that my breath was becoming too quick and too shallow.

"This is ridiculous," I muttered to myself. It really couldn't be that long, right? My last trip planetside was only... I racked my brains. It can't be ten years, can it? But it was. I'd not been outside, properly outside, for ten years. I'd done more extra-vehicular work in that time, but somehow, in a suit, with the right tethers in place, so I didn't drift away, that didn't bother me. But here, I'd have to rely on my shoes sticking to the ground. That seemed... a fragile faith.

Someone approached from ship-side. Dressed in uniform, I expected he was the *Metropolitan* pilot. He saw me there and frowned. "You alright kid? A Fresher, right? Just head out into the quad, someone will be along soon enough to direct you to your accommodation."

"Right, yes, thanks," my voice sounded too quick and warbly. "So, when do you head back up again?"

He cocked his head to one side. "These old buses only get used at start and end of term, but we've cargo pods that do supply runs every few days and there are daily mail flights. Why?"

"Oh, just wondering, thinking about maybe becoming a... ah... ship-based superhero. Fighting space pirates and the like."

He laughed. "Live the dream kid, but space pirates? Not in this part of the galaxy. Maybe further out, towards Galactic South? There's been a bit of trouble that way I hear. But we don't need any protection on school runs, and if we did, we have the Avenging Spider."

"The Avenging Spider?"

"Tom. The steward."

"Ah right, yes, of course. He hadn't told us. Does everybody get a... hero name?"

He checked his wrist pad. "Look, go ask the people in the quad. I'm no superhero, just a school bus driver. They can answer your questions; I just work here."

"Yes, of course, sorry." I slowly turned and stared

through the doors. The blue sky was still there, waiting for me. I didn't have to do this. I probably shouldn't do this. I'd kept my deal with Gravane, he'd pay me. And if I went off to live his life, I gave it two, three days, tops before the ruse was discovered, and I was slung out. I didn't really need that aggravation. I could just go back to my life, untroubled by pretending to be a superhero, undisturbed by unnaturally large skies.

And yet.

When I was able to drag my gaze from the terror of the sky, down to the crowd of people below, I couldn't entirely dismiss a sense of fascination. A crowd of people about my own age, laughing, happy, excited, dressed in all the colours of the spectrum, not just yellowy-brown. Some were flying, some seemed to glow, others were stomping around in armour. It was... astonishing. Amazing.

You see one station, you've seen them all. I'd never seen anything like that. To be part of something like that, just for a couple of days... I'd never...

I took a step through the doors, right to the very edge of the quad, still sheltered under the spaceport's lintel. Seventhirtyfour waved from a crowd of students across the quad. At me?

I clenched my fist against the shake in my hand, set aside the queasy feeling in the pit of my stomach, felt my toes curl in an instinctive attempt to hold on... and stepped into the quad and life as a trainee superhero.

CHAPTER 5
ACADEMY

The first thing to hit me was the heat. It was like walking into a drive room with poor thermal shielding, the place was a good five degrees above station norm, possibly more. There was a strange tang in the air too, like salt. Heat, humidity and salt on the breeze, someone had set the enviro controls very strangely.

I made the mistake of looking up, and the sky opened above me, it stretched in every direction, deep azure blue pocked with stray clouds, stretching off to infinity. It sucked the breath from my lungs, my exhalation lost in endless, open sky, running away from me.

I staggered, fought to breathe in, gasped a lungful of air, tasted the salt on the breeze again. Coughed, chest aching. I pulled my gaze downwards, past some startled looking students, to the ground. Instead of a reassuring metal plate, or a comfortable carpet, the ground was covered in concrete, dusted with a layer of golden sand. It felt strange and other, but at least it was solid. I focussed on it, let my breathing ease. There was nothing wrong with the air. Everybody else seemed fine with it. I just had to breathe, not think about it.

This is ridiculous.

I fought the urge to turn and dash back into the spaceport. In the long run, that wouldn't help. Centimetre by centimetre, I raised my eye-line, taking in my surroundings more slowly, trying to avoid information overload.

The quad was crowded with students of every species I could name, and a fair few I couldn't. To a being, everybody else seemed happy to be here. The air rang with shouts of excited greetings, and laughter. About a third of the students wore obvious but strange tech: weapons and scanners and armour. Another selection, maybe one in ten, looked... odd for their species: a human woman emitting a faint purple glow; a Welatak with tufts of fur poking out of the top of her saline suit; a Polifan covered in ruby-red scales, only his wings looked normal.

It was strange, but a strange I could cope with. It's a big galaxy and I'd seen all sorts of unusual walk through station hatches over the years. This was a greater concentration than I was used to, true, but it was at least normal strangeness.

Steeling myself, I raised my gaze further. Registered the trees dotted around the quad. Palm trees, maybe? Took in the buildings that surrounded us. To the right, a vast dome-like structure of plain concrete, at least seven storeys high at its midpoint. There were no windows I could see, but the doorway was wide and was surrounded by vibrant posters. According to a series of colourful sign posts, to the left, a cluster of accommodation blocks, dozens of them, stretched out of sight. Each was three or four storeys high.

Finally, ahead, the signage proclaimed another group of buildings as the main teaching blocks. At the centre was the building I'd seen in the advert. I remembered it being a soaring white tower block, slightly tapered towards the top, giving it even more height with false perspective. *Don't look up.* Windows on every face would make it light and airy inside, no doubt. A sweeping shallow ramp led from the quad up to the tower entry.

The students from the *Metropolitan* had joined a larger throng gathered at the base of the ramp. I set my shoulders and walked across to join them, concentrating on the scuffing sound my shoes made on the sand as I walked. The sky was there above me, waiting to claim me, but I wouldn't let it take me. A railing flanked the ramp, and I placed myself beside it and held on. I hadn't floated off the planet yet, but the gravity felt lighter than 1G standard, and I was taking no risks.

Seventhirtyfour forged through the crowd to join me, two other students followed in his wake. The Brontom beamed at me. "Thought we'd lost you there for a minute. Look who I've met! This is Pilvi and this is Dez, they just came in on the *Fawcett*, from out east. Pilvi scored top three percentile on the science section of the entrance exam, and Dez..."

"Didn't," said Dez. She was comically short next to the giant Brontom; I didn't recognise her species, but she was reptilian, all angles and scales, her tail flicked constantly as she spoke. "I didn't score well on any of the book stuff, but that's okay, I'm going to be more of an action superhero, I expect."

"Sounds like a plan," I said.

Dez looked up and up at Seventhirtyfour. "You're so lucky. Testing positive for psychic ability! You could have actual superpowers. All I can do is lightly swat things with my tail."

"Just because you don't know what kind of hero you will be, doesn't mean you can't be one," said Pilvi. She was human, about my age, blond, with a quick smile. "We're all here to learn; that's what counts. They'll find ways for all of us to be heroes, you'll see."

"She's right Dez," I chipped in "How does the advert go? 'Phooey to that!'"

Seventhirtyfour laughed. "That was just like Captain Hawk! Hey, maybe you have super-mimicry."

Ouch, that was a bit on the nose. Maybe turn that down a bit. "But joking aside Dez," I repeated her name, committing it to memory. "Don't tie yourself up into knots about it on day one. Unless that turns out to be your superpower."

Pilvi nodded. "Quite right," she said and flashed Dez a smile. "Hi, nice to meet you...?"

"Mirabor Gravane," I lied. "But call me... Grey?"

"Oh, nice," said Seventhirtyfour "That's halfway to a code name already. You could be the Grey Ghost or the Grey Avenger?"

I laughed. "Hard pass on both of those. I'm further behind than Dez. I don't even have a tail, and the only half-decent score I got in the entry exam was for Maths."

"Ah, that solves it then," said Pilvi "Enter: The Grey Accountant!"

Oh well, at least they weren't talking about my mimicry skills now.

There was a dull roar and a flash of white light from overhead, and like an idiot, I looked up. Reverse vertigo swept over me, my stomach flipped, and I fought to keep my breakfast in. The light source was a man, flying overhead, a trail of white light streamed from his white-blond hair. He flipped, end-over-end, and dropped like a stone, which didn't do my stomach any good, then decelerated quickly, coming to a stop in a blaze of light a metre above the ground.

"Welcome to the Justice Academy!" he said. The assembled crowd of students whooped with enthusiasm.

"My name is Sunbolt, and I will be one of your instructors during your time here. The few of you with *actual* superpowers, if you're good enough, might get to join my Advanced Meta Combat class. The rest of you, I'll try not to hurt you too much in Professor Red Ninja's Self Defence class."

Well, this had taken a turn. The crowd and I weren't sure how to take that.

"But today, we start with orientation." Sunbolt pulled a minipad off his belt. "We will divide into your accommodation groups and tour the facilities. Pay attention, listen for your name. First group: Gravane!"

He paused. "This will go faster if you respond. Gravane!"

I raised a hand. "Here."

Sunbolt stared at me, brow furrowed under his domino mask. Wait... did he know? Did he know what the real Gravane looked like? Was my ruse over already?

Caught between appearing guilty by looking away, and looking guilty by staring at my accuser, I felt my shoulders bob as I shuffled uncomfortably. Being outside had really put me off my game.

The light behind the eye-slits in his mask intensified.

"I've got my eye on you, Gravane. Your reactions will need to be quicker if you're going to survive The Life." Sunbolt's hair flashed with light, but he moved on. "4,923,016,734!"

The Brontom raised two hands. "Here! But please, call me Seventhirtyfour."

I was too relieved to listen to the rest of Sunbolt's list.

Seventhirtyfour gave me his four-thumbs up. "Awesome, Grey. We're in the same accommodation block!"

"Fantastic."

# # #

Our group of twelve followed dutifully along behind a teaching assistant calling himself Kid Jetstream. What followed was a blissfully indoors hour touring the main tower block of the campus, or the Hall of Heroes as Jetstream insisted on calling it. He kept up a flow of overly-hyped patter throughout; for the most part, I tuned it out. I tuned out Seventhirtyfour too, he was off making friends with the rest of our accommodation group, but I had more important things to think about.

You live a life on space stations, you learn the importance of how things fit together. If an air seal breaks, or conduits crash, you need to know how to get out of places quickly, and where it's safe to go. And if station Security might want to talk to you, it becomes even more important to know every hidey-hole and shortcut. After ten years, there were few people who knew space stations like I do.

My groundside instincts were rusty; non-existent, really. People on the ground had it easy, they thought the default setting of the universe was 'safe', just because they didn't live in a steel box hanging in a vacuum. It made safety features rarer, escape routes more obscure, and finding places to hide required new ways of thinking.

Worse, the Hall of Heroes seemed designed to baffle me. As we left the ground floor (canteens, shops, recreational zones), there was an access panel in the ceiling. I paused, trying to figure out what it was for, and Jetstream spotted me. "Ah, Gravane, you have a good eye. That's a teaching aid for the Introduction to Building Infiltration class; It's one of my favourite classes, important to learn how to sneak around if you are in a hostage rescue situation."

"Great," I said and crossed it off my list. No point sneaking in a place everyone knows is designed for it.

Jetstream showed us gymnasiums, sports halls and combat simulation zones. The walls were thick, the equipment sturdy, and while much of it was expensive and high quality, it all showed signs of misuse, breakage and repair. I mentally catalogued storage lockers, equipment scaffolds and disused corners.

Classrooms and offices above that. These levels showed more promise. Lots of odd corners and repurposed corridors up there. Several promising places to check out, though how many were teaching aids remained to be seen.

The top few levels were labs. We stopped at the corner stairwell before touring them. "The main labs are in the buildings behind the Hall," Jetstream said, gesturing out of the window to a group of sturdy-looking buildings some distance away. "The labs up here aren't used as much as they were in the first few years of the Academy. There were… incidents. It was deemed more sensible and less explosive to give the student labs a little more space. The labs up here, are… safer, but it's still best to watch your step. Try not to touch anything in here."

One of our group (Dean, possibly?) was looking out of the windows facing the other way. "Wow, look at the beach! Is that part of the Academy too?"

Jetstream grinned. "It sure is. This whole world is Academy property, and that beach, in particular, has been home to some legendary parties over the years. If any of you have surfing powers, I can tell you the tide here kicks up some great waves."

Possibly-Dean high-fived one of his buddies; they fell to party planning.

My attention was caught by another building on the lab side, further back even than the student labs, notably separate. A squat, solid building, surrounded by razor wire and the unmistakable shimmer of a force shield. "What's that place?"

"Tartarus," rumbled Seventhirtyfour from behind me. "It's a prison designed to hold supers."

"I thought that none of the graduates of the Academy ever became super-villains?"

"They don't," said Jetstream, his normally sunny tone subdued. "But we don't graduate everybody. Even this place has bad apples, sometimes."

A squat blue Zalex, Breetoxa, asked, "How many people there?"

"None, at the moment, thank the stars. It's not designed to hold prisoners long, we ship them up to Galactic Patrol as soon as we can. We are a school, first and foremost," said Jetstream. "But we've had some… bad people in there, in the past. Arsonists. Imposters. Thugs. We can't be too careful."

Jetstream looked at the door to the disused labs. "Do you know what, I think we've seen enough up here. Let's show you to your accommodation block." His tone brightened. "Race you downstairs!" There was a crackle of lightning, a whoosh of air, and he was already two flights down.

Laughing, the sombre moment broken, the group chased after him. I followed, more slowly, lost in thought.

Imposters?

# # #

A short, disturbing, jog across the quad, and Jetstream showed us to the accommodation block that the twelve of us would share. We had a communal kitchen and lounge on the ground floor, then individual rooms on the floors above. Seventhirtyfour and I were assigned the largest rooms, across the corridor from each other on the top floor.

My room was all but a palace. Bigger than any private berth in any ship or station I'd ever seen, it was packed with comfortable furniture, had its own separate shower room with... yes, actual running hot water. Sonic showers are great and all, but I hadn't had a real shower in years.

I stripped off in record time and luxuriated in the unmetered, unrationed water. It is a sensation like no other, and if my ruse was discovered right now, it would all be worth it for that one moment of pleasure.

After an extravagant amount of time, I draped a towel over my shoulders and wandered back into the bedroom. There were two suitcases on the bed. Not mine, obviously. They must belong to Gravane, transitioned here from the *Metropolitan*. Of course, he couldn't take his luggage off the ship, or he would have tipped his hand, so it had followed me here.

Gravane had told me to maintain the ruse as long as I could, but I wasn't kidding myself, that had meant while

I was still on Meanwhile Station. I'd gone way beyond the plan by this point, and I had no instructions on how to open his luggage. In fact, looking at it, I couldn't see where the locking mechanism was. I tried just prising it open, to no effect. I ran my fingers all over the case, and eventually, I must have triggered something.

"Password?" asked the case.

I only knew one, but it had worked before. I quoted it again, and the case obliged by popping open. Man, Gravane was lazy about security.

But oh, my stars, the stuff he had in there. I'd known Gravane was money, that was kind of the point, but the array of... stuff... in his case was jaw-dropping. Designer clothes, designer computers, top-spec comm devices, pad and... well... one or two items that looked distinctly like contraband. That was troublesome, but I'd work out what to do with that later. For now, I resisted the urge to put on a fashion show and pulled out the most casual clothes I could find. A pair of artfully distressed jeans, and a plain black t-shirt. The size wasn't far off, the t-shirt perhaps a little big.

I wasn't stealing this stuff, technically, just borrowing it, to maintain the illusion.

Somebody knocked at the door, and I jumped. Slammed the cases shut and stuffed them under the bed. I cast a quick glance around the room for incriminating evidence. Like what? I wasn't sure. Then went to open the door.

Seventhirtyfour loomed outside, filling the doorway. "Come on, Grey, I promised the girls we'd meet them for lunch."

"Who?"

"Dez and Pilvi. Come on."

I followed, suddenly feeling very light of heart, even knowing I'd have to cross the quad again. And then the image of Tartarus, squat and brooding, flitted across my mind... and my mood came crashing down again.

# # #

Lunchtime on the first day of term, it turned out, was a popular time to eat in the canteens. The first one we checked was completely packed, the second had a pair of bouncers in powered armour standing by the door. They took one look at the pair of us and waved us on. A glance inside that canteen as we passed showed everyone in there was decked out in visible tech of one sort or another.

Finally, we spotted Dez and Pilvi in the third canteen. Dez waved, pointed at two empty seats they'd saved us. Seventhirtyfour waved back, and we went to join the lunch line.

The diners were a sight to behold. Other than a few Freshers like us, everybody was in costume, and even the costumes which were individually quite stylish contributed to a nightmare of colour-clashes. Blue and green should never be seen. And certainly not alongside magenta, lime, stripes, spots and twinkly special effects.

And the sound was as bad. Even above the general hubbub of conversation, there was a noise of... no, I can't really liken it to anything. There was a buzzing of electronics, a beeping of monitors, a clicking and ticking of clockwork, a hiss of steam, and that was just from the left side of the room, which seemed to have the concentration of the technical heroes. Over to the right, there were strange other-worldly sounds, of powers I didn't really understand just idling, while the possessors of those powers ate garlic bread.

Except for one pale guy in an opera cape, who I think was supposed to be a vampire?

We paid for lunch and threaded through the crowd to our seats.

"This place is amazing!" Seventhirtyfour said, raising

his voice to carry.

"It certainly is," I shouted back.

Dez gave me a grimace. "I don't like it, I have very sensitive ears."

"I know what you mean. I don't suppose anyone has any sound-damping powers, do they? We're all superheroes, right?" I laughed.

The Zalex sitting beside Dez looked up at that, cocked his head to one side, then vanished under the table. Which was odd, I thought.

"How do you like your dorm room?" asked Pilvi.

"Oh, it's great. I've been ship-bound a lot, recently, I'd forgotten how good a proper shower feels. And the view is pretty impressive too. How's yours?"

"It's okay. I came from Marwick, an Agri-world, so we have plenty of space and water. The dorm room feels a bit small after what I'm used to, but it's warm and comfortable, so no complaints really."

"Can't believe how busy it is in here," I shouted.

"It's great isn't it?" asked Seventhirtyfour.

"Sure, I guess."

"Everybody is just excited to be here," said Pilvi. "Thrown together, meeting new people. Oh! Where are my manners? Grey, Seventhirtyfour, this is Avrim," she indicated the lanky Polifan that sat beside her, his wings folded in close to his back. "And under the table is… actually, I didn't catch his name, but he seems nice, probably."

Dez folded herself over to look under the table. "What *is* he doing?" she asked.

I held out a hand to Avrim. "Grey," I said.

"Hi." He shook, nodding politely.

"What's with all the factions?" I asked. "I noticed when I came in, all the guys in armour over there, all the glowing ones over there. The ones with wings over that way..."

"Not all of them," pointed out the Polifan.

"Ah but you're in the Fresher group," said Dez.

The Zalex emerged from under the table with an armful of small black boxes. *Where had he gotten those*? He began to circle our table, placing boxes on the ground about ten centimetres apart. Dez hopped down from her chair and followed him. "What *is* he doing?" she asked again.

"I've read that the Academy encourages people with similar power sets to work together," said Seventhirtyfour "It helps people new to their abilities learn the ropes, get some mentoring, that sort of thing."

I frowned. "I guess that makes sense. But don't you want people with different powers to get used to working together, cover each other's weaknesses?"

Seventhirtyfour nodded enthusiastically. "I agree. What's the point of having a team-up if you can both do the same thing?"

"There are classes on team-ups though," said Pilvi.

"I suppose that's..." I stopped, realising I was shouting, which I had been doing before, but now it wasn't necessary. The thunder of the canteen around us had faded to a background whisper. I looked about and spotted the Zalex grinning like a lunatic.

"Sound-damping," he said, proudly, pointing at one of the boxes.

"Dude! That's amazing. Thanks. Did you just have those gadgets on you?"

"No, only just thought. You said sound dampen. I thought: boxes."

"You just made those now?" asked Pilvi.

"Is what I do. 'Phooey to that'? Superpowers. Gadget, dude."

"Now 'Gadget Dude', that's a superhero name," said Seventhirtyfour.

"These little things do that?" said Dez, she lay flat on the floor, tail curled around, studying one of the boxes. She reached towards it.

"No touch," said Gadget Dude, but it was a little too late.

Dez had poked the box with a claw tip. The box sparked, fizzed, popped, and the sound of the canteen rolled over us again. Gadget Dude looked forlorn.

"Ow," said Dez. "Sorry."

I couldn't help but laugh. "Don't worry, I guess we'll just make do with the noise. But that was genuinely impressive, Gadget Dude."

The Zalex bowed, clearly pleased with the praise and his new code-name. Together, he and Dez gathered up the boxes again.

# # #

After lunch, we decamped to one of the student bars.

Avrim offered to buy the first round, and I went with him to help carry the drinks. The crowd seemed to part for the Polifan, people stepped out of his way, gave him space. It made getting served quicker, but Avrim had an expression like thunder.

"Can I ask...?" I said.

He growled, but more at the world, than me, I think. "It's what I was afraid of. Perhaps it was a mistake coming to the Academy after all, but my Aunt Veritas said it would be fine."

"Your aunt?"

"She's on the staff here, works as a Counsellor and teaches Ethics classes."

I picked up our drinks. It turned out eighteen was the legal age for alcohol here, and Gravane was old enough, even if I wasn't. "The students are avoiding you because your aunt is a teacher here?"

"Not quite. They're worried I might have the same powers as her."

We carried the drinks back to our table. "What power

does she have that have people so nervous?"

"It's impossible to lie to her."

"Ah." *Danger*! *Danger*! I stumbled, managed to not spill the drinks.

"What's Grey looking so panicked about?" asked Dez.

Avrim set out the drinks in front of Dez, Pilvi and himself. "He thinks I might have the power to compel truth, and he has some deep dark secret."

"I… that is…" I stumbled.

"Oh, sit down, Grey. I don't share my aunt's power and wouldn't care about your misdemeanours even if I did."

"Okay." Dammit, every time I started to relax in this place, I stepped in another puddle of hydraulic fluid, I'd be tripped up and on my back in no time at this rate. And I definitely wanted to avoid Avrim's aunt.

"I'm a little bit curious, though," said Pilvi. "What's your dark secret, Grey?"

"I… don't have superpowers. I'm just normal." *Change the subject, change the subject, change the subject.*

"Don't get so hung up on superpowers," said Seventhirtyfour. "Most of the students here don't have them. Just look at us. I *might* have latent psychic powers, and Gadget Dude is a natural Builder, the rest of us are normal."

"Normal means different things for different worlds," said Pilvi. "I know more about farming than anybody in this room, I bet. On my world, that's the least interesting thing about me; everybody on Marwick knows farming, it's what we do. But there are worlds where our agri techniques could revolutionise people's lives. Stop famines. Save entire civilisations. If the Academy lets me do that... that's important."

"It's not just the big stuff, you know," added Seventhirtyfour. "My people are known as fighters, soldiers, disposable, faceless. If I can show them that the Brontom can be different, can stand up and be noticed as *individuals*... that's why I'm here at the Academy."

This got a murmur of agreement from the group.

"Of course," he rumbled as an afterthought, "beating up some supervillains would be cool too."

Dez joined in. "It's just like that silly advert says. We're not here to gain superpowers. We want to find the place in all the galaxy, where what we can do matters. Where if I'm me, and you're you, and Avrim is a non-truth-enforcing Polifan, just as hard as we can be, we can make a difference. Help people."

# # #

That evening, I lay on my comfortable bed and stared at the ceiling. I found myself looking again at my reasons for being here. I'd thought I could join in, have a relaxing few days being ridiculous pretending to be a superhero, spend some time with people my own age without the daily pressure to find my next meal. I thought being here would be a fun new game. The costumes, the code names, the 'Introduction to Grapnel Maintenance'. That was all still extremely silly. But the spirit. The intent. The ambition. Their reasons for being here had nothing to do with being silly.

I wasn't sure they were doing things the right way, but all of them, even grumpy Avrim, were here because they earnestly wanted to help.

Was I just mocking them by being here, for my reasons? That was an uncomfortable thought.

Another uncomfortable thought: Dez's comment about being herself as hard as she could be. To be able to be yourself as hard as possible, you had to know who you were, and maybe, my own answer to that question was... complicated.

I was an imposter, bound for Tartarus.

A soft but solid knock on my door. This time Seven-thirtyfour managed not to loom, though he still blocked the doorway. He looked if anything, slumped.

"Did I wake you?" he asked, voice low and deep enough to feel in my toes.

"No. Is something wrong?"

"Can I come in and sit with you, just for a bit?"

Something was clearly bothering him. "Sure, come in, what is it?"

He slumped into one of my easy chairs. "You'll think me silly."

"Maybe, but I still want to know."

"I was... look, this is my first night sleeping away from the family barracks. The first time I've tried to sleep in a room by myself. I was just..."

"Lonely?"

"Yeah."

"I get that. The first time I had to sleep away from my family..." I paused. I'd found an airlock, pulled an exo-suit off the wall and used it for bedding. Eight years old. Hungry, cold, alone. The only thing that kept me going that first night, and many nights after, was a hot coal of anger in my chest. Knowing my parents would never miss me. That wasn't the story to reassure Seventhirtyfour though. "It gets better."

"Thank you. You're a good friend, you know."

I had no answer.

"Registration tomorrow," he rumbled. "You have your courses all picked out?"

I didn't even know I had options. "Not yet."

"Yeah, me neither, they all look so good, you know? I think I'm just going to cram in as many courses as I can the first few days, then drop what's not working."

"You can do that?"

"Sure, well, except the mandatories. All the courses

this first week are just supposed to be tasters. But if there's anything in particular you want that's popular, best to make a point of signing up to that. There's no guarantee spaces will open up later."

From the little of Gravane I knew, it seemed unlikely he would have made his course choices himself. I grabbed my (his) pad off the bedside table and logged to his (my) student account. I skimmed his course selections. Yeah, I didn't think they'd suit Gravane, and they sure as heck didn't suit me. *Jetpack Basics*? *I don't think so*.

I spent a little time shuffling courses on and off my list. Rescueology was full, sadly. I'd wanted to find out what it was.

I looked up from my pad at a low, loud rumbling. Seventhirtyfour was asleep in my armchair.

# # #

He'd retreated to his own room by the time I woke up in the morning.

Registration day.

It was probably my single biggest hurdle. If they ran biometrics, I was screwed. If they quizzed me about Gravane's personal life, I was screwed. If they had information on Gravane that I didn't and referred to that, I was screwed. Honestly, if I wasn't in Tartarus by lunchtime it would be a miracle.

Could I duck Registration completely? Unlikely, but I might be able to dodge it for a bit. Even doing that would draw attention, though, and that was the last thing I wanted.

I needed to get a look at it, find out what I was up against.

An access panel on the third floor led to a maintenance space that provided a route onto a low roof for the building next to the main gym. I almost turned back at the first spots of rain on the back of my hand, but I noticed an open window across from me. I screwed my eyes shut and ran four paces across the roof to reach the window. I hit the wall, found the window edge with my hands and scrambled through.

Under a roof again, I opened my eyes and let my breathing and heart rate normalise. I was on a window ledge up high near the ceiling, and the view was obscured by an equipment rig. That was easily solved; I threw myself off the ledge, caught the equipment rig one-handed, and pulled myself over and on top of it, working my way along until I got a better view of what was going on below.

I was surprised at how many students there were. I'd expected it would just be our group of Freshers, but there were more of us than I'd realised. There must have been hundreds, maybe a thousand. Three long queues of students trailed through the gymnasium doors, snaked around, leading to three trestle tables where three harassed-looking staff members, two humans and a Polifan, dealt with the students in turn.

The maths was simple, this many students, this few staff, they couldn't spend more than a minute or two with each, or they'd be here for days. I could get through a minute or two without being discovered, surely? Right? Of a list of bad options, it felt like the best one.

Resolved, I clambered around full circle to look for a way off the rigging. There, in the shadows a few metres away, a dark figure was hunched over on my rigging. His face was covered by a three-quarter mask, all I could see of him were glowing red goggles, and a frown that had been chiselled into place.

We stared at each other for a long, long moment, then he flourished his black cape, and seemed to fade into the darkness among the rafters.

"This place," I muttered, as I clambered to the edge of the rigging and navigated my way to ground level.

I joined a queue, spent an hour shuffling through the gym as the queue moved onwards. I used the time to access the stellarnet from my wrist pad to revise what I could about Gravane and his family. I doubted it would be enough to make a difference, but I'd be a fool to not at least try.

"Hello?" said a woman's voice.

I looked up from my wrist pad; I'd reached the front of the queue. A smiling Polifan woman sat behind the trestle table, gestured me to a seat. "Good morning. My name is Veritas. What can I do for you Mr...?"

Veritas? Oh hell.

CHAPTER 6
LESSONS

I shut my mouth so hard, my teeth clicked.

Veritas's eyes twinkled. "Interesting, that's not the question that stumps most people." She jotted a note on her pad. "Let's try something easier. What do you want me to call you?"

Say Brian, say Brian, say Brian. "Grey."

Damn. Her power was real.

"It's an abbreviation of Gravane," I added, picking my words very carefully. "But I would rather you called me Grey." So, I could talk around the truth at least.

"Very well, 'Grey' it shall be." She leaned forward, tapping on her pad to bring up Gravane's details. As she skimmed the record, her wings twitched, and I caught the scent of cinnamon and fresh-baked bread.

"Quite the academic curriculum you have selected. Are you sure you want to be a superhero?" she asked.

Yes, of course. "No."

"We are associated with the University of Tau Vega, so credits you earn here can be transferred across if you decide to pursue that path."

"I do want to sample what the Academy offers." *Truth*. *Truth*. *Truth*. Short sentences were easier to keep true.

She must have known I was evading. Hiding something. But she must be used to it, can you imagine what it must be like to only ever hear the truth? Horrific. Nevertheless, we worked through the course selection, and together, we built my syllabus. While the conversation remained focussed, I was safe, but as we approached the end of the list, I felt the dread of approaching chit-chat.

"So then, Grey, that's all sorted," she said.

"That's useful. Thank you. Um." Was it too soon to run?

"Can I ask you something?"

No. "Yes." Oh, of course, because she *could*.

"You don't fit the normal profile for students here, and that's saying something, as we have quite the broad intake. What made you choose the Justice Academy?"

I couldn't open my mouth, not even to try to tell her I had to go. There was no telling what would come out if I did, except that it would be true. I flashed her a thin-lipped grimace and fled.

Smooth.

# # #

Classes started that afternoon, first up, a course I'd selected only because our steward on the *Metropolitan* mentioned it. Grapnel Gun Basics with Tom the Avenging Spider.

We met in a classroom on the eighth floor. The class was organised into two concentric semi-circles of consoles surrounding a wide-open space in the centre, with the teacher's desk beyond. We filed in and took seats at one of the consoles each; I chose one in the back row near the door between a human woman, dark hair kept away from her face by a jewelled headband, and a young male Cholbren with dark red shoulder fur. There were maybe two dozen of us, all strangers, and as far as I could tell not a power amongst us. The Cholbren kept glancing upwards as Tom spoke. I followed his gaze; the class was taller than I'd realised, and the light arranged in such a way that the ceiling was kept in shadow.

"As a superhero, you need to be mobile," said Tom,

sitting cross-legged on top of the teacher's desk. "If you don't have movement powers, how do you address that? Running? Too slow, and way uncool, dude. Car? Skimmer? Vehicles are useful and all, but sometimes you need into places they just don't fit. Personal jetpack? Great if you have it with you, but clumsy and cumbersome. Flight ring? This isn't comic books." He looked wistful for a moment.

He unclipped his grapnel gun from his belt, held it up for us to see. It looked like a heavy pistol with a claw attachment on the barrel aperture. A line of thin metallic cable hung from the back, leading to a spool attachment on his belt. "This... is a galactic classic. A Klorr Industries 2000XK. Capable of propelling the grapple claw to a maximum vertical range of 25 meters. Across a horizontal plane of 150 in single atmosphere; though watch for the cross-winds. The cable will hold two tonnes if you are connected to a sufficiently stable anchor.

"In later classes, we might study models with gravity clamps, or drone-smart deployment solutions, but *this* is what it's all about."

He flexed and hopped, going from cross-legged to crouched on the table in one fluid motion. He pointed the grapnel at the ceiling and fired. There was a puff of air, and a hiss of cable releasing, much quieter than I'd expected, then a clang from the shadows that hid the ceiling.

Tom grinned. "Just don't forget to hold on!" He pressed the retraction stud on the gun, and he shot upwards, vanishing into the darkness above.

Spotlights flicked on, all pointing upwards, to show that above us, the classroom was crisscrossed with steel bars that spanned the entire room. The Avenging Spider, crouched on one of the bars, called down to us. "Today, we're just going to practice the very simplest aspects: latching on, ascent and descent."

His teaching assistant wheeled in a trolley with racks

of grapnels.

Awesome!

# # #

Afterward, shoulders aching, and with an honestly-earned sheen of sweat, I headed for the stairwell. I had a free period and was looking forward to a shower after my exertions. Before I could get there, I spotted my green four-armed shadow.

"Grey!" He was clutching a stack of textbooks to his chest but still had a hand free to wave. "How was your first lesson?"

"Hey, Seventhirtyfour. Good. A lot more practical than I'd expected, and grapnel guns are great fun. What are you on your way to?"

"'Superheroics: A History' with Doctor Phenomenal. This guy's famous, he literally wrote the book, you know."

I still couldn't quite get my head around the idea that superheroes existed, let alone had existed long enough to have a history. "Have fun with that, sounds a bit dry for my tastes."

"You're missing out. There's so much to know about where we've come from that can really point us to where we're going."

I let him continue but didn't really listen. I was too distracted by a flash of feathers I'd caught in the corridor behind him. A female Polifan. Veritas.

My encounter with her was too fresh, and I knew that I must have raised her suspicions. I shuffled sideways to keep the massive Brontom between me and her. I didn't think she'd noticed me yet, so if she wasn't heading this way...

Ah, of course, marvellous.

"Do you know what, Seventhirtyfour, you've convinced me. I need to learn some history. Which classroom was it?

This one? Excellent." I ducked through the door, Seventhirtyfour followed.

He was excited because, of course, he was, and he headed for the front row, middle seat. I pined briefly for the back row, but I slid in beside him.

"So, has there been a long history of superheroes then?" I asked in a whisper.

"Oh sure. Longer than most people realise. I mean, you probably think of Atomic Force being the first superhero, I bet? That's just on the human side, there's supposed to be a Brightish superhero who predates 'tommy by like a millennium and a half!"

"How can I never have heard of any of this?"

"You've never heard of any of this?"

"Um, well... Tommy? Obviously? A real idol of mine growing up, he's what made me want to apply here..."

"I bet! The way he took down Ryan Orion and the Belters? It's the first documented case of the Reflection Inversion being used to defeat four villains at once. Breathtaking."

'Ryan Orion and the Belters' sounded more like a covers band than a group of villains to me, but Seventhirtyfour clearly thought they were a thing. "Pretty impressive. But, I mean, sure, Tommy is a given. But there's a whole Academy for superheroes, how is it they aren't major news all the time?"

From nowhere, a voice said "That... is an excellent question!" And then, behind the lectern, the air shimmered and a red-finned Welatak wearing a purple and yellow saline suit faded into view. "I am... Doctor Phenomenal!"

Seventhirtyfour grabbed my wrist in excitement with both of his right hands.

"And during this course, we will talk about the history of superheroes and why, even now, with all of the excellent students passing through our Academy and going on to save, on occasion, whole planets, there is not a greater awareness in the galaxy at large of our activities and why it, therefore, behoves we humble practitioners of the superheroic arts to record, study and celebrate those that went before us, while simultaneously writing our own amazing deeds into the annals of superheroic endeavour!"

"He's such an inspiring speaker, you know?" Seventhirtyfour rumble-whispered into my ear.

"Impressive breath control, certainly."

Doctor Phenomenal gave us a stare which, I'm told, can wither plants.

"Sorry!"

"Sorry."

His breath control was probably the only thing to impress me about the lecture. Doctor Phenomenal spoke non-stop for an hour, and I swear, only used half a dozen sentences. Seventhirtyfour was practically bouncing with joy by the end, but I couldn't keep my attention focused. Knowing about these ancient superheroes didn't help me. Maybe that's why I'd never heard of them before.

"If we're moving on to chapter two of the textbook next time, it should be all about the early super team-ups," Seventhirtyfour told me as we made our way out at the end. "We're in for a treat!"

"Sorry Seventhirtyfour, I think this clashes with Secrets of the Quick Change, and I want to give that a try."

"Oh. Well, we all have to find our own path, you know?"

"Yeah. Hey, there's Dez! I didn't notice you in this class."

She was lying on the bench in the back row but uncurled and sat up as we approached. She gave an angular shrug, her shoulders looked like they popped out of their sockets, then back in, to manage it. "I wasn't, not really. I came in earlier to have a nap at the back, the class was empty when I laid down..."

"Oh, but you missed an amazing lecture! Doctor

Phenomenal took us through the first chapter of his book! Such a privilege!"

"Books? Pft. My people don't really do books, we're more a practical get out there and have a go sort of species."

I hung back and let them chat. Seventhirtyfour needed a friend, and I didn't know how long I'd be able to be there. Better if he made other connections.

# # #

We rounded out day one with Superhero Self Defence; it was one of the mandatory courses, and the Freshers were split into groups of about fifty for it. Our group met in the main gym, now cleared of the tables from Registration.

Dez, Seventhirtyfour and I joined a ragged line of students against the long wall. Pilvi joined us soon after. The girl with the jewelled headband from my Grapnel class gave me a half-wave and I smiled in reply. Last in were two more familiar figures, Avrim and the short blue Zalex from the night before, the one we'd named Gadget Dude. He seemed completely oblivious to his surroundings and was instead studying a small device in his hands. He twisted and folded it, making tutting noises. Avrim gave him occasional guiding nudges.

The pair made their way to join us. "Glad to see you," said Avrim. "Someone else needs to take a turn watching Gadget Dude; keeping him from walking into, or off, things... is exhausting." He rolled his shoulders, and I caught a faint tang of ammonia from his wings.

Gadget Dude looked up at the sound of his name. "Avrim!" he declared in surprised delight.

"Do you hear that?" asked Dez. "Faint music?"

"I don't hear anything," rumbled Seventhirtyfour.

"It probably hasn't reached you up there yet," said Avrim.

"Shh! I'm listening!" said Dez.

I was too. I couldn't hear anything at first, but after a few seconds, there was *something*. More of a beat than a tune. The volume rose, the tempo increased. Dez started tapping her foot along with it.

"It's kind of dramatic," said Pilvi.

There was no mistaking it now, it was coming from speakers in the walls, a stirring tune, intense, building to a crescendo. As the music burst open, so too did the gymnasium doors, and a bolt of white light erupted through it. Sunbolt. He spiralled around the ceiling, filling the air with white sparks of light. As the music gave one last flourish and cut out, Sunbolt came to a halt, hovering in front of us, fists on hips, energy coruscating down the lightning bolt designs on his uniform, long white hair glowing almost too brightly to look at.

A few of the class cheered, Sunbolt acknowledged them with a slow nod.

"Well then, noobs," Sunbolt said. "Professor Red Ninja has asked me to assess your combat abilities, to determine if you would survive your first mission as superheroes. The Academy wants very much to keep you safe and my job is to help the Professor make sure you don't embarrass yourselves or the Academy." He looked us over, with a very doubtful expression. "Let's see if we have anyone worth my time. Who's got powers?"

Seventhirtyfour half raised a hand, he had only tested for latent ability after all, and Gadget Dude put his hand up too. The rest of us just shuffled our feet.

Sunbolt glided over, arms crossed, hovering directly in front of Seventhirtyfour. "Oh ho, what do we have here, a super-powered Brontom? You may be worth my time after all. What do you do, big guy?"

Seventhirtyfour smiled his broad, open, smile. "Well, sir, I tested positive for latent—"

But Sunbolt cut him off. "'Latent', ugh. What a

disappointment. Well, come on, you'll do. Front and centre. Now, class. I call myself Sunbolt because, after a freak accident on a Solar Research Station, I gained the ability to shoot sun-bolts out of my eyes. Everybody watch. You, Brontom, I'm going to shoot you with my sun-bolts, you need to try to dodge, okay?"

Seventhirtyfour nodded, and a burst of bright white energy hit him in the stomach. He collapsed in a heap, gasping for air.

"Rubbish!" said Sunbolt. "I gave you a warning, I used the weakest blasts I could, and that's the best you can muster." He looked back down the line of us. "Who was the other one? You, right?" he pointed at Gadget Dude. "Well you're a smaller target at least, so, you have that going for you. Come on, hop to it. What are your powers?"

Gadget Dude opened his hands to reveal the project he was working on. It was a small mechanical bird, it whirred as it flapped its wings and launched itself haphazardly into the air. Gadget Dude pointed to it fluttering towards Sunbolt and smiled. "Gadget," he said, then pointed to himself. "Dude."

"Oh. A *technician*. Great," said Sunbolt. "So, dodge... now!" Sunbolt whipped his head left to right, and his energy beam sliced the mechanical bird neatly in two, before striking Gadget Dude on his shoulder and sending him spinning backward into Seventhirtyfour. The two halves of the bird hit the ground and shattered.

Sunbolt shook his head in exaggerated mock dismay. "Oh dear, oh dear, oh dear. Come on, who's next? Nobody? I'm going easy, if you can't cope with me, a real supervillain will eat you for breakfast. Come on, let me help you. You, Wings, you're up, that's almost a superpower."

But Pilvi stepped in front of Avrim. "No," she said. "Me next."

Sunbolt shrugged. "Right you are. Any powers?"

Pilvi dropped into a crouch, balanced forwards and ready. "None at all," she said.

He laughed at her. "Well don't you look fierce. Good for you. Okay then... dodge!"

Pilvi whipped her right hand to the side, throwing something small off to her right. Everybody, including Sunbolt, glanced over to see what it was, and as they did, Pilvi lunged forwards.

She put her entire body weight behind her balled fists, roaring as she leapt. The angle was wrong, too high for her, but she connected, landing a glancing blow to Sunbolt's hip. He was forced back, but only a few centimetres, he was tougher than he looked. Pilvi, off-balance, sprawled to the floor but even so, there was no doubt she got the better of the exchange.

She'd made her point. And Sunbolt knew it.

Right there, he could have gotten us on-side. If he'd played it right, taken the temperature of the room, congratulated Pilvi, a bit of self-deprecating humour, he could have pulled it back. Gotten us to believe he really was trying to help us and wasn't just a bully.

"Right," he snapped "Pair off and take a training blaster, we're going to practice dodging."

I went straight over to Pilvi. "You okay?"

She winced. "Think I may have broken my wrist," she confessed. "Was like hitting a wall. Or his head."

"Let me help you up, we'll get you to the med centre."

"Thanks, Grey. Don't you want to stay and practice 'dodging'?"

I shook my head. "I think I've learned all I'm going to in this class today."

# # #

We found the med centre in the basement of the Hall of Heroes. There were a few other students waiting to see the med tech, all nursing minor injuries of one sort or another.

The red-furred Cholbren from my grapnel class looked up as we walked in, he was holding his left arm awkwardly. "Sunbolt?" he asked. He must have been in the previous group.

"Yeah."

"What an ass."

A student I didn't recognise joined in. She was a tech hero, holding an ice pack to her forehead, the dented helmet to her armour sat between her feet. "I had him last year. Believe it or not, he gets better. Once you get past his alpha, big dog, phase, the injuries tail off in a week or two. He can be an effective teacher if you don't get on his wrong side. He tagged you with a sunbolt to the arm?" she asked Pilvi.

"I punched him in the hip."

"Yeah, you're toast. Might as well ask the med tech if they do loyalty cards for this place."

"Great."

I held the pad for Pilvi to fill in her details, then we sat to wait her turn.

The med centre felt nice and familiar, perhaps being underground was like being on a space station. Both safely insulated from the outside world. The plain concrete walls were even painted a nice yellowy-brown colour. Positively soothing.

There was something a little off though. Something that had been bothering me about the Academy since walking onto the *Metropolitan*. The place was fine. The furniture, the equipment, the buildings, all of it was completely adequate if a little patched-and-repaired. But the number of students here, the kind of price some of those students could afford; the place should have looked better. Where did all the Academy's money go?

To put Mirabor Gravane here, some money must have changed hands. Not that he wasn't a worthy candidate; that was just the way corporate entities and schools interacted. The Gravanes wanted their son here, they would make sure some funds went into the Academy. They would show an interest, no matter what Gravane himself thought about his parents, they would protect their investment. The Academy would get a sizable donation and the Gravanes would put an agent or two in the school.

All this unprocessed air was clearly affecting my brain.

Why hadn't that occurred to me before? I'd worried that some mistake of mine would get me found out, but, no. Of *course*, there would be someone here looking out for the real Gravane. Student? Teacher? Both?

Pilvi broke through my rapidly accelerating thoughts. "Grey? Are you okay? You've gone pale."

"Fine." I needed to get out of my own head or I'd go crazy. Grasped for something to say. "It was pretty impressive, standing up to Sunbolt."

"We're training to be heroes, to protect people. Might as well start as we mean to go on. Besides, my youngest brother used to get bullied at school; I've no patience for it."

"You have a brother?"

"Three, I'm the eldest. You get in the habit of looking out for them. Here." She pulled her minipad off her belt, juggled it one-handed to bring up a photo of her family. "Petrus, Ahti and Vesa."

"And who's that, your sister?"

"No. That's Kaarina. My girlfriend. Well, ex, now, I suppose."

"Ex?"

Pilvi shut off her pad, clipped it back on her belt. "Yes, long-distance, it's difficult. I miss her, but we agreed to be realistic about it. If we both still feel the same when I get back... I don't know, though, will I even go back? Marwick doesn't need my skills, I can't be a hero there."

"You took down Sunbolt, you're a hero in a building

full of heroes. I'm pretty sure you can be a hero anywhere."

She laughed at that. "But it's your turn now."

"My turn for what?"

"I just shared my secret origin, now you need to share yours."

The best lies start with the truth. "Don't tell Seventhirtyfour, but I didn't really want to be here. The Gravane corporation decided they needed their own superhero, I guess, and now... here I am."

"I did wonder, you don't have the bright-eyed earnestness."

I shrugged. "I'll work on that. The Academy is an interesting place though. More so than I'd realised when I stepped onto the *Metropolitan*. I think I could learn a lot here."

"And...?"

"If you're looking for me to declare I now want to be a space alien superhero, sorry."

Pilvi grinned at me. "We can work on that. I promise not to tell Seventhirtyfour, but I don't promise to let him go easy on you. He'll get you in a cape before the end of term, I bet."

"Save me from the capes!"

# # #

Once the med tech had wrapped Pilvi's wrist and given her some stims, and once we were confident that Sunbolt's class was over, we went in search of the others.

The most likely place for them to be was the bar, the Gamma Bomb, and the reason we suspected it: it looked like *everyone* was there. The doors and fire exits were wide open, and people filled the hallways around the bar, spilled out into the quad and the party was just starting. Somewhere in the mess of people, a live band was playing an upbeat rock number, their singer belting out the song as though her greatest dreams had all come true.

I'd never seen its like. You can't live on space stations for ten years without seeing a dense crowd or two, but that usually meant that departures were locked down because of some fault or other. A crowd this big were usually well on their way to an angry mob. Not so here, these people were happy, no joyful; a crowd gathered to celebrate youth, hope and the start of new endeavours.

It filled my chest with a contact high from life, I grinned at Pilvi, she grinned back.

"How are we going to find them in that lot?" I asked. I had to lean in close and practically shout in her ear.

"Don't know! Want to split up and look?"

"Stick together, or we'll need to find each other too."

She gave a thumbs-up, and we stepped into the throng. My fingers itched, just a little, a crowd this dense, if I had a mind to, I could make a killing with a little dipping here or there. But I didn't need it, for now, I was set for money. Gravane had been as good as his word, and my credit stick had a nice healthy level on it. Besides, I couldn't steal from these people, not unless I really needed to.

The biggest worry in a crowd of trainee superheroes is crushed feet. About a tenth of the students were decked out in their power armour, and that stuff is heavy. Even the lighter-weighted alloys could crush toes with a miss-step, and not everyone favoured the sleeker look. One behemoth stepped in front of us; highly polished brass, cogs and gears ratcheting as he moved, steam escaping from vents in his shoulders. He put a gauntleted hand up to stop Pilvi, I stepped to her six, in case she needed backup.

"I hear you punched Sunbolt," he said, his voice amplified but modulated by his suit, making it audible, but robotic.

"He started it," said Pilvi.

"I bet," he intoned. "What's your name?"

"Pilvi."

He unlatched his helmet visor, pushed it back. "Nice to meet you, Pilvi. I'm the Golden Juggernaut but call me Simon. Can I buy you a drink? Feats of heroism like yours need celebrating."

"Okay, why not? Grey? I'll catch you up."

"Sure thing."

Simon lowered his head to speak into his mic, amplifying it. "Fellow students, today, this day, a hero was called, and a hero answered. I give you, the vanquisher of the vainglorious, the puncher of posers, the smiter of Sunbolt: Pilviiiiiiiiiiiiiiiiiii!"

I doubt his words carried far, but far enough, the chant went up, "Pilvi! Pilvi! Pilvi!"

Laughing, I joined in but stepped away. Pilvi deserved to enjoy her moment, there was nothing I could add. I returned to my search.

The room was dark, and the crowd swayed to the music, ebbing and flowing in a tide that made progress slow. The first face I saw that I knew was the girl from my grapnel class. She saw me notice her, smoothed her hair back from her face, smiled at me. The tide of the crowd moved us apart again before I could do anything but smile back.

Eventually, I found Seventhirtyfour, Avrim and Gadget Dude tucked away at a table in the back, near the stage. It was far too loud for conversation, but the band was great, the singer was amazing. I slid into a seat at the table and enjoyed the sensation of sitting with friends listening to good music.

It was a feeling I'd never really experienced before. I'd worked with teams on stations across the galaxy, shared downtime with them on occasion, sat in bars and cafés when music was playing, but most of the time the people I worked with were older, in some cases much older.

They were people with whom I had socket wrenches and welding masks in common. Nothing more. There was association, but not camaraderie. Sitting there with three trainee superheroes, though, it felt something like a home. How had that happened?

The band took a break between numbers and Avrim leaned over to me in the quiet. “You recognise the singer?”

“Should I? Is she famous?”

“It’s Dez.”

“Shut up.”

“Look for yourself.”

I stood, craned to see past the crowd, and there on the stage was Dez. She smoothed back her yellow head crest and leaned into the mic. “For this next one, we’re going to take it down a notch, play an old Cholbren favourite *The Waters of Forever*. It’s a beautiful song, and it starts… with a shimmer of drums.” The drummer obliged, and Dez sang.

I collapsed back into my chair. “Wow.”

“She’s great, isn’t she?”

This place. There was a magic to it. Thirty-six hours we’d been here, and already Seventhirtyfour, Pilvi, Dez… they belonged. Avrim had family here. Gadget Dude had a new name, a new identity. This place absorbed people, adapted, found a way to fit them in.

And then there was me. Sooner or later, one way or another, I was going to leave. I’d have to. Maybe it was better for them if I made it sooner.

CHAPTER 7
SPORTS

I couldn't just steal a ship or buy a ticket off-world; both would draw the kind of attention I wanted to avoid. A bit of quiet nosing around the spaceport the next morning ruled out the mail pods; they were automated and not fit for biological use. I needed a passenger flight, one big enough to sneak aboard without getting spotted, and they weren't as frequent as I hoped. My first chance wasn't for a long month.

It was a sobering discovery. I'd spent the last two days on auto-pilot, enjoying the novelty, dodging disasters as they came. If I was going to be here long term, I needed to get more serious about it. My goals were simple: get as much as I could from my time at the Academy and get away again without spending time in Tartarus, or worse.

I kept my head down and got on with lessons, tried to dodge feathers whenever I saw them in case Veritas *was* looking for me and kept my profile as low as I could manage it. Classes ranged from the interesting ('Tactical Combat Analysis') to trivial ('Parkour Basics') to the disappointing ('Yellow Wood: About Heroic Vulnerabilities'). That part of the plan went well enough, I devoured the learning on offer, particularly where I could apply it to my own life.

My plan to pull away from socialising, on the other hand, struck a large green four-armed stumbling block.

One day it was "Pilvi's having a movie evening in her accommodation block." The next "We're all going down to the Gamma Bomb again tonight." Or "Board games with Gadget Dude!"

It wasn't as though he didn't have other friends, but for some reason, he always wanted me there too. Did his latent powers include some sort of mind control? All I can say for certain is that somehow, I always ended up going along.

"Great news!" Seventhirtyfour said. We sat in the communal kitchen of our accommodation, a couple of our housemates preparing their breakfasts at the counter behind us. Seventhirtyfour was onto his third bowl of cereal and his second cup of coffee. "I've signed us up for Power Ball."

"You did what?"

"Don't worry, it's all inside."

"Why would that matter? No, I meant, I don't know what Power Ball is."

"You'll love it."

"The fact that you're not telling me what it is, makes me think you know I won't."

"It's something fun for us all to do together every couple of weekends. Team building. Practical tactical exercises. Puzzles."

"Oh for the love of... just tell him!" shouted Dean from over by the toaster. "It's a sport, Grey, a superhero sport. Like a cross between hockey, dodgeball and sudoku."

"That's pretty hard to imagine."

Seventhirtyfour cocked his head, considering. "It's a fairly accurate description, actually."

"I see," I lied. "And when you say 'us', who did you mean?"

"You know, the gang? Our group? Me, you, Pilvi, Dez, Avrim and Gadget Dude? Oh, but that reminds me, I need you to tell Avrim that he's on the team."

"Me?"

"He'll take it better from you. You're very persuasive."

"I can't persuade him, I still don't know what it is." I mean I probably could, but that wasn't really the point.

"You have a free period this morning?"

"After 'Superheroics and the Law', yes."

"Great, get Avrim to meet us in the Dome then, and we can have our first team strategy session."

# # #

The Dome, as the name suggested, was the large dome-shaped building on the quad. It was the Academy's stadium. At its centre, a vast circular field with several small platforms suspended above it, each of the platforms had a console in the middle. Across the field, pockets of other students were practising, which mostly seemed to involve knocking a small spherical drone around the field with batons or standing on the platforms doing something with the consoles.

The six of us gathered on the benches at the edge of the field, Seventhirtyfour unpacked his own drone and bats. He switched on the drone, which rose gently into the air to about waist height. Pilvi gently put a hand on Gadget Dude's shoulder before he started disassembling it.

Avrim sat on the second row and let his wings unfurl. "I'm only here because this is supposed to help prepare for the end of year practical exams," he said. The ammonia scent of irritation from his wings was particularly sharp.

"It does?" asked Dez.

"Anyway," I cut in, "who wants to tell me how this all works?"

"The problem with a sport for superheroes," Seventhirtyfour said, "is how to make the game fair for all. When they invented Power Ball they were looking for something where strong players, fast players, smart players and tough players could all contribute. When everyone can have such different levels of strength, speed, reach and so on, what you need is an equaliser. That's where the drone comes in."

He tossed me a bat, then dragged the drone ten paces away, so he was standing in the middle of a pair of goal posts. "I'm going to knock the drone towards you, all I want you to do is score a goal; get the drone past me. All players can strike the drone with their bat, but as goalkeeper, I'm also allowed to block your shot with any part of my body."

"Okay."

Seventhirtyfour tapped the drone and it drifted in my direction, slow enough that I could give some thought to my strategy. The goalmouth was large, but Seventhirtyfour covered much of it. Knocking the drone into one of the corners at some pace seemed my best bet. I wound up my swing, and...

THWACK!

The drone vanished off to my left, spinning uncontrollably, at right angles to the direction I intended. "What?"

Dez laughed so hard she fell off the bench.

Seventhirtyfour pressed a button on his control pad, and the drone zipped back to him. "There's a force field on the drone; the harder or faster you hit it, the more unpredictable the direction of travel. A gentle tap like I used, and it flies true, but it's easy to intercept. A stronger strike, particularly a super-strong one, there's no telling where the drone's going."

"Okay, so, the solution to superhero sports is to bring everyone down to the same level? Seems like that defeats the purpose of it being a *superhero* sport."

"That's why the game has Puzzlers," said Pilvi.

"Right! That's my favourite bit, you know?" Seventhirtyfour pointed up towards one of the platforms and the console on it. "Each team will have one or more players whose primary job is to solve puzzles on those consoles. Whichever team solves fastest can choose different bonuses, like turning off the shield on the drone or making the goals bigger. It means teams need brains as much as power: you need Power Plays so the rest of the team can use their powers."

"My powers. Sure."

He beamed at us. "Great. Now we have that all cleared up, we need to run some practice, find out who's best in which position: Goalkeeper, Puzzler, Strikers and Interference. Now, I think, obviously, I am probably the best choice for Puzzler, because I know how the puzzles work, which is a big advantage. First off, let's try... Avrim in goal, Grey, Dez and Gadget Dude as Strikers, Pilvi, Interference?"

"I'll try," she said, waving her still-strapped-up wrist.

"Great! Let's play Power Ball!"

# # #

"I'm about to solve the last puzzle," Seventhirtyfour called down from his platform, "get ready for a Power Play... now!"

Dez tapped the drone, a little too hard, slicing it over towards me. Pilvi read the move and was already charging me down, baton held high, her jaw set in grim determination. Over her shoulder, the goal posts shifted as the Power Play went into effect.

I swung at the drone, but even as my bat connected, I knew I'd swung too hard again. With an electronic screech of protest, the drone rocketed skywards, caught the edge of one of the Puzzling Platforms, bounced randomly again, accelerating towards Seventhirtyfour. He threw himself backwards, toppled over the edge of his platform, fell to the ground with a heavy thud.

I rushed over to him. "Are you okay?"

Seventrhityfour gave a one-handed thumbs-up. "All good." He gasped, caught his breath. "Maybe we try Grey on Puzzles."

# # #

Below me, the rest of the team lazily knocked the drone between them. Pilvi passed to Avrim, who knocked it back to Seventhirtyfour. Gadget Dude was nominally on Interference, but he only waved his bat at the drone as it sailed past. Dez sat on the goal line checking her social media on her wrist pad.

I moved another of the puzzle pieces on screen. For reasons I wasn't clear on, it changed colour. I'd been working on the puzzle for ten minutes now, and I was still no closer to a solution. I wasn't even sure what the solution I was trying to get to was.

"Okay, Grey, I think it's time to call this," said Seventhirtyfour.

"Wait," I said. I slid another piece up the screen, and this time all the puzzle pieces turned green, flashed, and vanished. Was that what was supposed to happen? "I think… I think I solved it!" Five icons lit up on screen, giving me my list of Power Play options. I couldn't remember what any of them meant, but they were all supposed to be useful. I picked one at random.

The lights across the Dome all went out.

"Excellent choice if any of us had sonar or infravision," Dez said. I got the impression that the rest of the teams practising were less impressed.

"Grey?"

"Yes, Seventhirtyfour?"

"Let's try you in goal."

"Sounds good."

# # #

The end of the second week saw the start of the Power Ball season proper. Seventhirtyfour dragged me over to the Dome early, and we were far from the first to arrive. The place was already buzzing and only got busier as we waited for the others. It was the weekend. You would think that people would be off doing their own things in their own way. But it turned out that most of the students and staff crammed themselves into the Dome in preparation for the start of the league.

It also turned out that we were one of dozens of teams signed up to participate. While Seventhirtyfour goggled at everything, he was so excited to be here, I had plenty of time to skim through the listings.

I was still trying to decipher the boards when Avrim and Dez came up to join us.

"Hey guys," Dez said. She was wearing a Power Ball t-shirt, a large foam hand over one of her claws, and a cap nestled on her head crest. "Have you visited the merchandise store yet?"

"Morning Dez. Do you know what the icons next to the team names mean? I asked Seventhirtyfour, but he's a bit over-excited."

"They show team size and make-up. Teams can have four to six players, so each icon shows whether the player is a Power, a Tech or a Skill hero.

"Okay. Hmm. So… most teams are all one type by the looks of it?"

"Yeah. The Academy doesn't really have formal factions, but for practical purposes, you must have noticed, there are."

"Did you see, there's a team on that board called 'Balls of Fury', that's a joke, right?"

The name cut through Seventhirtyfour's excitement because he said, "Oh no, Grey, they're deadly serious. They lost out on the championship last year, but the team that beat them have all graduated now; the Balls of Fury are the ones to beat this year, you know? It's a small team, only four players, but they are the best of the best. Do you think they're here yet? I need Wrecking Ball's autograph to complete my collection."

"You're really into all this aren't you? So what name did you give our team, I can't see us on the list..."

"We're not on this board, these are the top-ranking teams, the unseeded teams are on the board over there. There we are. 'By The Numbers'." He looked embarrassed. "Because, you know, I'm Seventhirtyfour... You hate it, right? It's okay we can change it later, but I'm not very good at coming up with names. It's not something we Brontom really do."

"It's as good a name as any, Seventhirtyfour, don't worry about it. We're at the very end of the second board. Does that mean...?"

"Yeah, we're the lowest ranked team. But that's okay, we aren't going to win, I just wanted to be part of it."

"Oh well that's encouraging," said Avrim. "Here I thought I was the only one who knew our chances, but it seems like everybody does. How very reassuring."

"Good morning Avrim!" Seventhirtyfour enthused. "Have you seen the others?"

"They will be over shortly. Pilvi is attempting to keep Gadget Dude from tampering with the scoreboard. It seems we are very much off to a flying start."

"Go and get them, please, we need to have a team talk, in case we're up first."

Avrim gave a winged shrug and wandered off to go and collect the others.

"Actually, who *is* playing today?" I asked.

"That's the thing, it's randomised. There are four teams on the field during a game, and this way, there's less chance that pre-existing alliances can affect the outcome."

"Does that work? I'd just think the big teams have more alliances planned."

"Well, yeah. But it does help. A bit. You know?"

"Great. And I'm assuming from our placing on the

boards, nobody's tried to ally with us?"

"Right! You're really getting the hang of this."

A great roar went up from the crowd as the first match-up was posted. I had a small knot in my stomach as I looked but our team name was not amongst those called up.

"Interesting match," said Seventhirtyfour. "All four teams are from the tech faction, so there's nobody obvious for them to gang up on. The Technauts have a good record, but they lost their star player last year when he took a hero gig on Ceynakk. The We're Not Black Holes squad are all second years... they had a fair result last year, so with experience on their side... I reckon they may be the ones to watch in this match."

The six of us took seats high up on the south end to watch. Play was much faster than our practice games, and the Technauts' Interference player was brutal, his tackles hard, and he constantly harassed the Black Holes' Puzzler.

The Technauts' Puzzler finished on his first console, then rocket-jumped to a higher platform.

"There's nobody marking him!" Dez said. "Here we go!"

The lights in the arena switched to red, and the announcer intoned "Technauts: Power Play!"

The goalmouths for all the other teams expanded slightly, and as the other three teams scrambled into defensive formations, the lead striker for the Technauts wound up a mighty hit, there was a crack, and the ball flew unerringly into the back of the Not Black Holes goal.

The crowd erupted. Dez went wild. "Did you see that? Whack! Whoosh! That's the way it's done! Woooo!" She waved her foam finger.

"This isn't much like we practised," I said. "Nobody mentioned rocket boots."

"The Tech students get to bring their tech," said Pilvi. "Just like the Power students have their powers."

"There are certain natural advantages that can't be disabled," added Avrim, flexing his wings. If the scent of cinnamon meant what I thought, he was enjoying himself.

"Like being able to fly, right."

"Sure, it's not perfect, but come on, look, it's exciting!" protested Seventhirtyfour.

"Goooooooooooooooooooal!" shouted Dez. "Guys, you're missing it, the Technauts are on fire!"

After that, the Not Black Holes had no way back. They managed to claw a goal in the last few seconds of the game, but the Technauts' lead was too big.

I took advantage of the break between games to visit the bathroom. After, I decided it might be a friendly gesture to buy us all drinks, so I joined the long queue for the concession stand.

I was standing there, in the queue, hands in pockets and regretting my charitable urge when Dez dashed up to me. "Dude! Where have you been! The next game is called, and we're up!"

"We're up?"

"We're playing, us against the Balls of Fury! And two other nobody teams of course, but, the Balls of Fury! Balls! Of Fury!"

"Oh, right."

"Don't just stand there, come on!"

# # #

We caught up with the others by the players' entrance. Seventhirtyfour sat, head in hands, his spare arms flailing. "Oh no! This is a disaster! We can't play today, we're not ready. Grey barely knows the rules!"

"It'll be fine, Seventhirtyfour," said Pilvi, "we're only here to have a bit of fun, it doesn't matter if we lose, even you said that."

"I know what I said! Now's not the time to remind

people what they said!"

Gadget Dude patted him on the knee.

"Can you at least suggest positions for us to play?" asked Avrim. "That would be something."

"Right. Right. Yes. Positions. Well, we need our best Puzzler if we have any hope of keeping up, and I guess that's me. Grey is... best in goal."

"Right."

He nodded. "Avrim, Interference, obviously, keep high, and try to keep the other puzzlers distracted."

"Obviously."

"Dez, Pilvi, Gadget Dude, keep moving, and look for your chances."

"Right."

"I'm so excited."

Seventhirtyfour took a huge, calming breath. "Okay, great. We can do this. Let's go do this. Remember people, By The Numbers!"

"That's not the most encouraging battle cry," mused Dez.

# # #

I spent the first half of the game padded up in front of our goal with nothing to do. The Balls of Fury had fallen back on faction bias and had kept the pressure on the tech team, the Circuit Breakers, scoring goal after goal against them.

The Balls were impressive to watch, their two attackers, Fireball and Mirror Ball ruled the pitch, and always seemed to be where the action was. The Balls' keeper, Wrecking Ball, a Germile who simply had to stand in front of the goal to cover it, was untroubled throughout. Their puzzler, a Zalex bizarrely called Golf Ball, solved more quickly than I'd seen Seventhirtyfour solve anything.

But the Circuit Breakers' puzzler was faster still,

managing to keep all the others at bay, and despite Golf Ball's best efforts, he couldn't get the lead he needed to trigger a Power Play.

Still, by the time of the break, the scoreline told it all. Six goals to the Balls of Fury, nobody else had come even close to scoring.

"Well, that's it, we've lost," said Dez, lying panting on the ground.

"Yes," said Avrim, and Gadget Dude nodded forlornly.

"Come on, By The Numbers, we can still do this!" Seventhirtyfour tried, but we all just looked at him, and even his head dropped. "Okay, we can't; they're better than us."

"By a country mile," said Pilvi.

Seventhirtyfour huffed, and then sank to the ground. "Oh, what's the use?"

He looked so beaten, his enthusiasm battered and spent. It was just wrong.

He sighed the biggest sigh I've ever heard. "So disappointed. It would have been awesome to score even one goal against the Balls of Fury."

I perked up. "Oh! If that's all you want, yeah, we can totally do that. I thought you wanted to win."

"Well, sure I wanted to win! But... no... wait, what do you mean we can score a goal against them?"

I hedged. "Well, not for sure, but I'm pretty confident. It'll mean changing things around..."

Dez sat up. They were all looking at me now.

"Remember, this isn't for the win... but... Don't worry about the puzzles, we don't need them. None of us have powers that the Power Play would help with, right?"

"Well, I suppose so..."

"Right. So, Seventhirtyfour, I need you in goal; we have to assume Power Plays will still happen, and we need as big a body in front of the goal as possible if only to make other goals more tempting. Avrim, when I give you a high sign, forget the ball, forget the other teams, I need you to focus only on Golf Ball. Harass him up to the limits of the rules, okay? If we can stop him solving a single puzzle, all to the good."

"I can do that."

"Dez, Gadget Dude and me, we stick on Fireball and Mirror Ball hard, don't worry about the others, but crowd them as much as you can.

"Pilvi, from what I've seen, you're our best shot, so our best hope for the goal. Hang back, don't get involved, conserve your energy, and look for your moment. When the time comes... hit that ball with everything you've got and put it past Wrecking Ball and into the net. Can you do that?"

"Well, no, not without a Power Play. Wrecking Ball is bigger than their goal!"

I grinned. "Leave that to me."

Seventhirtyfour gave his four-shouldered shrug. "It's worth a go. Let's do it. By The Numbers!"

We all sort of mumbled a "By The Numbers" response, which seemed to please Seventhirtyfour immensely.

We did well, for the first couple of minutes. With effectively five strikers in play we got hold of and kept the ball, at least for a while, but try though we might, we couldn't get a convincing shot at goal. Dez came the closest, but she over-hit in her enthusiasm, and the drone careened wildly around the Dome afterwards.

I took the moment's distraction to get close to Diode, one of the Circuit Breakers' strikers to have a quick word. "You want to take them down a peg, right?"

He pretended to ignore me, but I didn't let that stop me. "We're neither of us winning this, but I bet you'd like to spoil their day, right? If you can get a Power Play, we can get a goal. It's not much of a victory, but you know it'll annoy them."

The ball was back in play again, and Diode ran after it; I let him go for now. He probably needed a little more convincing yet.

Moments later, Fireball knocked the drone to Mirror Ball, who sliced it into the top corner of the Circuit Breakers' goal.

The two Balls high-fived, and Fireball threw a stream of flame into the air, a technical violation, but the ball was out of play, so the judges let it slide. From their goal, Wrecking Ball roared. "Fury, yeah! Fury, yeah! Fury, yeah!"

Diode caught my eye, nodded sharply.

I gave Avrim the high sign.

We dug in, as the clock ticked down. There was time for the play, but not much. Avrim went to work on Golf Ball, a close fly-by, some name-calling, even a shoulder-ram when the ball flew close enough to justify it, and Golf Ball cracked. He stood at the edge of the platform, and in the staccato manner that Zalex have, he shouted a stream of invective at Avrim. Avrim, literally, rose above it all.

But with our puzzlers out of play, and Golf Ball distracted, the Circuit Breakers' puzzler only needed to move ahead of one other, and he took his chance. He solved one puzzle, then grapnelled from one platform to another, and solved a second in, well, seconds.

The arena lights went red, and the announcer called "Power Play: Circuit Breakers!"

Diode took the ball and fired the jets on his armour, with a roar of flame he flew full speed at the Balls of Fury goal; the ball seemed glued to his stick. Fireball and Mirror Ball closed in, narrowing his angle, Wrecking Ball shifted his massive bulk, covering the goal mouth, blocking any chance that Diode had to score. A practised and seamless move.

But at the last moment, Diode flicked the ball wide to me. For my part, it was all I could do to control its angle off my bat, so it went to Pilvi.

She didn't flinch though. As the Balls scrambled to change tack, she drew back her stick, and let fly. The drone sailed past Wrecking Ball's outstretched hand and buried itself in the back of the net.

The entire Dome erupted with noise, as several thousand people roared their approval. Mirror Ball shouted accusations at Wrecking Ball, who roared, pounding the ground so hard it shook.

Heady stuff.

Let's not dwell on the fact that the Balls went on to score twice more before the game was over. That doesn't matter. The simple fact of the thing is that in all manners other than the final scoreline, we beat the Balls of Fury that day.

# # #

In that first month at the Academy, I learned how much there was to learn. I tried courses in all sorts of things, sampled the technical courses, a few detective modules, attended workshops and lab sessions to see if I had any latent superpowers.

As the end of the month approached, my mind turned again to that passenger flight. My best chance of getting out of here. I knew I needed to start planning. Needed to sort out how I was going to get aboard, how I was going to remain undetected, but somehow, I never quite got around to it. In fact, I'd caught myself looking at the course syllabus for the second term.

Only a couple of days before I would leave, and yet again, I chose to rest in my accommodation block over reconnoitring the spaceport.

In my defence, between Combat, Power Ball and Grapnel, I was exhausted; bruised and abraded my muscles felt tight, yet somehow also strung out. I lent my full weight on the fire door to open it, pushing just seemed too much effort.

Seventhirtyfour was chatting to someone on the hallway comm. He looked up as the door opened.

"... oh, in fact, he's just here," he said to the comm. "I'll just forward you through to his room. Nice talking to you Mrs. Gravane."

I felt cold.

Seventhirtyfour grinned. "It's your mother."

CHAPTER 8
LIES

I sat in my room and stared at the blinking call-waiting light.

I could always not answer.

That would be the sensible thing to do, and it wouldn't necessarily be out of character for Gravane Jr either. But. If I ducked the call, that would just get her to sic her (admittedly so far presumed) spies on me. Of course, I couldn't just answer the call either. Even a hands-off mother would notice if someone she didn't recognise claimed he was her son.

No time for any artful solutions, this was going to be entirely low tech and might get me plunged into Tartarus anyway, just as it looked like I was going to get away with it. I opened the door to the bathroom, turned the shower on full blast, and draped a towel over the comm camera, leaving just enough exposed so that she would see the reason for no picture. I pressed the answer button and retreated to the shower doorway.

"Yes?" I called, figuring if I could keep the talking to a minimum, and covered with other sounds, I might, might get away with it.

"Well... what?" said Mrs. Gravane. I could only just hear her over the shower, so nipped out and turned the volume up, hopefully, the feedback would annoy her too.

"Mirabor, is that you?"

Well, that was a bust. Could I do an impression of

Gravane? How did he sound? "Yes?" I asked, trying to pitch my voice at about the same level of the shower, in a half-remembered take on Gravane's accent.

There was a long pause at the other end, it must have lasted about a week. And then she said, "Don't think you can fool me, young man."

And I died inside; slumped into my comfy chair. I'd miss it.

"I am well aware that you had a haircut," she continued.

Wait. What?

"These silly acts of rebellion are beneath you, but I suppose you have time to let it grow out again before you return to polite society. You are a Gravane. And you will comport yourself as one at all times."

"Sure," I grunted. Oh, that's right, Gravane's haircut to match mine. Well what do you know, that precaution worked. Of course, that meant there were spies somewhere on Meanwhile, which was freaky, and it made it even more likely there was someone watching here.

"Really," she huffed, "I can't talk to you when you're like this."

"Okay."

"Do be quiet, I have a conference call with the First Minister of Draygam VII in two minutes, and you remember how much he disapproves of tardiness.

"We require you to attend to an opportunity that has arisen on Bantus. One of our affiliates there is a client of this Justice Academy of yours and they have a situation that I believe requires family attention. I've spoken to your headmaster and arranged a field trip for you. Be a... superhero if you must, the school expects, and so on, but ensure that they know it was Gravane business. We didn't send you to this school for recreational reasons."

"Right," I muttered.

"Don't mumble, dear. I shall let you return to being

reactionary; just don't get a tattoo. Your headmaster will give you all the details about Bantus. Go make use of that degree of yours. Be a Gravane."

She cut the call.

Did that just happen? Did I get away with it? I looked around half expecting her to materialise out of nowhere and frog-march me off campus. I'd seen some things this month, my catalogue of the possible had expanded somewhat, so I double-checked. No, I seemed to be in the clear. Wow.

Not wanting to waste all that lovely hot running water, I stripped off and somewhat bemusedly went and had a shower.

So that was Gravane's mother. I could see what he meant about her, she really didn't have a parental relationship with him, no warm caring bond there. (Though, what do I know? Where are my parents, right?) She might not even have called if there wasn't business to conduct.

And she had just handed me the perfect excuse for getting off planet. All I had to do is go with the flow, sign up for this Bantus trip, then disappear at the first transit station I passed through. It would be simple.

So simple.

Back to my normal routine. Ready to roam the galaxy alone and untroubled again.

Unnoticed.

Unmissed.

Why did that feel so empty all of a sudden?

# # #

I requested an appointment with Captain Hawk for first thing in the morning. If ever there was a time to ride out my identity as Mirabor Gravane, it was the day after I'd spoken to my 'mother'. Who would even think to question me now?

Until then, I had time on my hands. I was too tired to go

out tonight but too wired to settle. I fidgeted in my comfy chair. Tried putting a movie on but gave up after twenty minutes when I realised I hadn't watched a moment of it. I needed to be doing something.

I called up the route to Bantus on my console. It was pretty far out to the galactic south; would take three jumps to get to it, about a week of ship-time, but I wouldn't be going all the way. The second station the route passed through was Aviary, a place I knew well. I'd worked there twice about five years ago and knew enough of its secrets that vanishing there would be no problem. I felt a slight pang that for a while Mrs. Gravane might think she'd lost her son, but when it came down to it, it was only the truth.

Speaking of Mirabor, his mother said something about using his degree. What did she mean by that? He was a couple of years my senior, but surely, he was too young to have a degree? A quick search of the stellarnet answered that; Gravane not only had a degree, he had a Master's degree in Galactic Tax Law.

Thank the stars nobody ever asked me about that!

But that raised a further question. What was going on on Bantus? What could possibly be happening there that they might need a superhero Tax Lawyer?

I opened a new stellarnet search window and set about finding out.

There must be tens of thousands of planets like Bantus; enough natural resources to attract settlement, not enough to fill the world. Its population concentrated around a single city, with outlying agricultural towns to support it. An unremarkable world, and one which didn't generate a lot of news. The first few articles I found that mentioned it at all, only did so in the context of increased piracy in that area of the galaxy. Even then Bantus was not central to the stories.

Even the most insignificant gravity well has some

people who care about it though, and those people tend to live there. It took some digging but eventually, I found access to the local Bantus news.

I set to skimming articles, watching broadcasts, using the meagre skills I'd gleaned from Professor Craft's 'Intelligence Analysis' class. I didn't find much; I'd only had four lessons so far. But, reading between the lines, I suspected that Bantus had an organised crime problem, and from more than one organisation. There was no mention of outright warfare on the streets, but I watched enough worried vox pops, the inference was clear.

One piece caught me; a Zalex who had stood up to a gang, talking about how hackers had accessed her company accounts, stripped them bare. Every credit she and her family worked five years for, gone in a blink. "Ripped away," she said.

I was very aware that directly below the console screen was the desk drawer where I stashed my Ripper.

Throughout the interview, she was holding her daughter in her arms. The girl wasn't wailing or crying, I'm not sure she really understood what was happening, only that it was bad. She could have been Gadget Dude's younger sister. She clung close to her mother, huge wide eyes staring straight down the lens at me.

I... yeah.

# # #

I'm not sure what I expected from Captain Hawk's office. At the back of my mind, I think I'd theorised that the imbalance in Academy money would show up there with platinum curtains and ludicrous works of art on display. But no, it was on brand with the rest of the facilities. Perhaps a little nicer, but still with that lived-in scruffiness. His assistant, Jeff, asked me to take a seat, and the sofa was comfortable, if saggy.

A couple of minutes later, I was called in before the man himself.

Captain Hawk sat behind his desk, in uniform, though his yellow cape hung from a coat stand by the door. Perhaps a little older, perhaps a little greyer than in the advert, he still held himself with quiet authority.

"Have a seat, Mr. Gravane. I believe your mother has spoken to you already."

I nodded.

"It puts me in a difficult position. The situation on Bantus is not actively dangerous, but it is sufficiently unbalanced that I am not happy about sending a student into it this early in your training. Your mother's talk of field trips notwithstanding.

"That said, the Gravane family have been generous to the Academy, and I am aware that this is family business, and you have a duty of responsibility. I appreciate the pressure that puts on you. But if you tell me you don't feel ready to represent the Academy yet, I will speak to your mother and turn down the request."

"It's okay, Captain Hawk. I'll go. It's family business."

He gave a sharp nod. "Very well. The round trip to Bantus will take two weeks, plus whatever time is required to resolve the problem there. I don't want you missing out on that much training time, so I have arranged for a member of the faculty to travel with you. He can tutor you on the journey, and if necessary, provide backup during the mission."

"That's okay, I don't want to inconvenience anyone."

"No, this is for the best." He gestured through the control field on his desk, and a holoscreen popped open showing his assistant outside. "Jeff, could you send Sunbolt in please?"

Oh, great.

"Good morning, headmaster."

"Sit, please. So, we must turn our attention to the situation on Bantus." He gestured through his desk control field again, and several images popped up above it. From my own research, I recognised views of the planet Bantus IV and views over its primary city. He flicked files across to my pad and Sunbolt's. "You can read these at your leisure, but to give you the highlights: Bantus is gripped in something of a cold war between mobster families."

Sunbolt's eyes flashed with white light. "A mob war? What are we sending a no powers Fresher like Gravane for? If you need some mobsters put down, let me pick a group of third years to deal with this, we'll be done before we can check into a hotel."

"I'm sure," said Hawk. "But this is a cold war, no outright aggression between the parties involved, and may require a little more finesse. There are, of course, plenty of category 2 and 3 henchpersons that could be blasted or punched, but if there is to be a more permanent solution, we need to look a little higher than street level."

"I bet," I said. "But what does... my mother think I can do about it?"

"There are three primary factions to be considered," Hawk said. "Each with its own interests and specialities. The Campbells, the Bowriders and the Tazforj. The Campbells run an army of thugs, they're street level, the normal muggings, drugs, protection rackets. The Bowriders are a little more sophisticated. They employ burglars, smugglers and pirates. There are fewer of them, and even fewer of the Tazforj. They are the office criminals. Hackers, blackmailers and industrial espionage."

I remembered the Zalex girl in the video the night before. Her family must have crossed these Tazforj.

"The system is largely stable because there are strict lines of demarcation. Mrs. Gravane feels that if you can destabilise the situation, we can pit one family against the others, bring the situation to a head, as it were."

I frowned. "And bring on that open conflict they're so far avoiding? I guess I can see how that would hurt the crime families but aren't innocent people going to get caught in the cross-fire of that?"

Hawk looked uncomfortable. "I am merely presenting your mother's plan, as I understand it," he hedged. "She feels that the Tazforj are the most vulnerable to your powers.

"Their resources are primarily of the book-keeping variety, and where there are records, they can be taxed. Your mother wants you to consult with the Bantus government and give them some suggestions on restructuring their tax laws to squeeze the Tazforj."

Sunbolt shook his head. "That is the least superhero thing I've ever heard."

I hated agreeing with him, but I kind of, sort of, totally did. "But that's idiotic. She might as well be poking a reactor with a radioactive stick. Sooner or later it's going to explode in your face. Assuming changing tax laws would have any effect at all."

"Your mother seemed confident that you would find a way."

"Right. Yes. Sure."

"Second thoughts, Grey?" Sunbolt asked.

"Perhaps. What happens if I decide not to go?"

Captain Hawk leaned forwards, fingers laced. "Nobody would blame you," he said, in a tone that should have been reassuring. "You can simply continue with your studies as though this question never arose."

That wasn't what I was worried about. One way or another, I was getting on that ship. "No, what happens to Bantus?"

"I would talk to your mother, perhaps offer alternative services. You know your mother best, what do you think she would do?"

What indeed? It seemed likely that she would simply proceed with her plan and flood the place with tax lawyers. But, what would she do if her son disappeared on the way there? Would she send Sunbolt blazing into battle?

"I'll go," I said. "But..." Where was that sentence going? But... I'd solve the problem on Bantus and sneak away on the way *back*? I could hardly tell him that. And even if I went to Bantus I couldn't solve the problem like Mirabor Gravane might and didn't know how to solve it as 'Grey'.

"Yes, Mr. Gravane?"

"But... Oh! How about you send some other students too? I mean, I don't want to get accused of favouritism. Private tutoring? My own mission? It doesn't look good. Questions about Gravane donations. Probably best avoided. But I'm sure Sunbolt is more than capable of handling the training for a few of us as well as he can handle me?"

Sunbolt snorted. "I could handle the whole Freshers class, but I'm not playing babysitter to dozens of noobs." Annoying, but he was helping my point, so I let it pass.

"Sure, and I wouldn't ask you to. How about half a dozen? Me, Pilvi, Gadget Dude, Avrim, Seventhirtyfour and..."

"I'm not dragging your little gang on some holiday jaunt."

"Captain Hawk? What do you think? If I'm not up for the challenge on Bantus, that's a nice spread of talents to help me, without having to rely on Sunbolt to bail me out and spoil the learning opportunity. And with a group, nobody could suggest there was favouritism."

Captain Hawk nodded. "It's an interesting thought. Yes, I think we can swing that," he said, jotting down the list of names. "Maybe you have the Wisdom of Solomon as a power. You wouldn't be the first."

That seemed to be a reference to something, but it went straight by me, so I just nodded.

"Now, hang on," began Sunbolt.

Hawk cut him off. "No, Mr. Gravane is right, this way, five students will get a crack at the Bantus problem, a chance for all of them to learn something."

"I meant to include Dez," I said.

"No, I think five is enough. A good compromise," said Hawk.

Dez was going to kill me. Still, at least Seventhirtyfour would be excited.

# # #

I gathered them at our favourite table in the Gamma Bomb, bought a round of drinks, and pitched the plan to them.

"So, we would have to miss classes?" Seventhirtyfour said.

Pilvi waved her now-recovered wrist at me. "And be stuck with Sunbolt for at least two weeks?"

I held my hands up. "It won't be so bad. Sunbolt is a jerk, but we can learn things from him. If you overlook his obvious and varied character flaws, he does know what he's talking about, we will just have to work together to drive the lessons in a more useful direction."

Avrim shook his head. "Easy to say, Grey, but in a cramped indoor environment, I can't fly, my chances of avoiding a blasting are nil. I appreciate you thinking of me, but I'm sorry, I don't think I can help on this."

"Then I can go in Avrim's place," said Dez.

"If I go in there and renegotiate, the deal might get worse."

Seventhirtyfour added. "And I don't need combat classes. Right now, what I need is help with my psychic abilities and Sunbolt can't help with that." He looked distraught.

I looked over at Gadget Dude, but he was clearly in

creating mode; he had emptied his pockets onto the table and was connecting and rearranging circuits and wires, and who knew what else.

"This is our chance to be superheroes," I tried.

"No, this is a chance for you to build favour for the Gravane legacy, by rewriting tax law," Dez said.

I squirmed. "No, that's what my mother wants me to do, I told you, that's not what I aim to do."

"But you can't tell us what you *do* plan," said Avrim. "Why am I even... no, I said I'm not coming. I'm not coming."

I felt deflated. This had been such a good idea. But I could hardly force them, and their objections were all totally valid. I sighed. One last try. "The people of Bantus need help. I can show you the articles if you want, the place is caught in a war between organised crime families, and sure my mother sees the solution in a business sense. She thinks we can... tax bullets or something, and save people while turning a profit," I said, though I was reasonably convinced that Gravane's mother was only seeing the profit. "But while that may help the corporations, the government of Bantus, even, it's not going to do much to help the actual people.

"The people of Bantus don't need lawyers, they need someone to stand up for them. They need someone willing to stand in the middle of this war and say 'no'. To stare down each of those crime families and make them blink.

"They need superheroes.

"But no, I can't tell you what we're going to do, I don't know what we're going to do. The what, it's not important. What's important, what's important is the why. That we take a stand and we do what's right because it's right."

They were all staring at me. Pilvi blinked. "Where did that come from?"

My hand was shaky, my head buzzing. "I don't know," I confessed, "but I meant every word."

"Yeah, I can tell." She shook her head. "Oh, go on, I'm in. It was a good speech."

Seventhirtyfour grinned. "Welcome to the Justice Academy, Grey. I wasn't sure how seriously you were taking it, but clearly, I should have had more faith. I'm in too. How could I not be?"

They both turned to look at Avrim. "Nothing's changed," he said. "Look it was a good speech, but I'm not... it's not enough to... you're ganging up on me, ask Gadget Dude!"

Gadget Dude looked up, his latest device complete. He held it up towards Seventhirtyfour. "Help," he said. "Not miss classes, wear hat!"

We exchanged glances. Gingerly Seventhirtyfour accepted the device from Gadget Dude.

"It's sized for my head," he said, and before anyone could advise against it, he put it on. It was a snug fit, rested just above his ears. It looked like a crown, made from a thin chain of circuits and sensors, held in place on his scalp by spindly arms. Gadget Dude's creations were often amazing, sometimes baffling, but for some reason always extremely fragile.

"It's... nice?" offered Pilvi.

"It feels... weird. Oh." Seventhirtyfour's shoulders spasmed, his whole body jerked. He made a series of short gargling sounds. His eyes blinked rapidly, rolling back in his head.

"Seventhirtyfour!" Pilvi stood up, clearly wanting to take the crown off but not daring too in case it made matters worse. Avrim jumped to his feet, his wings unfurling reflexively. Gadget Dude just stared, looking surprised and horrified.

I couldn't leave Seventhirtyfour like this. I reached over and snatched the device from his head. I expected a shock, some feedback, tingling, but felt nothing. Something wasn't right.

Seventhirtyfour slumped forward managing, just, to avoid bumping his head on the table.

Dez hopped up beside him, proffered a drink to Seventhirtyfour.

He took a big gulp to steady himself. “By the great clone vats of Brontom Prime,” he said, his voice ragged.

This was all very...

“Gadget Dude’s device, it triggered a flash of psychic power!” said Seventhirtyfour. “I saw... the future!”

“What?” said Avrim.

“I don’t know, a possible future, anyway,” Seventhirtyfour hedged. “We all have to go. There is evil on Bantus, and we can only defeat it if Avrim is with us.” He flounced, gesturing wildly like some fortune telling witch in a pantomime.

Okay, that settled it, this was Seventhirtyfour’s idea of a scam. Clever... but seriously over-done. Time to rein this in. “Don’t try to talk, we need to get you to a medic and get you checked out.”

“But I...”

“No, seriously, don’t try to talk, there could be... damage. Guys, look after Gadget Dude, he didn’t mean for this to happen.” Or expect it. Or deserve the flak he was going to get for it.

Whatever the crown was supposed to do, it clearly wasn’t a fortune telling device. As I led him away, Seventhirtyfour snagged the crown, folded it carefully and slipped it into a pocket.

He straightened up as we got into the corridor. “I bet Avrim comes now,” he said, pleased with himself.

“Maybe so,” I said. “I hope nothing bad comes of it.”

That took the wind from his sails.

“Look,” I said “I appreciate the sentiment, but you can’t just go around tricking people. And not just because you are really, really bad at it. If Avrim comes now because he believes your little 'prophecy' and he gets hurt because of it, how are you going to feel?"

He did a rather impressive four-armed slump. "You're right. That wasn't very superhero was it?"

"No. There's a time and place for a big fat lie, but it's not between friends or family." That made me wince, internally. I was probably going to hell for that. I was infinitely worse than Seventhirtyfour.

Mind you, I was also a lot better at it than him. Truly, if I had any superpower at all it was...

Oh.

"Grey are you okay? You have a very strange expression all of a sudden."

"Oh yes. Yes. Families don't lie to each other."

"You've made your point. I'll apologise to Avrim."

"Hmm? Oh no, not that. Seventhirtyfour you are a genius, I think I know how to fix this."

He looked confused. "Fix it? Avrim...?"

I grinned. "No, not that. I think I have a way to fix Bantus IV. With a big fat lie."

CHAPTER 9
EXCURSIONS

How had I talked myself into this?

For ten years I'd set my own goals, my own timetable, my own destinations. If I got into trouble, I could always cut and run, no need to face consequences. There was always a new station to go to, people who didn't know me. Starting over was easy.

All I wanted was to leave the Academy, right? I rode my luck as far as it could go, longer than I thought possible, and it was time to start over. Perhaps I *should* ditch Sunbolt, Seventhirtyfour and all the rest at Aviary? Let them sort out Bantus. There was no easy out once I sank into that gravity.

But that was the thing about gravity, everything in the universe affects everything else. Bantus already had its grip on me, and I was falling towards it, whatever I wanted.

We would leave on the exact same flight that I'd intended to escape on. There was some irony. I wouldn't even have to hide. But that meant I had one evening to decide what I needed from the Academy, and the plan for Bantus required a few props.

The plan. Hah. There was a long way to go before I could justify that as a name, but I knew how it started, and I would have more than a week to work out the details.

The plan started with jewellery, and I hit the campus print shop to make it. I wanted something simple and distinctive, a pin, something nice enough that people would wear it, but not so flamboyant that they might save it for a special occasion. I started with a smiling face design but pared it back until it was just the smile. I printed off a dozen in shiny bronze pins and took them down to the Gamma Bomb. I left them lying around for people to find.

I wouldn't find out if the idea worked until the morning but wouldn't then have time to print all the copies I needed. I took a gamble and printed some more. A lot more. One in gold, three in silver, and a few thousand in bronze. I watched the numbers on my credit stick plummet. Oh well, being moderately well off for a fun month had been an interesting change of pace. At least the school would be paying for our "field trip" flights, presumably sponsored by the Gravanes.

I left the program to run overnight and jogged back to the accommodation. Packing was a problem. I wasn't coming back to the Academy after Bantus, so whatever I took with me, I'd basically be stealing, and I'd long since sailed past my normal limit on what I'm happy to steal from anybody. Enough for a meal and somewhere to sleep? Much more than that. But I had to look the part. I took one of Gravane's business suits plus accessories. That included one of the mini-pads and a personal comm. I left the other tech behind.

I added my Ripper to the case; my one actual possession. I still felt I was missing something.

One last sortie back to the Hall of Heroes and the Grapnel Maintenance workshop. The old model PS-10N that I'd been working on in class was stored in the cupboard at the back. I spent a quiet hour finishing the repairs, then clipped it to my belt.

Well, if I was going to be posing as a superhero at some point, I needed my equipment.

# # #

I took breakfast in the canteen, sat alone, watching the crowd. I chose the neutral ground canteen, wanted one last taste of the bonkers atmosphere when the factions mingled, I doubted I'd ever see its like again. A purple-skinned human hovered cross-legged opposite me; he could have sat on the chair just as easily, but that was the thing with the Powers crowd, they liked you to know they were special. I asked him to pass the salt, and he did it telekinetically. Show off. The whirr of servos caught my attention, and I watched a knight in cybernetic armour thread his way between tables to join a crowd of his fellows in the corner. I spotted Diode from the Circuit Breakers amongst the group, gave him a wave. He didn't respond.

# # #

After breakfast, there was just time to pick up my printing, several kilos of costume jewellery, stow it in my luggage, grab one last shower, and then it was time for the off.

Seventhirtyfour met me in the kitchen. "Cometh the hour, cometh the Grey Warrior," he said.

"Needs work."

"Grey Hood? Captain Grey? Doctor Grey?"

I laughed. "I haven't made it through year one yet, I think it's a little early to claim a Doctorate."

"You're about to go into action as a superhero, Grey, you need a name, at least. Maybe a costume too, but at least a name."

"No costumes, no names. If all goes to plan, I'll be keeping my identity secret until the very end anyway."

"Oh!" said Seventhirtyfour. "Wait here."

He dashed back up the stairs to his room, returned a couple of minutes later with a pair of glasses. "Here, Grey, you'll need these."

Plain black frames, I tested them, yes, prescription free. "Why?"

He beamed. "Trust me, Grey."

"Sure, why not? Glasses. Okay, Seventhirtyfour, all set now?"

"Lead on, Grey Leader."

I squared my shoulders, took a breath, and stepped into the quad. Last time. This was the last time I'd have to do this. Once I got done with Bantus, I was going station side and staying there. Humankind was not supposed to live in the wide open outdoors. Or at least this one wasn't. Head down, I forged across the quad, Seventhirtyfour hustled to keep up.

Halfway across the quad, too focussed on my destination and not my route, I collided with another student.

"Sorry," I said, gaze firmly planted on the ground.

"Are you okay?" asked Seventhirtyfour.

"Oh hi, it's Grey, isn't it? We're in Grapnel Basics together?" I looked up. It was the girl with the jewelled headband.

I adjusted my glasses. "Hello, yes, that's right, and you're... Sky Diamond, isn't it?"

"Lucy, please." She smiled. "Nice glasses."

"Thanks. I don't need them." Why would she want to know that?

She smoothed back her long dark hair behind her ears. "They are still nice though."

"Thanks and I like your..." I stopped. "You're wearing one of my pins."

"Oh, is this yours? I found it in the Gamma Bomb last night." She moved a hand to remove it.

"Keep it, it looks better on you."

"Thanks. Are you going somewhere?"

"Yes."

"Oh."

"Just a short trip. I'll be back in a couple of weeks."

"He's being modest," rumbled Seventhirtyfour. I'd

forgotten he was there. "He's leading a special mission to Bantus, direct orders from Captain Hawk. Top priority."

"Wow, really?"

I rubbed the back of my neck. "I… can't really talk about it, yet."

"Well when you can, I'd like to hear about it."

"Sure. Of course. We'd… probably better get going, we have a flight."

"Okay, Grey. I'm glad we bumped into each other."

"Me too. And sorry about that, again."

I followed Seventhirtyfour to the spaceport. For some reason, he was whistling a jaunty tune as he strolled.

I punched him on the arm. "What are you so happy about?"

"Nothing at all, Grey, nothing at all. Although… I'm a little disappointed she recognised you while you were wearing the glasses."

# # #

The trip to Aviary was unremarkable. Sunbolt's lessons were not as bad as I feared. For the most part, we worked from our own assigned texts and avoided asking questions unless we really needed to. His answers were terse but usually accurate. Fortunately, neither of the ships on the first two legs of the journey provided space for combat training so apart from some brightly-lit glares, we avoided his worst excesses. Otherwise, he kept to himself, and we were happy that way.

Aviary was just as I remembered it. Meaning that it was like every other station out there. Well, mostly. Run by a Polifan corporation, the top level was a wide empty space where you could really stretch your wings. Avrim took to the air, while the rest of us grabbed a coffee between flights. Sunbolt sat slightly apart from us students, not separate, but distant enough to make a point.

"Grey," said Pilvi.

It was time. "Yes, I know, I promised you more details before we reached Bantus. I've been thinking long and hard on the journey so far, and I can only see one way for this to play out. We need to split up."

"Now wait a minute," said Sunbolt.

"I've checked the population data on Bantus and it's clear, they don't have Brontom or Polifan inhabitants, Seventhirtyfour and Avrim are going to stick out when the mission needs to be covert. You're going to draw attention, and I figure we lean into it. Sunbolt, I want you with them. The three of you are going to do exactly what superheroes do: go on patrols, stop some muggings, rescue some people. I want people to notice you, I want you to make the news cycle if you can." I flicked a file from my wrist pad to them. "Here are a few local journalists who might take the bait. I want the three of you to be big news on Bantus."

Seventhirtyfour's chest was swelling, this was the job he was grown for. "But," I said "I don't want you engaging the crime families directly. If you stop muggings, you'll ruffle the Campbell's feathers, but that's the limit. Don't do anything too big. I want people thinking about you, but not targeting you. Not yet."

"And what will you be doing?" Sunbolt asked.

"Me, Pilvi and Gadget Dude will blend in easily enough. We'll take a later flight, travel on assumed names, and then I'm going to approach the Bowriders."

"Your mother wanted you to target the Tazforj."

"They have hackers who could slice through our identities in no time. The Bowriders we might be able to fool, for a while." I really didn't want the Tazforj looking too closely at me, or my double layer of fake identities. "Pilvi will back my play there. Gadget Dude, I need you to provide tech support."

Gadget Dude nodded and passed me a small box. It had

a wind-up key on one face and a large red button on the top.

"Great. Thanks?"

"I don't approve the plan," said Sunbolt.

"Pardon?"

He folded his arms. "If you split up, I can't monitor all of you. I am the responsible adult here, I can't let you go into this alone."

"You can. I thought Captain Hawk was clear, you're here for when I get in trouble. You don't get to override me before we've even started. I think I just made it clear, of the two groups, yours is in more direct danger. Look after Seventhirtyfour and Avrim."

"I will speak to the headmaster."

"Fine. Do that. In the meantime, I will be rearranging our flights."

He stormed off in one direction, I chose the other.

At the reservation terminal, I pushed the reservations for me, Pilvi and Gadget Dude back a flight. Our new journey was a little slower and we'd arrive almost a full day after the others. Perfect.

I took a moment, stared out of the big observation window to the planet above. Blue and gold, a world of oceans and deserts. A smear of lights along one coastline would be a large city, Worrastasa, I think? A Polifan world, like the Aviary itself.

I grabbed a water tube from a nearby vendor and took a moment to enjoy the solitude. I was all alone in the crowd again. Over behind the vendor's cart was an access panel to the maintenance tunnels, I knew. Twenty seconds of distraction, and I could be in there and away. No superhero in the galaxy would ever find me.

I finished my water and walked back to the group.

# # #

By the time we got to Bantus IV, I was convinced

my plan wasn't going to work. But it was still better than 'mother's' plan because I knew significantly less about tax law than I did about being a superhero. And it was rapidly becoming apparent I knew nothing about that.

Irritatingly, Sunbolt was better equipped in that department. The news headlines on Bantus were all about a new trio of heroes who were cleaning up the streets. At first, I was worried that they were over-playing their role, but when I read the articles behind the headlines, I was reassured that they really hadn't done so much. Worked the public relations, a few low-key but news-worthy heroics. I was sure I had Sunbolt to thank; Seventhirtyfour would have been too keen, and Avrim too reluctant, Sunbolt would have been the one to walk the line. I'd call him and thank him, but I really wanted to keep our teams separate. Probably nobody was watching them, but it would be a shame to spoil the planning by calling attention to the link between us.

Of late, my life seemed to be ruled by people who may or may not exist and may or may not be watching what I do. It's not a fun way to live, I don't recommend it.

I checked us into a chain hotel near the spaceport. The receptionist was a friendly Zalex woman, who I think took something of a shine to Gadget Dude, though I'm no expert on the dating rituals of the Zalex. I do know that Gadget Dude shaded to purple every time she smiled at him. I took that as a sign of something.

When we got up to our rooms, I left Pilvi and Gadget Dude unpacking. I was too fidgety and nervous to wait, so I clipped my grapnel gun to my belt and headed straight back out, taking a bag of the jewellery with me.

The late evening air was cold after the nicely temperature-regulated ship. Really, what's so great about outdoors anyway? Going out in Bantus wasn't as stressful as navigating the quad at the Academy, thankfully. Yes, there was open sky between the buildings, but the people of Bantus had contained all that open air by creating footbridges between buildings, stringing cables across roads, by putting up brightly-lit advertising boards and by having a naturally dark and overcast climate. I didn't like knowing that the sky was up there but found it easier to tune it out with the combination of neon and bustling street scenes.

This part of Bantus was an urban sprawl, the streets filled with people despite the lateness of the local hour. The roadsides were lined with small stalls or carts, selling food, drinks, trinkets, souvenirs. People bustled constantly, on their way to bars and nightspots, on their way home from late shifts. The few vehicles I saw attempt the streets weren't heading any faster than walking pace and the pedestrians seemed disinclined to let the cars through.

I stood for a while and watched an argument between a driver a stall holder, who had set up shop seemingly in the middle of the street. The driver was making the point, quite vehemently, that this was a road, not a market, while the vendor countered with an offer on a discounted hot dog. I got the impression they had been here for a while and were stuck at something of an impasse.

I watched for a few minutes, before dipping my hand into my jewellery bag and dropping a few of the cheap pieces on the roadside. Nobody seemed to notice.

Next, I stopped by a souvenir stall and studied their wares. Apparently, the Trejo Tower was a popular tourist spot here, I think I'd even spotted it from the ship as we'd come in to land. But it was staring out at me from the stall too, in dozens of plastic replicas of various scales, it was on tea towels and t-shirts, baseball caps and mugs. All the cheapest and nastiest type of tat. I bought Pilvi an 'I climbed the Trejo Tower!' baseball cap, and while I was waiting to pay, scattered a few more of my jewellery smiles nearby. Cheap as they were, they were better quality than the stuff on the stall.

And so, it went. I circled the area, stopping at bars, shops, taxi ranks, anywhere that people might linger a little, and at each, I seeded my smile. I didn't cross the main plaza but edged around it where the sky was less intimidating. Wherever I lingered to study café menus or laugh at the street entertainers, a few more pieces of jewellery found their way from my bag.

When I came across a crowd staring up at the sky, I braved a glance upwards to see Sunbolt and Avrim lazily circling the plaza, making a show of being out on patrol. I grinned to myself, and while the on-lookers gossiped about the superheroes, I slipped cheap jewellery into their pockets and bags.

My supply was severely depleted after a couple of hours of wandering, and I turned my step back towards the hotel. The trip out hadn't been all about the smiles. I'd also gotten a sense of the street layout around the hotel. I'd spotted a few potential bolt-holes if everything went badly wrong, and against my better judgement, I'd plotted a few roof-top runs that would be quicker than street level. I didn't mind heights, but the roofs, well running on top of them, generally meant they weren't above you, as the Great Architect had intended.

I turned down an alley-way that I'd spied earlier would make a good shortcut, and almost ran straight into a reminder of why I was there.

I'd let the general bustle of the place distract me, but Bantus was ruled by criminal families, and there at the end of the alley, were three people who I assumed were associated with the Campbells, working over a tourist. Souvenirs and shopping lay scattered about, as they shoved him back and forth.

I retreated before any of them noticed me. I couldn't let myself be seen before I was ready to stage-manage it.

But... damn.

I glanced back around, in time to see one of the muggers knock their victim to the ground. The victim wailed in fear and pain as one of the others kicked him in the stomach.

Dammit.

I couldn't be seen, couldn't. But I'd been hanging around Seventhirtyfour too long, and I couldn't let this pass either.

Muttering about the general idiocy of superheroes, I pulled my scarf up to cover most of my face and pulled on the cap to cover most of the rest. If I moved fast... I wasn't planning to take on the muggers, just getting their victim out of there. Fortunately, I was still carrying the grapnel gun, so in theory, I could be in and out in a blink.

I could hear sobbing punctuated with kicking.

Now or never.

I ran fast and quiet, no battle cry to draw attention while I covered the open ground between us. It cost the victim another kick, but it greatly increased the chances we'd both get out of there alive.

No science or strategy really, I barrelled at full speed into the nearest and cannoned him into his buddies. They went down in a tangle of startled swearing. I almost followed them but twisted as we fell so I landed on their victim, not them.

"Hold on," I growled at him, and pulled him up. The muggers were untangling themselves and drawing pulse pistols, as I aimed my grapnel towards the rooftops. *Please work*. I pulled the trigger.

The recoil felt like somebody had stamped on my hand, it went numb, but I held on for dear life. My aim was way off, and the rocket claw sailed over the roof ledge that I'd aimed for, but a heartbeat later, I heard a clank. I prayed it had caught on something... and flicked the switch to reel us in.

My rescuee's grip tightened painfully around me, as we both hurtled sky-wards. Hopefully, the frightened wail came from him too, but, yeah, it's fifty-fifty.

Almost before I could process, we were moving, my shoulder slammed into the edge of the roof, and we were carried up and over.

Pulse fire rippled across the roof edge. Chips of the concrete sparked and burned. *Too close.*

I checked that we'd both made it intact. And then as my rescuee had a bit of a weep I looked about for a way off the roof, angrily and deliberately not looking up. If I looked up, we were both likely lost, and I wasn't going to let that happen. I fought the shakes, wasn't sure if it was my sensible fear of open sky or the sudden dump of adrenaline, but either way, I couldn't afford it now.

I'd lost my baseball cap in the escape, but the scarf still covered the lower half of my face. "This way, if you want to live," I said in my best vigilante growl.

The man, the teenager, he was about my age, swallowed hard, then nodded. "Who are you?" he asked.

"I'm the Grey..." Accountant? Ghost? Avenger? None of them sounded right.

"The Grey?" he repeated.

Great, now my superhero name was the same as my assumed secret identity... I'd have to work on that.

"This way," I repeated, and we ran.

Two blocks over, and I led us down a fire escape, another two and we came down to ground level, my first thought was to merge with a crowd. I didn't think the muggers were still chasing us, they were opportunist thugs, not after this guy in particular. I figured we were probably safe already, but get amongst a crowd, and they definitely wouldn't chase after us. Then I remembered I was supposed to be a shadowy vigilante keeping a low profile. Either way, I couldn't go running through a street scene.

I stopped just before the exit to the alley. "You should be safe from here," I said, still pitching my voice to a growl. My throat was starting to hurt. As I talked, I fired the grapnel gun again; it caught on a walkway two stories above me, and I zipped upwards into the shadows, disappearing into the night like a ghost.

At least in my mind.

I got back to the hotel, I don't quite remember that journey, but I did.

Pilvi looked shocked when she saw me, I must have looked a state. "What happened?" she asked. "Did something go wrong?"

I shook my head. "I'm fine." But I wasn't feeling it. I was feeling shocky, nauseous, and was barely holding the shakes off. "I'm going to bed," I mumbled and retreated in fair order to my room.

I slumped to the floor, back against the door, and just shivered. I couldn't understand my reaction. This was hardly my first time running from people who wished me harm, that was a semi-regular event. It was the first time someone had ever shot at me though, that was probably part of it. And being outside hadn't helped. And the look on my rescuee's eyes, as though he was putting all his faith, his life, into my hands...

I wasn't sure I was cut out to be a superhero.

I showered, which calmed me a little and fell into bed, but sleep was a long time coming.

# # #

The next morning, it was time to swing into action, but thankfully not as a superhero. I was going to be back on much more comfortable ground today, I was going to be telling my big fat lie. And the target of the lie was the leader of the Bowriders, a Cholbren by the name of Wardegar Bowrider.

He had been the obvious choice for several reasons. Firstly, of the three crime lords, he was the one that was easiest to locate, he owned a bar called the Smuggler's Cove on the east side of the city. Secondly, the Bowriders were the most likely to take the bait... the Campbells might just beat me up on principle, and the Tazforj probably had more resources to fact check the lies. Plus, the Bowriders were probably the closest to the type of person I was claiming to be. They'd relate and making the story relatable was half the scam.

I asked Pilvi to go business formal, and I unpacked Gravane's suit. It looked good on me, plain, simple, but obviously expensive. The only remarkable feature of either of our outfits was the smile jewellery we wore prominently on our lapels, mine shining in gold, hers in silver.

Gadget Dude would monitor us using some micro-transmitters he'd whipped up. He wasn't coming in with us, but if things went badly wrong, he could contact the others.

We took a cab across town and went to a coffee shop opposite Bowrider's restaurant. We ordered drinks and sat while I watched out of the window.

Pilvi was quiet, subdued, she hadn't said much in the cab over and didn't seem to be in the mood to chat now either. I gave her my best reassuring smile, but she grimaced in reply.

"This is not going to work," she said at last.

"It will work," I said, with confidence I didn't feel. "This first meeting, we're not selling them on anything other than the fact that we exist. Which clearly we do."

"I don't know that I can 'sell' even that, I'm an awful liar. I've had to write down the fake name you gave me, or I'm going to forget it."

"As long as you've not written it anywhere that Bowrider is going to see," I said, and I checked the back of her hands for pen marks. "Besides, I'll do all the talking. I don't need you to lie, I just need you to be there so that I am not just a lone nutter."

"No, we're just a *pair* of nutters."

"That's the spirit!"

I paused, because I'd just seen a car pull up, and three people get out. One of them was Wardegar Bowrider himself.

"Okay, he's here, we'll give him time to settle, and then head over. Remember, no need to talk, but if anyone asks your name, just tell them you're ..."

"Kaisla Mistral."

"Right you are," I grinned.

We crossed over to the Smuggler's Cove. It was near the end of the lunch-time rush, so the place was busy, but beginning to thin out. The waiting staff were cleaning, reading credit sticks, and pushing the bon hommie to try and squeeze a bigger tip. The Cove itself had something of a pirate theme, I guess because dressing up as pirates was easier than as smugglers... what do smugglers even wear? But it was well done, classy even, no cheap plastic parrots or eye patches, just wenches and corsairs and... I wasn't sure what the two Zalex staff were wearing, presumably traditional Zalex pirate clothes? I'd ask Gadget Dude later.

Wardegar Bowrider and his cronies were sharing a drink at a private table near the back. *Burglars, smugglers and pirates.* These were people not to be trifled with, used to getting their own way, and travelling through life unchallenged. I couldn't ignore the threat they represented, but I couldn't let it intimidate me either.

We let a waiter show us to a table, I made sure that my seat faced Bowrider. I took out a pad I'd prepared earlier, slid it across to the waiter. "When you get a moment, if you could show that to Mr. Bowrider, it would be in all our best interests." I gave her a winning smile.

I ordered the 'Weigh Anchor', a sharing sampler of

starters and a glass of mineral water. Pilvi just went for a coffee.

The waiter took the pad over to Bowrider's table, handed it to one of his henchmen, and pointed back at our table. For our part, we didn't react, sat calmly awaiting our drinks. No eagerness, non-threatening, calm, cool, professional. On the outside anyway.

The henchman looked at the file on the pad, shrugged, and was about to pass it back to the waiter, but before he could, Bowrider beckoned it to him, curious. *Gotcha*. I pushed down my elation. That was only one step.

A few minutes later, the waiter approached us and told us that Mr. Bowrider would like to see us.

"Of course, thank you."

I stood, and Pilvi followed me across the room.

Bowrider waved us to sit. As we did, he tapped the pad. "This is genuine?"

"It is." It wasn't.

"I notice you have left one rather important piece of information off." Bowrider slid the pad back across the table towards me. I noticed him notice my pin as he did. Did he recognise it? I thought perhaps he did.

"Naturally. It is a calling card, not a sample."

Bowrider laughed. "Well as a calling card, it lacks the rather tricky issue of names. Not your name, not the name of the station, or the names of any of the ships you claim to be shipping through there."

I folded my hands on the table and smiled. Everything calm and studied, every movement controlled. If you can't control your surroundings, control yourself, that's lesson one of running a scam. "Then allow me to correct some of that. My name is Michael Andrews, this is my colleague Kaisla Mistral. The ship which no doubt caught your attention is the Fortune's Favour, a light transport registered to the Gravane corporation, and, yes, that manifest is accurate. The prototype security drones are valuable, and you certainly don't want them being supplied to Bantus security."

Bowrider drummed his fingers on the table. "All of which is very nice, but without the name of the station, it doesn't really help me."

I gave a short, seated bow. "Indeed. My organisation..."

"Oh, your 'organisation'," he interrupted.

"My organisation feels that particular bit of information should have a price attached. We have approached you as none of us wants Bantus security to get those prototypes, and your organisation seems best placed to prevent it. However, the Tazforj might also suit our purposes, so perhaps, if this is of no interest...?"

Bowrider sat back, grinning broadly, relaxed suddenly. "Ah, so this is a shake-down. I confess Mr. Andrews, I wasn't sure what to make of you at first, but now that's clear, I think we all know where we stand. Go on then, amaze me. What's the price? How many thousands of credits?"

I did my best 'startled and offended'. "You misunderstand. My organisation does not need money. We can accrue that very nicely for ourselves. What we desire is a meeting of all four crime families of Bantus IV." I saw Pilvi's eyes widen at the number 'four', but Bowrider missed it, thankfully. "Because it's time we stopped the Gravanes. They are bringing superheroes to our quiet little world, and they are decidedly bad for business. And that is something we can only do together."

He looked at me like I was crazy (points for him, I guess), but he didn't interrupt or contradict me. I'd just told the biggest fattest of lies and he hadn't called me on it.

I stood. "Now. I will leave you to decide that price. My number is on the pad. Once you have decided, either way, please do contact me. If you choose to ignore this, then we will be speaking to the Tazforj. Ms Mistral, let us leave these gentlemen to their lunch."

It took every iota of self-control to not run from the Cove, but I walked very carefully, and with a very precise and determined gait, out of the restaurant. To my astonished relief, the only person to follow me was Pilvi.

"What..." she began.

"Not yet," I whispered back. Time for that when we got back to the hotel.

# # #

We took every shortcut and switchback I'd worked out, took and changed taxis twice until I was completely sure we hadn't been followed. And then we cut through shops, took a tram, and reached the point when I nearly got us lost. Only then did we head back to the hotel. Pilvi spent the entire time clearly itching to ask questions, but also clearly understood they had to wait until we got somewhere safe.

The moment I closed the door to our suite behind us, she turned on me.

"What the hell was all that?"

"Okay, so it didn't go quite the way I said it would," I admitted "but it went pretty well, I thought. We got his attention, that's the main thing."

"Did you just tell him we were a fourth crime family?" Pilvi poked me in the chest, hard.

"No. Absolutely not." I backed away a little, around the table, she advanced as I retreated. Gadget Dude watched us both, bemused.

"It's possible," I admitted, "that I *implied* the existence of a fourth crime family, but I never actually said it was us. Of course, if you made that leap, then hopefully they did too. The lies you tell yourself are always more convincing than the ones someone else told you."

"But there is no fourth crime family. There's just us!"

"Wellll... that's only true in the strictest sense. Look,

the names I gave for us were false, even if they don't assume that, a simple directory check will confirm it. Neither name registered on Bantus... which is kind of weird for a name like 'Michael Andrews' don't you think?"

She stared at me, looked ready to poke me in the chest some more, so I continued quickly. "The suits were plain, nothing to go on there, but we were both wearing a pin. I did the talking, so... gold outranks silver... maybe Bowrider will think it's some sort of rank insignia. If it is, he'll have his people look for more..."

She looked horrified. "And you dropped hundreds of those things last night."

"It was more like a couple of thousand in the end, but, yeah. Most will end up down drains or in the waste, but some will get picked up, and I made them cheap enough to not be worth handing in, but pretty enough to wear. So, some people will wear them."

"Maybe, two or three, maybe," she said.

"It was one in twelve when I tried it at the Academy. So... let's say it's more like one in twenty that see the pin and like it enough to put it on. If Bowrider goes looking, he will start seeing our pin, the rank insignia of our crime family... all over the place."

"Even if it works..."

"Actually, it did work, I saw three of them myself out today, and we don't have an actual crime family to do the legwork. Once Bowrider starts looking, sending out his people to go looking, they're going to find several, maybe many, more."

I watched her work it out. "But," she said slowly "that means you've just inducted dozens of people into a crime family that doesn't exist without them knowing it."

She'd stopped chasing me for the moment, so I took the chance to retreat to a comfy chair and grab a drink from the mini-bar. "I know," I said, grinning. "Genius, right?"

"No! Not genius! Bowrider is a thug, he's going to pull in one of those innocent bystanders and ask them questions, questions they won't know the answer to. It's going to get people hurt."

I shook my head. "Not likely. Bowrider is a businessman. He has all those waiting staff in the Cove working for him, they're part of his family, but nobody expects them to know anything. He knows there's no point pulling in any of the bronze pins, he wants a silver or a gold for information."

Gadget Dude poked his silver pin dubiously.

"Look," I said "if we'd tried this with the Campbells, yes, a real risk, they *are* just thugs, but I'm betting that Bowrider has more class than that. And besides, so far, we're a curiosity to him, we've implied some stuff, sure, we've offered some, admittedly dodgy, but seemingly useful information. The better play for him now is to keep on our good side, until he knows more about us."

"That's a pretty big bet on a guy you've met for five minutes."

"I'm betting on me, not him."

She slumped into a chair next to me. "All the same, maybe we should call Seventhirtyfour to keep an eye on the Bowriders to make sure they don't hurt anyone with a pin."

"No, we can't do that, sorry. The others are an implied threat hanging over all organised crime on Bantus. If they start targeting just one or two families it breaks down. We have to make them, and the Gravanes, a big enough reason for all the families to agree to meet."

She sighed. "And why put your family name out there?" she asked with an air of resignation.

"Mother wanted me to make sure that people knew the solution came from the Gravanes. She was really clear on that."

"How can you be sure they will even go for it? We're talking about the three most dangerous people on the planet who are already at each other's throats. Why would they even willingly go into the same room as each other?" asked Pilvi.

"Because they do. On some level, they must. You don't just fall into a situation with such clear boundaries as Bantus has. They must meet, on occasion, to agree on limits, spheres of influence." I'd realised that as soon as Captain Hawk outlined the arrangement. "And the idea that there may be a fourth power base out there is exactly the kind of thing they would deal with. Chances are they will want to crush us, quickly."

"Brilliant."

"But we need more than that. If all we do is foster a new spirit of co-operation amongst the organised crime families, we've pretty much failed."

"That much we can agree on," said Pilvi. "So, what's next?"

And there was the question I'd really been dreading because truth be told, I didn't have an answer yet. I'm a small-time grifter, my specialities are distraction and petty theft. Every instinct I had was that the solution started with getting the main players in a room, but after a week of going over this again and again, the end hadn't crystallised.

We needed to take them down at the meeting. Or get themselves to take each other down. Or get the police to arrest them all. Or... something.

"Wait, you really don't have a plan!" I heard Pilvi from a long way away.

Then Gadget Dude said in a whisper "Grey creates."

I blinked. "Okay. Okay, here's what we do."

CHAPTER 10
DIVERSIONS

First thing was to craft the perfect follow-up message to Bowrider. Something with enough encryption on it that any Tazforj watching, and of course they were, would be curious enough to hack. Gadget Dude leapt on that, creating a series of rotating encryption keys that would need parallel... *something* to break. I didn't really understand and was worried it was too difficult to hack.

"Not difficult, *interesting*," said Gadget Dude.

The actual message was my part, and a fine line to walk. I needed it to read one way by the Bowriders, and another by the Tazforj, but still look like it was a message written normally. The first draft turned out weird and stilted. The second draft was better, suggesting that there was an established alliance between the Andrews clan and the Bowriders if you read it without knowing the details of our meeting, but still came off a little full-on if you had been there. The third draft got it, but if any of this came to trial, I didn't really want to call too much attention to 'Andrews' for legal proceedings, so I took one final pass to vague it up a bit.

"It needs something. We should include some technical specifications of those prototypes. Gadget Dude, can you write something techy?"

He shook his head. "Gadgets art, not science. Follow song, not specifications."

"Really? You don't plan the things you make?"

He put a hand to his heart, then head. "Feel, not plan. Like Grey."

"I suppose the message works without it. Never mind."

Pilvi coughed. "You know I'm a science nerd, right?"

"You are? I thought your background was farming?"

"Grey, what do you think farming is?"

I knew a trap question when I heard one. "Tell me."

"It's biochemistry. Botany. Meteorology. Drone optimisation. I've spent more time in a lab than in a field. Give me an hour of research, I can give you something convincing."

"Perfect. We'll do it all again in a couple of days if the Bowriders don't set up the meeting before then. I want the Tazforj thinking the balance of power on Bantus is starting to shift. If they break the encryption, they should start to worry."

It was a good start, but was it enough? I'd circle back around to that once we'd got the Campbells on the hook.

# # #

After some agonising, I decided we needed the second team to help with the Campbells. And I needed Pilvi to put herself in harm's way. I would have been wary of a plan that did either, a plan that did both... Pilvi was up for it though.

She made it back to the hotel the next morning. "We did it just like we'd rehearsed, I walked down a few suspicious alleys until one of the Campbell goons jumped me. Yes, I managed to resist the urge to break his nose and let myself get 'rescued' by Sunbolt. You owe me big for that, by the way."

"Yes, sorry."

"And then we made sure the mugger saw us conspiring together before Sunbolt blasted him unconscious."

"Great. Were you able to do it more than once?"

"Four different criminals now think there's a woman

in league with the superheroes. Do you think it'll get back to the Campbell leaders?"

"I would have thought so. That's why you had to do it a couple of times. Once word gets around and is corroborated, the bosses should hear about it. The bigger sticking point is will they recognise you at the meeting? We'll burn that bridge when, if, we get to it."

# # #

Bowrider contacted me two days later. "It's on. Tomorrow morning, 10 am."

"Excellent news. My organisation has a pitch which I think you will all find fascinating," I said.

"This had better be worth it, kid."

"You can be sure it will be profitable all around. I have arranged for us to use the conference centre at the top of Trejo tower. I thought neutral ground would be best, and we can all see things coming from a mile away."

"I'll spread the word."

Now I needed to book Trejo tower, and it wouldn't come cheap. For the first and last time, in the direct service of Gravane interests, in a place they expected Gravane to be, I wanted to try to access Gravane's bank account. If he used a different password for access, as he should, it'd be a bust. Worst case, I could tap Seventhirtyfour, he was the genuine billionaire superhero in our group, but I wanted to push my luck if I could.

Gravane's bank used high-grade security, the Ripper wouldn't be able to slice through it all, but I let it concentrate on the biometrics. I had the account information already, and maybe, maybe, the password. The Ripper pinged, and tentatively, I punched in Gravane's password.

I goggled at the balance, this guy really *was* loaded. I could have emptied his account then and there but didn't. I had no need of the money, beyond the needs of my current project.

It took a little extra cash to arrange it all last minute, but the Trejo company obliged; I took the top two floors, including a restaurant with excellent views of the city around it. Fine by me as long as the roof stayed on. I made sure they gave me a receipt. Perhaps someday I'd be called on to explain the expenses and every credit of it was going to be spent on Gravane interests, not mine.

I then gave the staff very strict instructions: serve the first round of coffees and then retire to a safe distance. I told them it was because the meeting was confidential, I didn't admit it was because I expected the meeting to turn violent. One way or another.

I looked to Gadget Dude and Pilvi. "Ready?"

"This is all going very fast, Grey."

"It has to. We don't have the numbers or the resources to sustain a long con. The more time they have to look at us, the easier it is for them to see right through us."

"I think Avrim would have the right words just now."

"Probably. Ready?"

"Ready," said Pilvi.

"Ready as ever," said Gadget Dude.

# # #

The representatives from the Campbells arrived first, twenty minutes early. I met them in the lobby with a smile and a warm handshake. My smiling pin had been polished until it glistened, and they all noted it. "Thank you for attending. Your involvement in the endeavour is extremely important. Come with me, we've laid on refreshments upstairs, you can get yourself comfortable while we wait for the others to arrive."

Hector Campbell, leader of the family, returned my greeting with a growl. Not one for pleasantries, it seemed. "These damn supers are the problem, not some fat cat corporates on a different world. We're here because we're not getting left out, but you better have something to sell other than spaceships and prototypes."

"My word, yes, I quite understand. Rest assured, I think you'll be quite pleased you made the effort to come along today. But, let us wait for everybody to arrive. Shall we?"

The key here was to appear calm, relaxed, non-threatening and non-threatened. It was not an easy sell when we got into the elevator together. All eight of the henchmen that Campbell brought towered above me and looked like they could snap me like a twig. I made a point to smile and nod at each one as we travelled upwards in uncomfortable silence.

When we reached the restaurant level, Campbell's goons spread out, and methodically and professionally searched the place. Opened every door, looked inside every cupboard. Searching for, I'm not sure, weapons? Listening devices? Hidden police? There was none of that to find, just me, Gadget Dude and the serving staff. I'd asked Pilvi to wait downstairs until her moment. And the cameras rolling to record this meeting were across town with a zoom lens and directional mic; one of two reasons to pick a nice up-high meeting venue.

I think the serving staff were a little freaked but weren't directly molested, so persevered.

I gave Campbell a wide smile. "I trust everything is satisfactory?"

He nodded, and lowered himself into an armchair, while his goons took up tactically strong positions around the room. He gestured for someone to bring him coffee. Sniffed the drink, then took a swig, and beckoned for more.

"Excellent," I said and collected a cup for myself. I fought off nervous shakes and took a sip. Decaf for me, I felt it best.

The Tazforj arrived at the precise moment that the

meeting was scheduled for. I gratefully beat a retreat from the restaurant and took the elevator down to greet them. Bayor Tazforj brought only two of his family. He was a fair-skinned Zalex, and like Gadget Dude was not prone to long conversation.

"Glad you could join us, we have important work to do here today," I said with a smile.

"Show to meeting," he replied.

This time in the elevator, I was the tall one, but somehow, still managed to be intimidated. The Tazforj were not the friendly soft-spoken Zalex I'd gotten used to hanging around Gadget Dude. They seemed to exude an air of frosty superiority, and while I assayed a smile at the first of them, it broke on his hard edges. Still, I had to plant another seed. I turned to Bayor. "It is a pleasure to finally meet you Mr. Tazforj. Wardegar has spoken of you often."

He didn't rise to the bait, but I saw an eyebrow twitch.

They swept out of the lift ahead of me. Bayor nodded to Hector, and took a seat near, but not very near him. The other two moved around the edge of the room placing small devices against each of the windows, a small box with an arm out of the top that extended out to touch the glass. Gadget Dude called them 'Warblers', designed to vibrate the window glass to stop people listening in simply by pointing a microphone at the glass. He assured me the microphone he had given to Seventhirtyfour wouldn't have a problem though.

I took the seat next to Bayor, placed what looked like a mini-pad on the armrest near him. "It really is a magnificent view from here," I said.

Bayor turned his back to me and spoke to Hector Campbell.

I left them to it, checked the time on my wrist pad. Where was Bowrider?

Campbell stood up. "If you called us here to waste

our time, little man, you've made a bad mistake. I came for Bowrider, if he is not even going to show up, then I am leaving. Boys." He looked me dead in the eye. "Break his legs."

There was a chorus of "Yes, Boss."

The elevator door pinged, and Wardegar Bowrider strode out, grinned like the swashbuckling pirate he was. "What's this, someone starting a party without me?"

Campbell held up a hand, and his goons paused, stepped back, much to my relief. He glowered at Bowrider. "I've wasted enough of my day on this already. I don't have time for your damn theatrics."

Bowrider sketched a quick bow. "My apologies, affairs of state and all that." He hopped over the back of a chair, folding himself into it with fluid grace. I hadn't seen it when I caught Bowrider relaxed at his restaurant, but he was a showman, this was supposed to be my stage, but he was pulling focus effortlessly. There was a style there to be studied and emulated. I started taking mental notes.

He looked around the room. "I see you felt the need to bring moral support with you, very wise."

"Nobody here alone," Tazforj said and shot me a glance.

"Right you are," I said with a smile. Confirming the lie that I'd put around that I was in cahoots with Bowrider. "Gordon, could you dim the lights." And then taking it back for Bowrider, letting him think I was talking about Gadget Dude ('Gordon' for this gathering's proceedings).

The presentation lit up in the middle of the room, a group shot that I'd staged earlier with as many people I could persuade to stand in one place wearing our pin. In a moment it wouldn't matter, but I needed a quick subliminal message to reinforce that the Andrews family wasn't just me Gadget Dude and Pilvi, even if it was.

"We at the Andrews family are here to offer you the opportunity of a lifetime, as market leaders in... public relations and marketing..." and let them fill in what the pause meant. "If you sign up with us..."

"What the hell is this?" Campbell was on his feet again, fuming. "You said you had something important to show us Bowrider, and this? This is what you brought us here for?"

I had him, almost there, just another little nudge. I pressed the remote in my pocket to signal Pilvi.

Bowrider shot me an angry glance but held up placating hands to the other mob bosses. "Gentleman, I know you're busy, perhaps we should skip the preamble? Let's just get to business."

"Yes, sir," I snapped to, flicking through dozens of slides I'd prepared for just this moment.

Tazforj stood up too. "Tell monkey to stop act. Not fooling us. He with you."

"What are you trying to pull Bowrider? What are you trying to sell us?"

"No, no, I assure you, the Andrews family is a wholly independent..." Yes, we were almost there, just needed...

The elevator door opened, and Pilvi stepped out, her Andrews pin sparkling in the spotlight.

"Boss, it's her! That woman working with the supers!"

"*You* brought them?" demanded Tazforj.

Campbell roared. "Kill everyone!"

# # #

The best way to end the conflict on Bantus was dedicated police work, political pressure and time. None of which were available. The only way I could think of to finish this quickly was to get the bosses of the families in prison. And the only way to do *that* was to get them out of their comfort zones and turn the screws, make them react the way I wanted them to.

Campbell was a thug, he expected and respected physical intervention. Sunbolt, Avrim and Seventhirtyfour supplied it. He was angry before he even arrived, he was by far the easiest to set off.

Tazforj at first glance was the hardest, but they were all about secrets and plots and hidden conspiracies. Present him with one and he'd reject it, let him *uncover* it, and he'd lap it up. And when threatened they were going to react just as badly as Campbell, if with more sophisticated tools.

And finally, Bowrider. He needed a show, he needed a challenge. We were too alike really, and he was the hardest to find a button to push. I'd let the others do it for me. Backed into a corner, he'd fight hardest of all.

So there, in a fishbowl above their town in plain view of anybody looking, and more particularly in the view of the cameras and microphones that Seventhirtyfour was running, three very clever, very serious, very dangerous men had a moment of stupidity.

They had spent years watching each other move around the criminal underworld of Bantus, suspicious of each other, protective of their own piece of the pie.

Cooler heads, on a calmer day, would have seen through the tissue of lies I'd given them, but right there in that single moment, Tazforj thought Bowrider had some grand trap waiting for him, Campbell thought I, and by extension Bowrider, was working with the superheroes, and Bowrider was wrong-footed and found himself fighting for his life.

# # #

"Pilvi! Down!"

She rolled behind a couch, while I elbowed one of Campbell's goons in the face and went to ground too. From the safety of the projection booth, Gadget Dude lobbed a flash-bang grenade.

Confusion to the enemy was the plan, but this was the first serious fight I'd been in, and it wasn't like the practice battles in the gym. This was chaos. I instantly lost track of all the major players. I hoped they would stay in one place long enough. Pilvi would have locked off the elevator as she was coming up, so nobody was leaving that way for the moment. There were fire exits and stairs, but... my planning went out of my head when one of the Tazforj slumped to the floor next to me; he was unconscious and bleeding badly.

One of the Campbells loomed over me, knife in hand. "You next, kid."

I kicked out, hard, to his kneecap, he staggered, and I took the moment's grace to get to my feet; if I stayed on the floor, I was dead. I risked a glance around me, but just caught movement, anger, violence, I couldn't really process it. Campbells had numbers, Tazforj had tech, Bowrider had skill. I had no idea who was winning. I just needed to stay alive and have the fight last long enough for the police to arrive.

The goon, limping slightly, lunged at me, leading with the knife-point, I grabbed for his wrist, caught it, pulled, twisted, threw. Just like I'd practised in class. The goon fell forwards, but I felt a line of fire across my ribs. I'd been too slow, he'd cut me, even as I over-balanced him. He lost the knife though, and instead of going for it again, he turned, fists clenched.

Pilvi struck him from behind with a lamp, low, taking his knees in a classic Power Ball tackle. He tumbled to the floor and Pilvi and I dragged each other towards Gadget Dude's bolt hole.

The fight was starting to thin now. Bowrider was standing surrounded by fallen Campbells, but he wasn't alone. Hector Campbell and his last two goons, circled him, trying to find an opening. Bowrider spared me a venomous glance. No doubt I wasn't his favourite person right then.

The Tazforj seemed to have fallen early. There was one by the door, the one that had fallen by the window and...

wait, where was Bayor?

I looked around frantically if he got away... there he was, lying on the floor behind a sofa a few feet away. And then he moved, and I realised he wasn't out of the fight, he was sneaking around towards where we were hiding, with some monstrous construction of a handgun.

He looked up and saw me staring at him.

There was a clatter of boots on the stairs. Seventhirtyfour had called the cops before the fight even started, and they were miraculously getting here right on time. I could hear them shouting.

Bayor stood up. "Not beaten by child," he spat. He levelled the gun right at me.

From behind me, a blur of blue as Gadget Dude lunged forward. He barrelled into Bayor, and his momentum carried them towards a window. They bounced against it, Gadget Dude holding Bayor's wrist, keeping the gun away from them both.

I clambered to my feet. "Hold on, Gadget Dude." Pilvi was right behind me.

There was a flash of energy from Bayor's hand cannon, a snap of noise like the whirring of a band saw, then a crash of glass as the window shattered. Gadget Dude recoiled, let go of Bayor's wrist, he stepped back.

"No!" I shouted. I ran towards them but there was too much ground to cover. I could only watch as Bayor Tazforj put his free hand to Gadget Dude's chest and pushed. My friend toppled out into open air, hundreds of meters above the ground.

Bayor turned his pistol back towards me.

"No."

There was an explosion of hot white light as Sunbolt burst through the window, sunbolts blazing from his eyes. Bayor dropped his gun as it heated in the blaze.

Sunbolt hovered in the centre of the room, eyes

smoking, hair a cascade of glowing energy. "Put your weapons down and surrender to the police," he demanded.

Bowrider and the two remaining Campbells dropped their weapons and put their hands up.

I scrambled to the window, but even before I got there, there was a sharp smell of mint, and the beat of massive wings; Avrim rose into view, awkwardly carrying Gadget Dude.

"Seriously," Avrim told him, "you have to stop doing that."

Gadget Dude grinned. "Again! Woo!"

Relief flooded through me. I reclaimed the thing which looked like a mini-pad, my Ripper, from the chair where I'd left it. Hopefully, it had ripped a tidy sum from Bayor's credit stick.

It was over.

I looked down at Bayor Tazforj. "You weren't beaten by children," I told him "You were beaten by superheroes."

CHAPTER 11
HOMECOMINGS

The police on Bantus questioned us for a week.

We stuck to our version of the truth: we'd hired the restaurant for a business meeting and were shocked and frightened when a fight broke out amongst those terrible people. I could tell the detectives weren't very convinced, but the footage that Seventhirtyfour sent them, the presentation from the meeting, every shred of physical evidence showed that our only role in the fight was as victims. I think they wanted to keep us longer but eventually caved to diplomatic influence from the Academy and political influence from the Gravane corporation.

The heads of the three crime families were going away. Perhaps only for a few weeks, depending on how the lawyers wrangled it, but it would give the people of Bantus a respite at least. I was worried that it might yet lead to fighting in the streets, but the power vacuums left by Campbell, Tazforj and Bowrider seemed limited to the ranks of their organisations for now. I'd call it a win, even if I wasn't sure what I'd achieved long-term.

Regardless, I got a thank you note from Gravane's contact on the planet, so, tick. I'd done as Mrs. Gravane asked.

I had one last job to do before we left.

My Ripper had worked on Bayor Tazforj's credit stick throughout the fight. I couldn't get to his main account, but as I hoped, he was the sort of guy that liked to carry flash cash on him. Twenty thousand credits. An insignificant drop by the Tazforj organisation's standards, sure. But enough to get someone back on their feet once all their funds were wiped out.

I took Gadget Dude with me on one last tour of the city, finishing up in the artisan quarter, where dozens of small craft industries plied their trades. The sort of places that made things by hand despite the availability of cheaper mass-produced options.

The smell of wood and varnish in the cabinet maker's storefront was remarkable. Not the ozone and grease of home, but still pleasant. Wardrobes and dressers lined one wall, exquisitely produced, each an individual work of art.

The Zalex woman who ran the store came and stood near me. Not enough that I felt crowded, but so I knew I could call on her if I had a purchase in mind or questions to answer. Behind her, her young daughter sat on the store counter, playing with off-cuts of wood, stacking them into towers, then knocking them over.

"These are very impressive," I said.

"Listen to song," the Zalex woman said. "Wood knows what to be."

"I wish I had a place for this wardrobe, but I'm going off world tonight. Do you have smaller, decorative pieces?"

She nodded. "Wait, fetch."

I ambled over towards the display counter. Gadget Dude stayed by the wardrobe, put one ear against it, nodded appreciatively. I guess he liked the song.

"Hi there," I said to the daughter. "What's your name?"

"Ix," she said, then her eyes widened. "Same badge!" She pointed to my smile pin, still stuck to my lapel, then at her jacket, which had four of the bronze pins stuck to it.

I laughed. "Here, you can have mine to add to your collection." I unclipped it and passed it over.

She received it with great reverence, then pinned it to

her jacket.

"Actually, I have something else for you. Well, for you and your mum. Can I give it to you?"

She nodded solemnly.

"I saw you and your mum on the news before I came to Bantus. I want you both to have this." I put my Ripper on the counter, still primed with Tazforj's cash. "I hope it helps."

I gathered up Gadget Dude, and we bailed, before Ix's mum came back.

# # #

"And that's when I knew we couldn't stand by any longer, that we were needed here," Sunbolt told the assembled journalists and photographers at the spaceport. Avrim and Seventhirtyfour silently flanked him, both looked a little embarrassed and awkward with all the attention. "But the call to action is never-ending, and now I must journey on to the next world crying out under the heel of injustice." The white light in his eyes and from his hair blazed.

"Uh-huh. And do you have any comment that your action was associated with and financed by Mirabor Gravane of the Gravane Corporation?" asked a journalist. In my imagination, she was all hard-bitten and chewing gum in a no-nonsense way, but I couldn't see her in the crowd from where we were.

I turned away, hunched my shoulders, put on Seventhirtyfour's glasses. "Time to get out of here," I told Pilvi and Gadget Dude. "I don't mind the name being associated with the mission, but I don't want any captioned photos."

We made our flight unmolested by the press and enjoyed the first leg of the journey back to the Academy without Sunbolt's tutoring.

# # #

The first time the six of us got to compare notes about our field trip was back in a café on Aviary. I had just enough left on my credit stick to buy coffees for everyone, I'd end my time as a trainee superhero as I started it. Sunbolt sat slightly apart from the group, far enough to make the distinction, but close enough to join in. I mirrored him, close enough to feel a part one last time, but far enough to create some distance.

"You were amazing," rumbled Seventhirtyfour. "The three of you against a dozen hardened mobsters? It's what the Academy is all about, you know? Taking what you do best, whether it's a superpower or not, and helping people."

"And then keeping your head down until the guy with actual powers turns up," Sunbolt drawled.

"I'm just glad Avrim was there to save Gadget Dude," said Pilvi.

"Avrim save? When?"

"Do you think that's what your prophecy was about, Seventhirtyfour?" Avrim asked.

Seventhirtyfour choked.

"I guess it has to be, right?" said Pilvi.

I let their conversation wash over me, kept quiet and sipped my coffee. My pretence had gone on longer than it had any right to. I should have been found out weeks before, and any day I delayed now was going to increase that risk. Put myself at the bottom of the Academy's gravity well again, there was no way I'd make it out without blowing my cover. It was time.

Seventhirtyfour put two hands to his temples, the lower pair gripped the table. He crossed his eyes and muttered. "I see... I see..." The others laughed, egging him on. He gasped, and spoke in a tumble of words: "I see Grey with a black eye, but it's not Grey?"

"Truly your powers are amazing. You're predicting someone other than Grey will get a black eye at some point in the future?" asked Sunbolt. "However could you know?"

Seventhirtyfour, I think I'd miss the most. Considering he'd unwittingly chased me into the Academy, I had a lot to thank him for, one way or another. That he just assumed we were friends from day one, his endless enthusiasm, he had the biggest heart of anyone I'd ever met. It was such a shame that on our one and only mission we didn't get to spend time together.

I stood. "I'm just getting a refill. I'll be right back."

I crossed the café, ducked out of the back door, left the life of superheroes, and of Mirabor Gravane, behind me.

# # #

First order of business was to get off Aviary. They would likely search for me eventually, and it was probably better if I was far away before the search started.

A quick jog across station to find the service lifts. Slide in behind a pair of workers managing a wheeled cage of parts. Duck down a service shaft to avoid the security door. A bump on the grate at the end, while lifting the bottom edge with my fingertips, and I was out into the docks.

Always busy, always bustling this is the part of the process that most travellers don't see. Most people assume it's all automated, and sure the heavy lifting is all done by autonomous pallet-skiffs and semi-intelligent loaders, but every step of the way is managed and monitored by people. Eye-balling conveyors, double-checking everything from destination tags on individual bags to load distribution on heavy freighters. In charge of all the comings and goings, of people, cargo, and ships, was the Polifan dockmaster.

I knocked on the bulkhead beside the doorway to his office. "Hi Luada, how's tricks?"

He looked up from his terminal, scowling. "Get back to wor... wait... is that little Andy?"

"Right you are, boss," I lied. "You're looking good, Lu.

Have you lost weight?"

He patted his ample stomach. "Med techs tell me if I want to keep air-worthy, I need to shed a few kilos yet. He got in a right flap about it." I remembered his poor jokes and booming laugh. "But look at you, you've added more than a few kilos and centimetres since you were last here. What was it? Eight years ago?"

"Only five, boss. Feels like a lifetime, though."

He held up a finger for me to wait, tapped on his terminal. "Flight AQ-291 is cleared for departure," he said into the mic. "No rest for the wicked. So, what are you doing with yourself these days?"

"Oh, this and that. Nothing permanent. Actually, I was hoping you might be able to help on that front. Are there any ships hiring? I've got itchy feet, was hoping to send some sky by them again."

"Maybe, maybe. I assume you do more than just run messages these days?"

"Lots more. Most recently I've been working for a corporation doing… event management. But I'm looking for some solid crew work. Destination doesn't matter much." Just as long as I didn't end up crewing the flight back to the Academy.

He spoke into his terminal again. "Hold flight KD-909. Check that, I have a green. KD-909 is cleared." He scratched his chin. "Damndest thing. I'd almost forgotten, but a couple of days ago, I got a message about you. And for you."

"For me?"

He tapped a few times on his terminal. "They didn't ask for you by name, just a picture. Said you'd likely be looking for a ship. I didn't recognise it until now, still thought of you as a gangly runner underfoot."

My shoulders tightened. "Can I see the picture?"

"Of course, here." He twisted the terminal to face me. Not great quality, looked like a zoom of a security photo, but there was no mistaking it was me, dressed in Gravane's business suit; taken on Bantus, recently.

"And somebody sent this to you?"

"Not to me specifically. The recipient list was long. I recognised dockmasters for a few stations in this area."

Hell. "What did the message say?"

"Just to keep an eye out for you. And to give you a vid file to look at, if I saw you. You in trouble, Andy?"

"For a change, not really."

"You want the file?"

"Let me have a look at the list of recipients." I skimmed it. Most of the names meant nothing to me, but the addresses, I recognised enough of those. This had been sent to every station within a couple of jumps of Bantus. Someone who knew I'd been there wanted to get in touch with me. The fact that they weren't looking for Mirabor Gravane, or Michael Andrews by name... that said something. No idea what, though. "Give me the file."

He flicked it to my wrist pad. "You still want that crew job?"

"Hold off on that. Let me watch the video first. Thanks, Lu."

# # #

I found a quiet, dark area of the docks and opened the file. A tinny voice said, "Please state your name for verification."

Which name? So many to choose from. But the person in the picture... that wasn't me. As far as most people looking for the person in the picture knew, that was "Mirabor Gravane."

The screen faded to black, a single word in white text emblazoned across the centre:

Liar.

Something very cold gripped my chest. What was this?

The word faded out, and the shape of a face slowly faded in to replace it, filling the screen, distorted because the camera was so close, but there was no mistaking who it was. The real Mirabor Gravane. But not in the state I'd last seen him. This Gravane's face was smudged with dirt and sweat, his lip was split, his chin reddened with dried blood. One eye was swollen shut, the other was blood-shot and unfocused. His head bowed toward the camera, making his forehead appear massive, then something, someone, pulled his head back up again, and not kindly. Gravane's face contorted in obvious pain, all in eerie silence. There was no audio on the image.

It faded to black again, before more text faded in.

We have him, but nobody believes us.
Fade.
His life is in your hands.
Fade.
Five million credits.
Fade.
Two weeks.

What did Gravane need right now? A superhero?

He didn't need me, that was for sure. If I hadn't left my Ripper on Bantus... without it, I couldn't bypass the biometrics on Gravane's account, I couldn't get at his money to pay the ransom. I had nothing. The most I'd ever scammed in a week was a few hundred credits. I wouldn't know where to start making five million.

There was no way to bargain or bluff. I didn't know who sent the message, from where. The sender information was fake; I could have spotted that even without the training in Prof Craft's class.

Perhaps I could just vanish. They had no way of knowing

the message had even reached me. The kidnappers' problem was that despite their claims, with me in the frame, Mirabor Gravane didn't appear lost. They didn't have leverage. But if I vanished... would they go back to plan A and tap the family again? Or would they cut their losses? They clearly weren't above harming their bargaining chip.

And if I couldn't risk vanishing. Where would I go? Where could they be sure to contact me again?

Right.

# # #

"Grey! You agree with me, don't you?" asked Seventhirtyfour.

I hooked a thumb back over my shoulder. "I was just at the..." I said. "Wait, agree about what?"

"That all the fighting we did on Bantus should give us extra credit for self-defence. Sunbolt says we've not trained enough."

"Right," said Sunbolt. "I did the only real fighting, and even that was over in less than a minute. I'm not giving myself extra credit, so I'm certainly not giving you any. If anything, you losers need more mat time now than when you left. I have some very particular refresher lessons in mind for all of you."

I sat back down, defeated. I'd been so close to getting away, but really, there was no choice. I wasn't done with the Academy yet.

Pilvi leaned in close, whispered to me. "Grey, are you okay? You were gone a long time."

Just tell her. That would be it. Ask for help. They would all give it. "I'm fine. I... just had some bad news. Family stuff. Don't worry."

She put a hand on my wrist. "If you need to talk, I'm a good listener."

I gave her a tight smile. "Thanks. But... I need to process

it myself first."

"Okay."

# # #

Crossing the quad was more difficult than ever. I'd thought it was behind me. Thought I could go out on a high, but I was back and the feeling of triumph of Bantus was a fleeting memory. Instead, I was walking underneath that damn sky again, aching, bruised and stiff – Sunbolt had made good on his promise – and worried not just for me, but for Gravane's life as well.

This had all been a game once, right?

We scattered to our various accommodation blocks. Seventhirtyfour and I stumbled up to our level; he gave me a tired thumbs-up and went to his room. I needed a long hot shower.

As the door closed behind me, something hit me hard on the back of the head.

And everything went black.

CHAPTER 12
CONFRONTATIONS

The inevitable headache woke up before me and was there to welcome me when I came to.

I was in an awkward position, tied to a chair, and been there long enough that I'd stiffened up. I shifted, seeing how tightly I was bound. That let my captor know I was awake again.

"Where is my son?"

I turned my face towards the voice, and despite shooting pains across my temples, I opened my eyes. Gravane's mother sat in my comfy chair, quivering with fury. Standing behind her were two men in suits, I didn't recognise either of them, but I recognised their type. One step up from the Campbells on Bantus.

"I can explain," I said. But could I? I was trying for cool, collected, but even I could hear my voice was thin, strained and scared.

"Don't," she said, sharply. "Tell me where my son is, and we will only call the police. Try and play me, try to bluff it out, and this will go much worse for you."

I nodded. I was finding it hard to focus anyway, I wasn't going to be running verbal rings around anyone. "Message," I croaked "on wrist pad."

She nodded curtly, sent one of her men forward. He untied my hand to let me access the pad but kept a tight grasp on my wrist to prevent me from doing anything else.

Awkwardly I brought up the kidnappers' message,

making sure Mrs. Gravane's man could see each step of the way. No sudden moves. "Can I send it to the console?" I took her silence as assent and flicked the video to the screen for all to see.

Mrs. Gravane put a hand to her mouth when she saw the state of her son's face but didn't make a sound until the video ended. "Who. Are. You?" she demanded her voice brittle steel.

"I'm not with the kidnappers. I don't know what they've done, didn't know that Mirabor was in any danger. Not until this message arrived. I'm... nobody. Just someone your son asked to help him."

"Don't take me for a fool. You're here living his life while he is lost and hurt. Don't tell me you are *helping* him."

"I have another message, from your son. It explains me, I hope."

"Show me."

The screen lit up with Gravane's recorded message, the one I'd asked him to make when I agreed to his deal. I hadn't bothered to watch it before, but there we were, the two of us and his bodyguard, and with Gravane's freshly shorn hair, the likeness was stronger than I'd realised.

"Hello mother," he said, voice dripping with sarcasm. "If you're seeing this, we've been found out. Well done you. I want you to know this was all my idea; this guy is, if not innocent, at least not to blame.

"I know you and father have all sorts of grand plans for my life, but this is me telling you, again, that's not what I want. I have plans of my own, friends to catch up with, places to see, my own life to live. So, stick your plans. While your little spies are watching this guy, I will be heading in the other direction.

"I'm not being coerced, conned, tricked, I'm not drunk or on drugs. I just want my own life." He paused for a long time. Then he finished in a more conciliatory tone. "Look,

I'll call you soon, I'll explain, don't worry, I'm okay. And don't be too hard on the kid, he's just doing his job."

Mrs. Gravane held out a hand towards the image of her son, a tear on her cheek. "You don't know anything, do you?"

"I..."

"The ransom demand arrived within an hour of the grateful message from Bantus saying how successful my son had been. I didn't believe the ransom. Wouldn't. But I had agents check, and the 'Mirabor Gravane' on Bantus...

"But you have nothing to do with the kidnapping, do you? You're just another opportunist parasite living off the wealth of others. The irony of training to be a 'superhero' while you do it? How do you sleep at night?"

"It's not always easy," I confessed in a whisper. "Mrs. Gravane, I'm so, so sorry. If there's anything I can do... your son seemed a good sort, though I didn't know him long. And, of course, I'll leave, stop pretending to be him..."

"No," she cut me off.

"Pardon?"

She straightened up, composed herself. She didn't wipe her tears away, but she stopped crying, at least in front of me. "Rumours of the kidnapping are out there but are vying with your antics on Bantus for now. The company comes first. If word gets out that we are vulnerable, share prices will tumble. As ever, first, we must be Gravanes.

"There is also the matter of this deadline. That must be met, and the kidnappers contacted you, they wish you to be the go-between. Anything to make the return of my son safer. No. I will not risk it." She pierced me with a stare more painful than my headache. "You must continue your ruse, but this time in *my* employ. To the outside world, there is nothing to worry about, the Gravanes remain strong. It will buy me time to find my son.

"Do not expect me to be grateful. Your little prank has

cost me more than you, or my foolish son, will ever know. But we pay our dues. I will arrange for your expenses to be paid, and the going rate for his protection detail."

Something about that gave her pause. I was still reeling, had formed no coherent reaction, so I let her think.

"My son's protection detail, Mr. Hauberk, did he leave alongside him?"

"His shadow?" I tried to think. "I don't think so. I'm fairly sure your son said... Hauberk?... was being reassigned. I think your son even said you hadn't felt the protection was needed at the Academy."

"I see." There was a new light in her eye. She clearly thought that was important. Now, at last, she wiped the tears away and stood up. "Well then, Mr... Grey isn't it?"

I nodded. It was as good a name as any for her to use.

"Well then Mr. Grey, be sure to pass on my hearty congratulations to your colleagues. Their operations on Bantus were a qualified success. I will leave credit chips for each as a note of gratitude when I arrange your salary and expenses." She walked to the door, her two bodyguards pacing her. I strained my neck to watch. "You will contact me the moment you receive any word from the kidnappers."

She gave me one last lingering look, before gesturing her man to untie me. The other one opened my dorm room door, and in a voice pitched to carry to any eavesdroppers in the hall, Gravane's mother said "It was very good to see you, son, keep up the studies, I expect those grades to rise. And call home more."

Then she and her minions flowed out of the room, leaving me dazed, confused and in pain.

# # #

I gave some serious thought to packing it in.

I'd made a fool of myself, hurt Gravane's family, and Mrs. Gravane's description of me as an 'opportunist parasite' felt uncomfortably close to the mark. But she was right, if the kidnappers called, I'd need to be here. It's why I'd come back to the Academy, and nothing had changed about that. I had to stay, at least until their deadline passed.

I took aspirin for my head, then collapsed into my comfy chair. Everything was different now. Before, if I'd been found out, it would have meant time in Tartarus. Now, if I played this wrong, if the kidnappers didn't like what they saw, it could cost Gravane his life. Bad enough that agreeing to the switch put him in harm's way. I had no direct involvement in his abduction, but now, I couldn't shake the feeling that my actions could keep him alive... or not.

I had to stay. I had to keep lying to Seventhirtyfour, Pilvi and the rest. That was my decision. Eyes wide open. It had to work.

# # #

The first day back in class passed in a daze. We'd missed three weeks of classes; even with Sunbolt's tutoring, I was way behind. The book courses were bad enough, I had a ton of reading to catch up with, but the physical disciplines were worse. I'd relied on talent and instinct to stay ahead of the curve before, but now my classmates had technique on their side, and I'd gone from top of the class to languishing near the bottom, in just three weeks.

I sought out the gang in the evening, found them in the Gamma Bomb with similarly shell-shocked appearances. The bar was thankfully quiet, and even the jukebox was on low. It suited our energy levels, even Seventhirtyfour was slumped on the sofa, exhausted.

Dez, on the other hand, was full of energy and pleased to see us. Most of us. Okay, them. Me, she hadn't forgiven for leaving her behind. "So, come on," she asked the others. "I scoured the news for anything about Bantus, and there was nothing. You have to tell me how it went. Did you beat up many bad guys?"

"Sunbolt did most of the beating," said Pilvi.

"Seventhirtyfour and I did a little, for a couple of days while Grey was off playing superspy," said Avrim.

Seventhirtyfour lifted his head from the backrest. "Wait, we didn't make the news?"

"Not that I could find," said Dez. "But of course, searching for books and things isn't really my thing, not really. So maybe I missed it. But I thought it was odd."

"It's the sad truth of the superhero life," said Avrim. "Aunt Veritas told me over and over again: Don't go for the life if you're looking for fame and glory."

"But we knocked back organised crime on an entire planet. There were all those journalists questioning Sunbolt at the spaceport," Pilvi said.

Avrim gave one lazy beat of his wings. "Do the maths. How many inhabited planets are there in the galaxy? A hundred thousand?"

"Actually..." Seventhirtyfour began.

"Doesn't matter. To make it into the *galactic* news, you need to be more important than the most important story in a hundred thousand worlds. You need to fight for top billing with politicians, celebrities, natural disasters, scandals. Sure, we beat some gangsters, saved the day on Bantus. Check the news there, I bet we get a bullet. But two systems over? Who cares? We might get an 'in other news' on a quiet news day, but in a galaxy this big, there's no such thing as a quiet news day.

"We all have our reasons for being here, the reasons we tell people and the reasons in our hearts. I'm not saying any of those reasons are wrong, just, if you want to be famous, you will need to be more spectacular than just background heroics."

"Well that's disappointing," said Dez. "I wanted to start

a scrapbook."

"It doesn't matter," said Pilvi. "We're here to help people, right, Grey?"

I looked up from my wrist pad, caught checking it again. "Huh? Oh. Right. The last thing I want is my name in lights."

"You know you're checking your pad every time anything chimes within ear-shot? What message are you waiting for?"

"Sorry," I said, glancing at it one last time, before folding my arms so I couldn't see the screen. Unless I twisted my wrist and peeked at the corner. I didn't know when the kidnappers might try to contact me again. "It's something my mother was going to send. It can wait."

"That reminds me, thank your mother for the credit stick, I'm not in it for the fame, glory *or* cash… but I hadn't realised how expensive some of the textbooks were going to be this year."

Gadget Dude nodded enthusiastically. "Bought new things!" he beamed and held up his latest creation. It sported a tiny rotating satellite dish, an array of flashing lights, and two trailing cables, one yellow, one red. He bobbed it up and down and the cables fluttered. "See?"

"It's great, Dude. What is it?"

He cocked his head to one side, studying his gadget. He bobbed it up and down again, watched the cables twist and the dish turn. He nodded. "Good question!"

"Hey, Gadget Dude, I think Prof Mind Lord wants to speak with you," said Seventhirtyfour. "I showed him the psionic crown you made for me. Before Bantus? He reckons it *does* augment my abilities, and he wanted to know how."

"Wear. It helps."

"Yes, but how?"

"I don't think Gadget Dude is a very 'how' person," I said.

"Are you any closer to working out what your latent abilities might be?" asked Pilvi.

"No. I spent two lessons this afternoon trying different disciplines both with and without the psionic crown. We are fairly sure I'm not telekinetic, which is a pity, you know? But nothing definitive on the other psychic tests. I'm shattered, mind work is so much tougher than Brontom combat training."

Dez patted him on the knee. "Don't worry, you'll get there."

"Thanks. Hey, Grey, don't look now, but I think someone's looking for you."

I whipped my head around.

"Hi," said Lucy. She was standing behind me, holding a drink. "Sorry to interrupt, just wanted to say welcome back."

"Lucy, hi! Come, sit down. Guys, this is Lucy. Sky Diamond."

"Lucy is fine."

"Lucy. She's in my Grapnel class. Lucy, these are the guys. Seventhirtyfour you've met, but this is Gadget Dude, Pilvi, Avrim and Dez."

"Hello," she gave a little wave. "But really, I don't want to intrude."

"You might as well join us," said Dez. "This lot are no fun today, I need someone with some energy to talk to. I wanted to talk superheroing but they keep changing the topic. Do you have powers?"

Lucy sat, threw a glance at me, then answered Dez. "I fall between the factions, a bit. I have powers, after a fashion, because of this headband, which I suppose is Tech." She pushed her hair back, so we could all see the jewels. For the first time, I noticed a slight puckering of her skin around it; it wasn't decorative, it was attached to her scalp. "My mother runs the local postal shuttle on my homeworld, a little nothing place called Nymanteles. A couple of years ago, I was helping out on the ship, when one of the packages we were transporting off-world exploded. I was caught in the blast. This bit of shrapnel... bonded with me. We never did work out which package of the shipment it came from. Nobody ever claimed it."

"Does it hurt?" asked Pilvi.

"No. Not really. It tingles sometimes."

"Give powers?" asked Gadget Dude. He had that look in his eye that he gets whenever he encounters new tech. I put a hand on his shoulder to keep him back.

"Kind of. It's a limited tech empath ability, mental remote control. It doesn't work with everything; it does spaceships best, or, or vehicles of any kind really."

"That's cool," said Seventhirtyfour.

"I guess. I can't make them do anything that a regular pilot couldn't, or over-ride someone who is at the controls. But, I can pilot anything now."

"I'll have to remember that, if I ever need to make a quick getaway off-planet," I said. Not even joking.

She lit the room with a smile at that. "But while it's useful, it's not something that can be trained in class, so, effectively I take the same classes as a Skills hero. Grapnel is a lot of fun."

"It is," I said, but I was distracted by my wrist pad pinging. A new message on my student account, and since everyone I knew to talk to was sitting with me... "Sorry, I need to take this."

I vaulted over the back of the sofa, jostled my way out of the bar, and ran across the quad.

# # #

Safely alone in my room, I played the message.

Gravane sat on the floor of a room, slumped forward, I couldn't see his face properly; enough to be sure it was him, not enough to properly gauge his condition. He was alive at least, he was moving, if only a little. I paused the image, tried to extract information about the room; the floor was rough, stone perhaps, or undressed concrete, the walls were stone, too, worked rather than built. He was in a cave? Or bunker? The stone had a slightly orange hue. Nothing to identify a location, but I filed it away anyway.

I set it playing again, and the picture faded to black. Again, white text faded in.

Five million credits.
Fade.
Midnight tomorrow.
Fade.
Come alone. If we see anyone else...
Fade.
Gravane dies.
Fade.
Tell no-one.
Fade.

There was nothing about a location. Presumably, that would follow, and close enough to the deadline that they could pick the terrain and deny me a chance to check it out.

I would have to break one of the instructions. If they wanted their five million credits, I'd need to speak to Mrs. Gravane. I wasn't sure what the time difference was between the Academy and wherever in the galaxy she was, but I was sure she'd want to know. She answered my call within seconds.

She was sat at a desk, in front of a picture window, dressed for the business day. I flicked a copy of the message to her to watch but told her the limited highlights.

"Five million?" She looked worried.

"That's what they said."

"I can provide it. I just wonder why it is so little." She picked up a pad from her desk, tapped its screen a few times. "There. The funds should be available to you now. As for the rest, you cannot go alone, naturally. My agent there..."

"With respect Mrs. Gravane, but if you're planning to pay the ransom, aren't we better off just following the instructions? If we do, the only person at risk is me. If we don't, it's me, your agents and, not to be blunt, your son."

She waited a long moment before replying, her face a mask. "No. Your instincts do you credit, Mr. Grey, but no matter how much I wish my son's safe return, I cannot put another child at risk to achieve it."

Child? "I just faced down three mob bosses and their goons..."

"Against my instructions. I understand that you were unable to conduct the mission to my specification, but that does not mean I approve of the risks you took. And it certainly does not mean you have my permission to repeat them."

"Fine. Who is your agent? I can brief them."

Her mask cracked with just the hint of a smile. "I think perhaps I will keep that information privileged for now. It would be a shame if I told you and you weren't able to find them."

"That would be a shame," I said.

"I am afraid I must return to my duties. Call me the moment you have the location."

"I will."

"Be Gravane." She cut the comm.

I checked my account. Yes, she had deposited five million credits there, on the assumption that I would dutifully transfer them to the kidnappers. Which, of course, I would. But it was a lot of trust.

# # #

I can't tell you what happened in class the next day. I might as well not have been there. I spent the entire time checking my wrist pad for updates. Sunbolt sent me to the Med-tech after self-defence, I'd taken so many hits. Arguably, he should have sent me sooner.

I was pacing the dimensions of my room at an hour before the deadline when my wrist pad finally pinged. The message contained only a set of coordinates. When I checked them on Academy maps, they were for a point ten kilometres up the coast, well outside of Academy grounds.

I called up Mrs. Gravane's number but stopped before I placed the call. If I went with backup, if I broke with the kidnappers' demands, it could ruin it all. I could do this myself. Hand over the credit stick. Bring Gravane back. Simple. More people just added more unpredictability. What if they didn't back my play?

I could do this.

I set my wrist pad to Do Not Disturb. Mrs. Gravane would call me soon if I didn't call her. My plan was the next time we spoke, I'd have her son for her.

Ten kilometres on sand in an hour. I could run that, but I didn't have time to dawdle. I ran.

# # #

One foot in front of the other. Control my breathing. Don't look up.

I was lucky it was night time, on the campus proper, the contrast between the building lights and the night sky gave the illusion of a ceiling. I kept my gaze down, didn't think about it, ignored the twist in my stomach. I could do this.

Out on the beach, the last party of the season was in full swing; the nights were turning longer and colder. I smelled barbeque and alcohol, caught a snatch of the live music, it sounded like Dez singing her heart out. I didn't have time to listen.

I left the party behind, left the campus behind. My calves were starting to ache. Running on the beach was harder than I'd thought, more tiring than I'd expected. The slight incline, the shifting underfoot with every step. I had to concentrate. Keep my focus on the ground. On my feet.

Don't look up.

Time ticked away, but each step ate up the distance.

I was slowing down, starting to ache. Regretted the punishment in self-defence. Should have ducked more. Breathing laboured. Spared a glimpse at my wrist pad. Still had time.

My foot caught on something, and the world tumbled around me.

I rolled, over and over, scraped knees and elbows across the wet sand. I came to rest, flat on my back, winded and abraded. But worst, eyes open.

Above me, the dark infinity of the universe. Beneath me, damp sand. I was caught on the interface between the two, and the stars called, dragging at my chest, I was going to fall into the universe. I pushed my fingers into the sand, trying to hold on, trying to keep myself from falling, but the grains just slipped through my fingers. I scrabbled, dug, frantic. I couldn't... I had to save Gravane...

I was being... I couldn't right now... couldn't spare the time for this. But my breath was shallow and rapid, couldn't quite catch it. My whole body shook. The cold damp against my back. The scent of the sea filled my lungs.

I felt so stupid. But I knew, in my bones, that my life was in the balance.

A dot in the sky, moving. Moving towards the ground, against the pull of the sky.

Focus on it.

It grew closer, the dot resolved into the shape of a small shuttlecraft. It descended; not quite towards me but heading to the rendezvous point. That was the kidnappers' ship.

Focus.

I couldn't be late. Couldn't afford to miss them. I tore my gaze from the sky. Rolled over, planted one hand, then the other. Got my feet under me. Stood. Ran.

The shuttle roared over-head, sank below the dunes. I dug in and ran faster.

# # #

I crested the dune on leaden legs, looked down at the shuttle. Now I had some frame of reference, I could see it was a small-hulled passenger craft, not big enough for more than a pilot and a couple of passengers. The back hatch was open, and a man stood on the exit ramp, backlit by the shuttle's interior lights. I couldn't make out much detail; he was human, probably, dressed in dark colours, a leather jacket perhaps. His hood was pulled up, and as I drew closer, I realised he was wearing a mask underneath it, it covered his entire face: black with a stylised skull.

Legs aching with exertion, I made it to the bottom of the dune, crossed half the distance to the shuttle, before Skull-face held up a hand to stop me. I was close enough now to get a good look inside the shuttle; it had one occupant, a woman with long dark hair, facing away from me. There was no sign of Gravane.

I pulled the credit stick from my pocket. Held it out towards him. "I have your money," I shouted. "Five million, just like you said. And I'm alone. Just like you said. Where's Mirabor Gravane?"

"Close. Once we have the money, we will tell you his location."

I shook my head. "No deal. Show me he is alive. Or I walk out of here and you can kiss your credits goodbye."

He made no reply, only raised a hand to point at me.

"Show me Gravane," I said. "Show him, and this is yours. You walk away with five million, or nothing. It's your choice." How far could I push this? I wasn't sure, but I couldn't walk out of here without Gravane.

Skull-face curled his fingers into a fist and the beach between the two of us exploded.

I threw my hands up to shield my face and eyes as sand erupted upwards, filling the air. I felt the credit stick get ripped from my fingers and something hit my wrist like a hammer.

And then it was over; sand pattered down like rain. Skull-face lowered his hand and turned back towards the shuttle.

"Wait! What about Gravane?"

"You bought him six months of life. We will be in touch."

"That wasn't the deal!"

The shuttle hatch slammed shut; its engines whined to life. I went to my wrist pad if I could contact someone to track the ship then, perhaps... but my wrist pad was smashed beyond repair. Somehow it had been ripped apart leaving my wrist undamaged.

As the shuttle blasted skywards, all I could do was watch, defeated.

CHAPTER 13
INVESTIGATIONS

Mrs. Gravane was not happy.

"Our deal is done, Mr. Grey. Pack your things and leave the Academy. If my agent informs me you are still there at this time tomorrow, I will exert my considerable influence to ensure your life is a hell equal to the one you have put me through."

"Of course, Mrs. Gravane."

"And if your actions have cost my son his life…"

I should have bit my tongue. "They didn't."

She bolted to her feet, the camera's pan didn't follow quickly enough. When it caught up, she was staring death at me with red-rimmed eyes. "How dare you?"

"I'm sorry, Mrs. Gravane. Perhaps I should have..." I squared my shoulders. "No. I stand by my choice. It was the right thing to do. They never had any intention of sending your son back, I'm sorry, but it's true. They didn't bring him, didn't bring any evidence he was alive, even. They must have known I'd ask. They could have shown a video, even a fake one, but they didn't even bother."

The iron in her spine wavered. "How can you say such things?"

"You would say the same if we were talking about anyone but your son."

"I…"

"I understand, I do. I wanted Mirabor back, too. But I doubt he ever got within three jumps of the Academy. In a weird way, I think it makes it more likely they are keeping him alive though. They must know the next time they make demands they will have to provide proof of life that we didn't get this time."

"There will be no further payments." Her voice was cold, unbending. "A Gravane does not treat with people who so easily renege on a deal."

"Then think of it this way, we bought six months to find him."

Her mouth tightened into some terrible approximation of a smile. "We?"

"Of course. I want to help if I can. I know that some of this is my fault."

She lowered herself back into her chair, closed her eyes and lowered her head in contemplation. "Perhaps we will make a true Gravane of you yet," she said at last.

"Very well, Mr. Grey, I rescind my earlier demands. You are correct, we have bought time to act. And to act freely, the galaxy must continue to believe my son is safe and sequestered at the Academy. It seems your performance continues. If you are willing?"

"Sure. I mean, yes, I am."

So, again, a member of the Gravane family asked me to pretend to be one of them. They were a strange family.

# # #

I stood outside the Grapnel classroom the next morning, staring out of the window. Across campus, Tartarus's energy shield shimmered in the morning light, but for the first time since I arrived at the Academy, I had no reason to fear it. Even if my act was uncovered, I had a legitimate reason to be here, an actual job, no less. Which was weird, on several levels. But they wouldn't send me to Tartarus for it.

In fact, for the first time since I spoke to that drunk

on Meanwhile, as far as I could figure, I was… safe? That couldn't be right. There must be something I was missing.

A group of students came through the doors from the stairwell, at the back, Lucy followed them.

"Morning, Lucy," I said with a grin.

She walked straight past me, went to stand by the far side of the door to class. She turned her head away from me.

I crossed over to join her. "Are you okay?"

"I'm fine, thank you."

That was not the reaction I'd expected. In the Gamma Bomb, I'd thought… "Did Dez say something?"

"Grey, just don't. I don't want to do this, not here, not at all, really. I thought… but then you couldn't get away fast enough. It doesn't matter."

"Oh." What could I tell her about why I left? Nothing. And an evasion would be worse.

"I'm fine. I just don't want to talk right now."

"Right. Sorry."

Well, there we go, start feeling safe, start feeling cheerful, life had a way of disappointing you. Now would be a great time to move to the next planet.

Instead, Tom the Avenging Spider arrived with the keys to the class, and we all filed in behind him.

# # #

That wrinkle aside, life at the Academy fell into a routine.

As good as her word, Mrs. Gravane's money for my tuition came through like clockwork. My salary too. I'd never had so much free cash, and I put most of it away for rainy days I knew were coming.

At first, Mrs. Gravane called every few days. I'm not really sure why. I imagine she thought she was maintaining the illusion, but I think the truth was a little more complicated than that. She would ask me to go over my meeting with her son again, or the confrontation with his kidnapper or she would update me with the progress on the search for him. As time went on and leads dried up, she called me less, and when she did, the conversation would turn to my classes, or Gravane business affairs, or how the family was getting on.

I think for all Gravane's opinion of his mother, she missed him very much.

But the calls tailed off. Days became weeks, then became months. I think we both knew that her son was gone. Each time we spoke, I started to raise the issue of how much longer she wanted me to keep up the pretence, but each time I stopped myself. For her part, she never mentioned it.

# # #

I rated high in Criminology and Clue Analysis classes. Professor Craft told me I had a remarkable insight into the criminal mind; I thanked her for her kind words but didn't explain why I thought that might be.

To my surprise, I also began to excel in the combat classes. I hadn't really thought that sort of thing was for me after I spent most of the Bantus fight getting rescued. But I kicked butt, particularly at the unarmed disciplines. Despite that, I was going to drop them; I had no interest in fighting, and hopefully, when this was all over, I wouldn't need it.

But when I raised it with Professor Red Ninja, he said "Dunno if you'll be a hero, don't matter." He *looked* like his name suggested but didn't *sound* it. "Way I figure, if you're rich as a Gravane, people'll always come for ya. Reckon it'll be good t' know yer way around a scrap whatevers."

I had to concede, so I kept in the class. And as the months passed, I think I even earned some grudging respect from Sunbolt.

We were called up to play Power Ball half a dozen times, and as a team, we slowly got better, though we were never in danger of troubling the league leaders. Seventhirtyfour was our leader and cheer squad all in one, but from time to time, when chips were down, and we needed a clever last-minute play, they'd all turn to me. My ideas worked more often than they didn't.

"If we can beat the Glory Engines," Dez told me, "I'll even forgive you for not taking me to Bantus."

Two goals later, and I was back in her good books again.

# # #

The winter break came. As one of the two long breaks in the academic year, most students took the opportunity to travel home to see families. I got offers from both Seventhirtyfour and Pilvi to visit with them, but I opted to stay on campus.

I spent the first week studying. There was a chance I'd still be at the Academy come exam time and I didn't want to embarrass myself.

The next week I spent going over every inch of the Academy. During term, I'd toed the line, but now I opened every 'no entry' door, explored every maintenance corridor and access hatch. Found some places that I didn't think anyone else had been in years. I filed those away as useful nuggets. It was strange to think a school that taught building infiltration still had such places, but it was the difference between learning a subject and living it.

I was musing that very point, hanging upside down over a tenth-floor lab when two students crashed through the door below me.

The Winged Knight, an armoured Polifan, stumbled backwards, shoulder-mounted flares erupting randomly, throwing the scene into sharp strobe light. Lady Psion, a human telekinetic, followed him in. She was laughing, shielding her eyes from the explosions of light.

In staccato, Winged Knight stabbed buttons on his wrist control until the flares suddenly stopped. He extended his wings, sheathed in the same metal as his armour. "Just stop it, okay? Funny joke, ha-ha, but leave off!"

Psion just pointed at him, and Knight's wrist-mounted fire extinguisher engaged, gushing foam all over the floor.

I realised, slower than I should have, that Psion was telekinetically pressing buttons on Knight's control panel, firing off random gadgets. An obnoxious prank and there was no telling what Knight packed into his arsenal – sooner or later Psion was going to stumble across something dangerous.

I let myself drop to the floor, careful to land outside the foam zone. "Morning chaps," I said.

The Knight turned to me. "Step off, Phooey, this doesn't concern you."

That phased me for a moment. "'Phooey'? Oh, like the advert, because I'm a Skills student. I get that, that's clever."

The world twisted. Something grabbed my ankles, pulled them up, and I was caught, suspended in the air like some groundsider messing up in zero gravity.

"Like the Tech head said, Phooey, there's nothing here for you, move on." Lady Psion crossed her arms and smirked.

If Lady Psion hoped hanging me upside down would bother me, she was disappointed. "I would, but I seem to be floor-challenged right now. Look," I said "I can see you guys have a whole thing going on here, and that's cool. I guess. But flares and jets and fire extinguishers... somebody has to clean all this stuff up. If you want to aggravate each other over which is better, powers or tech..."

"Powers."

"Tech."

"Nice. Sure. Really grown up. If you want to argue the toss, then fine, but either tone down the collateral damage or take it to the gym. That's set up to handle this kind of thing."

Psion rolled her eyes. "Ugh. I was having such a good time, too." She flicked her wrist and propelled me in a loop around the lab, accelerating me towards the back of Winged Knight's knees. Knight realised too late what was happening and while he tried to sidestep my flight, it just put him skidding in the middle of his fire extinguisher foam.

I struck with bone-jarring speed, pain bursting in my left side as I clattered against the back of Knight's legs. If he'd been planted firmly, the impact would have cost me broken bones for sure, but off-balance as he was, instead we both clattered to the ground, sliding through the foam. Bruises, stiffness and embarrassment, I could deal with.

I slipped and slid, trying to get upright again, ignored Lady Psion's laughter, as she stood in the doorway, recording my efforts on her wrist pad.

"You look ridiculous," she said. "Come on, Techs, you going to let the Phooey get upright first? Flap those wings."

"Not going to give you the satisfaction," Winged Knight said, and folded his arms, lying back in the foam, unmoving.

"I'm off to post this on the campus info stream. Laters!" She put her back against the door to open it, and spiralled out into the corridor, laughing all the way.

Finally, covered in foam, I managed to right myself. I planted my feet and stretched out a hand to Winged Knight. "She's gone now."

But the Polifan didn't move. "I had that under control, Phooey."

I pulled back my hand. "I was just trying to help."

He stabbed buttons on his wrist control, and a micro-drone detached from his chest plate. It hovered in front of my nose, and as Knight prodded more buttons, it started making an electronic noise like a baby crying.

"Fine," I said, "I take your point. Next time I won't help."

"You better hadn't!"

The drone followed me around for twenty minutes before I finally managed to trap it in a supply cupboard. But Winged Knight seemed reluctant to let my attempt to help go unpunished, and over the next week, I'd occasionally encounter the wailing micro-drone again.

# # #

By the start of the third and final week of the winter break, I knew every inch of the Academy buildings (except Tartarus!) and had nowhere left to explore. I found myself with time on my hands that I had no obvious way to fill. For the first time in my life that I could remember, I experienced boredom. In times past, long before I could reach that point, I'd have been away onto another ship to find another station. But that wasn't an option this time, for all sorts of reasons. But mostly, because I knew in only a week, things would be back to normal and I could distract myself again.

I spent the first morning stomping around campus some more, but it's hard to maintain a proper sulk when avoiding screeching micro-drones.

In the afternoon, I applied to campus supplies and spent some of my savings on three tins of paint. The next day I painted my dorm room, a rather pleasant yellowy-brown colour. I found it really soothing. But it hadn't filled as much of the week as I'd hoped.

By day four, I had to find something to do or go out of my mind. So I dug out all of the information I had about Gravane's disappearance. All the stuff I remembered that his mother had told me, all the information I could find on the net, the rumours and conspiracy theories that had surfaced when he was kidnapped. Mrs. Gravane had had the best investigators that money could buy look into all this already, with the advantage of being able to follow leads on the ground, but this puzzle had never faced the nascent skills of a super-bored student criminologist.

So. Treat it like a class project. I requisitioned supplies and went to work. I made charts. Time-lines. I used up two boxes of highlighters and did that thing with pins and strings I'd seen in drama vids, though it wasn't a technique we'd covered in class, so wasn't entirely sure how it was supposed to help me. It killed a day but didn't get me any closer to finding anything useful.

I went back to first principles. In my meeting with him, what had he said, how had he said it. Was there anything there? The one thing that stood out as odd, and this wasn't a new revelation, I'd told Mrs. Gravane too, but when Gravane had been talking about why he had to go somewhere else, he had said that being sent to the Academy would take him away from "friends and... friends." That pause had suggested something more than just friends and it wasn't family, I was sure of that, so... a girlfriend? Or boyfriend? His mother had claimed not to know but given their relationship that was hardly surprising.

I scoured the tabloids and society papers that might cover Gravane and his circle of friends. Gravane was from a rich family; he had his share of stalkers and gold-diggers. I constructed a list, cross-referenced with people who were mentioned more than once. That pause, that pause was important and spoke to a connection. The list was long, but not impossibly so. I programmed a search tool to cross-reference the names on the list with their activity before, during and after Gravane's disappearance. I left that running, it would take a while to return results.

What else did I have to go on? The only other stand-out point for me was something that Mrs. Gravane had asked, about Gravane's bodyguard... Hordburg? No ...

Hauberk, that was it. She had asked about him and seemed surprised when I said he was supposed to be reassigned when Gravane came to the Academy. Mrs. Gravane had never spoken to me about it again, but she'd clearly seen something in that. Did she suspect an inside job? It seemed obvious that the best person placed to kidnap a person was his bodyguard. I set another search program. It was a big universe, and I didn't have much to go on, a last name and a general physical description. His association with the Gravanes seemed the most obvious 'in', so I added that as a factor to the search. Could I find where Hauberk was now?

Mrs. Gravane had never shown me the messages the kidnappers had sent her, and there was obviously no way to find those on the net, but they seemed to me like the third avenue of attack. I racked my brains for anything I could remember about them, from the little Mrs. Gravane had told me. It wasn't enough to do anything useful with, not yet certainly. Still, I filed it and pinned it to the case board.

The first of my searches pinged up its initial findings, I paged them to the room console, projected them onto the wall so I could see them, literally big picture. I went through the output line-by-line.

At some point, Seventhirtyfour popped his head around the door and asked if I wanted to come down to dinner. I waved away the distraction with a grunt and cross-referenced the latest output of the first search with the output about Hauberk. There was something there. I pinned that to the case board as important.

And then, after what was probably an hour, I realised that Seventhirtyfour must be back on campus. And it was probably dinner time, or it had been.

Stiffly, I stood up. My bones seemed to creak in protest. I was exhausted, and ravenously hungry. What time was it? I checked the pad clock and blinked in surprise. What day was it?

Good grief. I must have worked on this for 36 hours straight. No wonder I was tired. And hungry. Too late for the canteen now. Perhaps it had been more than an hour since Seventhirtyfour was here. Still, the dorm kitchen had supplies. I opened my door to head across the hall, and there was a micro-drone staring me in the face. A light on it beeped, recognising me, and then it started up that awful screeching noise, which felt like a drill to the brain. I stared at it for a long few seconds while I processed this development. Then I closed the door on the drone. Couldn't... face...

Suddenly was... unbelievably tired. Couldn't... think. I staggered across to the bed. Sat down.

And was asleep.

# # #

By the end of the first week of term two, I was feeling more myself again. I'd caught up on my sleep, the micro-drone stalking seemed to be tailing off, and while I didn't stop thinking about Gravane's kidnapping, I was able to contain it to my back-brain and my search programs for the most part.

I was enjoying my expanded curriculum, Rescueology, in particular, proved to be a pretty awesome course, covering practical tips for getting innocent bystanders out of all manner of traps, tricks and ambushes. At the back of my mind, I wondered if it might someday come in handy to rescue Gravane.

Seventhirtyfour and Dez had both signed up for the class too, and we'd managed to get into a team for the group project; we had to plan a three-handed rescue of a ten-year-old girl in a simulation scenario. The simulation had been designed to our specifications, so there was an established solution using our skills, we just had to find it, or something better. We held a lunchtime summit over a communal bowl of chips.

"Well the obvious solution," Dez said speculatively, dipping a chip in the ketchup "would be for Grey to keep the villain talking, while I sneak around the back and untie the girl. You saw how I did in that ropes and knots session. Mad skills." She flourished a chip to make the point.

"Maybe," rumbled Seventhirtyfour, "but if the girl is drugged, or uncooperative, you wouldn't be able to carry her away. I could, but I can't sneak up there to her. Grey may make a great distraction, but there are limits."

"Well okay," I countered, "maybe we can create some sort of diversion, pull the villain out of the room with the girl, then Seventhirtyfour doesn't need to sneak anywhere."

Dez nodded enthusiastically. "I like it! So, we just need to work out something that would call him away from his victim. Oh! Perhaps the simulation knows about my singing ability, does it say he has a favourite song? Check the file!"

Seventhirtyfour looked dubious but pulled up the villain file on his pad all the same. "Maybe I can find something non-musical too."

I went back to poring over the scenario blueprints, and Dez worked her way through the food, distractedly people-watching the canteen around us.

I was trying to work out which me the simulation was designed to work with. Mirabor Gravane and I had different skill-sets, and while I didn't think tax law was the solution here if the puzzle was designed to his strengths, not mine, we might actually be in trouble. That said, I'd spent enough time here, sat enough pop-quizzes and had enough evaluations that if it was actually now playing to my strengths instead of Gravane's... there was a tempting looking access shaft right above where the villain was holding the girl. Could I make use of that somehow? It seemed almost too well placed...

"Oh hey, that's a cute little drone," said Dez.

"Ugh. Ignore it, it's just the Winged Knight playing one of his hilarious jokes. He's an idiot. If it starts making a noise, just throw something at it, that usually works."

Dez shook her head. "Doesn't look like one of Winged Knight's designs..."

Seventhirtyfour's head snapped up, eyes wide. With his upper arms, he reached across the table, grabbed Dez and me, and yanked us over to his side. Meanwhile, his lower hands heaved up and tipped the table over. It happened so fast, I just had time for a surprised yelp... and then the drone exploded.

CHAPTER 14
TENSIONS

My ears were ringing, my vision blurred, there was blood. A shallow graze on my forehead that was bleeding profusely but wasn't serious. Dez was lying underneath me, she looked scared but unhurt. Seventhirtyfour had taken a couple of hits, deeper than mine, but from the little I knew about Brontom anatomy, nothing life-threatening. He gave me a grimace, slumped back against the over-turned table, but he seemed to be coping.

I stood up, carefully. I didn't think there would be any follow-up, but then I was having problems believing this serious of an attack in the first place. the Academy just wasn't that kind of place.

The canteen was in turmoil. You have a bomb go off in a place full of people training to be heroes, you don't get many people just running away in panic, but the reactions are still on a spectrum. Half a dozen people were running towards us, I think to offer medical help, but at least one of them was shouting about not contaminating the evidence.

They, sadly, were the sanest amongst the reactions. Everybody else seemed to be shouting at each other, the teachers were shouting for calm, some students were shouting to find out what was happening, but there were a few shouting accusations.

"It was a drone! I saw it, came right up to the Phooey table and blew up!"

"Some powered idiot not able to keep himself under

control!"

Voices escalated, I couldn't hear the details any more, just shouting and anger and fear.

There seemed to be a collective drawing of breath, and students pulled back, away from the centre of the canteen, and almost instantly I could see they'd polarised into tech and powered students. The two groups stared at each other, tension building. I hadn't realised how close all this was to the surface. But these were well meaning, good hearted individuals here to learn to make the galaxy a better place. This wasn't going to get out of hand. It couldn't.

But in that split second, that drawn breath, I suddenly had a vision of a prank, even something like I'd seen Lady Psion doing to the Winged Knight... one spark, and it would set the place off. There would be regrets and recriminations, but the Academy wouldn't be the same afterwards, even if it could continue at all.

I couldn't let that happen. Now before the tumult erupted again, I had to do something.

"Wooooooooeeeeeeee!" I shouted. A hundred faces turned towards me. One of them meant me harm, I was sure of it, but I wasn't going to let them take down the rest of us. "Sorry about that! I hadn't expected that! Faulty rocket grapnel... my bad. No harm done." I wiped blood from my eyes. "Well not much and only to me. Didn't mean to startle everyone. Next time, I'll remember to decant the propellant before trying to fix the firing pin!"

Tom, the Avenging Spider, appeared from somewhere in the crowd. He stomped towards me, anger dripping off him. "That you will, Mr. Gravane, and we will be finding some way to remind you of it too. Clean up that mess. No. See the medic first for that scalp wound, and then come back and clean up this mess. I'll be speaking to Captain Hawk about this." He drew up level with me and grabbed me roughly by the collar. He raised his voice. "Right you lot, show's over, get back to classes, we'll be sealing this end of the canteen until we get all this cleared, so no point staying here. Don't dawdle Mr. Gravane!" He shoved me towards the door.

Dez and Seventhirtyfour followed, protesting my innocence, but I caught their gaze and gave a firm shake of my head, and they shut up and fell in behind.

Tom kept up the forced march all the way to the Med Centre, but as he shut the door behind us, he sagged. "That was some quick-thinking Grey, thanks," he said. "Awesome job."

"Thanks, but... what happened there, Tom? I knew there were factions, you see them every day, but I hadn't realised how polarised it's gotten, how tense. The Academy, it's closer to exploding than I'd thought."

He shook his head. "I've seen it get worse this last couple of years," he admitted. "The Academy I joined was a laugh, nobody really took us seriously, we're training to be superheroes! It's ridiculous. But we had some big successes. A couple of our students went on to do some big things for some important people, and suddenly corporations moved in. Well, I don't have to tell *you* that."

"Sure," I grimaced.

"Since then, people have been taking what we do much more seriously. Applying pressure and targets to what used to be a silly little playground." Tom shook his head. "I'm too young to be this cynical, but money spoils stuff, no offence."

A med tech came in, tutted at me and Seventhirtyfour, and set to work on our wounds. They looked impressive but really weren't that deep or serious.

"That's as may be," said Dez, "but don't we need to be worrying that somebody just tried to blow us up? That drone didn't come from nowhere."

"Ah," said Tom, "so it was a drone? I thought I saw one. Well, that's bad news. That means there's physical evidence to be found, and we have a student body more than happy to CSI a real crime scene given the chance. Let me just call Prof Craft, she needs to get that place sealed up tight."

He went off to deal with that, and I turned to Seventhirtyfour. "Thanks, man, if you hadn't realised what was happening... those were some amazing reflexes."

Seventhirtyfour still looked a little dazed. "Not reflexes," he rumbled. "I saw it. Before it happened, saw what I needed to do to save you. Glad it worked."

"Woah," Dez said. "You can see the future, that's fricking awesome!"

Seventhirtyfour shook his head. "It's the first time it's happened. Except, well... maybe it isn't. I had a flash of something on Bantus too, put it down to coincidence and confusion."

"We need to hit the Casinos on New Blackpool!"

"No Dez, I don't think it's that kind of power. So far, it's only triggered on imminent and physical danger. I don't think I'm going to be working casinos over."

Dez nodded. "Sure, sure. But, something to work on? With practice, you never know. Or, well, I suppose you could know."

But I was distracted by Seventhirtyfour's exact words. "You saw what you had to do to save me, that's what you said?"

"Yeah."

"So, what you're saying is that this was an attack aimed directly at me then?"

"Yeah," he looked miserable.

"Well, that's just... peachy."

# # #

Tom told us to stay in the Med Centre while he went to meet up with Professor Craft at the scene of the crime. We stayed put. Seventhirtyfour was quiet, I wasn't sure if it was because he was injured, shocked by the attack, or working through the implications of his new power. I couldn't think of anything to say to help him with any of it, so I kept shut up too.

Dez's reaction was to go hyper. She paced, practically bounced, from one side of the room to the other, tail twitching, talking nineteen to the dozen.

"Okay, okay, okay, so Grey calmed everyone down and that's great, but we all know that wasn't an accident, and we're not alone, so does the bomber, and so will anyone who checks the security footage. And you just know that at least one of the techies has a camera on their suit running at all times. Well, we don't know, but we know, you know? People are only going to stay calm so long. We need to get ahead of the game, figure this out, before things escalate, right Grey?"

I nodded, only half listening, half chasing my own thoughts around my skull.

"Right!" said Dez. "So first we need to work out who the target of the attack was. Seventhirtyfour said it was Grey, but can we be sure? I mean band rivalry can be fierce, so it could be someone trying to off me to get a singing gig, but the drone was flying too high if they wanted to get at me. So, it's much more likely they were after you, Grey, or Seventhirtyfour. Both your families have money, right, so it could be either of you, I guess, but who could get pissed enough at Seventhirtyfour to want to blow him up? He's the nicest guy in the galaxy, but you, Grey, you can rub people up the wrong way, no offence meant."

"None taken, I..." I tried to stem the tide, but Dez just kept right on.

"Okay, so Seventhirtyfour was right, Grey was the target. Now we need to look at the people who might want to blow Grey up. Has he upset any groups of people with criminal tendencies and access to explosives? Of course, he has. Three whole families of alien mobsters on Bantus IV.

And one of them, the Tazforj? They had the technical know-how to pull off this attack, right? That must be it, it wasn't a student at all."

I caught the look of relief on her face, but I wasn't so confident. Any reprisal for Bantus should have come months ago if it was coming. And even if Dez had the right agency, it would have needed someone on the ground to direct the drone. A student was still involved. Well, or one of the staff, let's not make too many assumptions.

Dez started up again, but this time I tuned her out, did some thinking of my own.

Assuming this attack was directed at me, and both Seventhirtyfour and Dez seemed in agreement on that front, the question remained, was the target me, or Mirabor Gravane?

The Gravanes were big business and had their share of enemies, as the abduction of their sixth child showed. I could just be catching that grief. But my life was a complicated place right now.

It could be the Bantus mob, any number of people that Gravane had annoyed, anyone that I'd stolen from (though if so, it was an over-reaction). It could be a student at the Academy that I'd annoyed. Or it could be that the people who kidnapped the real Gravane were annoyed that there was a fake one running around.

My head was spinning. Too many options, none of them good.

There was a knock at the Med Centre door. Seventhirtyfour looked up, but made no move to answer, Dez dropped into a combat stance, but I shook my head and went to open the door.

Pilvi stormed in, gave me a wordless hug, before moving on to Dez and Seventhirtyfour. Gadget Dude and Avrim trailed after her.

"So," she said, "What are we going to do?"

"Do?" asked Avrim.

"Someone tried to blow one of us up, we aren't just going to let that go, are we?" Pilvi replied.

Avrim gestured widely, indicating the Academy as a whole. "We are in a building where absolutely everybody is studying to solve and fight crime, why does it fall to us?"

"Why wouldn't it?" chimed in Dez.

I held up a hand. "Avrim's right, we can't join the trample to investigate this, all that will happen is we'll get in each other's way. That won't help anyone."

Pilvi gave me a look. "How can you say that of all people?"

Everybody started talking at once, all except Seventhirtyfour, who looked around sadly as we argued. He hadn't said a word since telling us about his new power, but now he stood up and spoke. "No Grey, Pilvi is right, this has to be us. I feel it. I don't know if it's my power, or just... it feels right. We're going to have to deal with this. But you're going to need to tell us how."

They all turned to look at me.

I stared at them.

"Okay.

"Okay then.

"Fine." I closed my eyes. Took a breath, organised my thoughts.

"If we're going to do this, let's do this right," I started slowly, but as each idea sparked the next, my words tumbled over each other. "Dez is right, the security footage is our first priority. They're not going to show it to us, I expect, so we will probably need to get it ourselves, and the time to do that is now, while people are still assembling their plans. Gadget Dude and I need to get on that. I can get him access, he needs to get us the copy."

Gadget Dude waved a salute, then dipped into his equipment belt to gather parts.

I turned to Seventhirtyfour, he stood at parade rest ready to receive orders, like a good Brontom soldier. "Seventhirtyfour, Avrim," I said, "I need you to talk to the Powers faction. Priority is keeping things calm, but we need information too. Anything that they saw or overheard that might give us any intelligence.

"Pilvi, that leaves the tech heroes to you."

She nodded, jotting notes on her mini-pad. "I'll start with Simon," she said.

I shrugged. "Sure. Check with Gadget Dude for some other likely candidates. Smooth feathers and get the message across that we don't blame or accuse anyone on that side. Dez mentioned that one or more of the techies might have had a camera running. See if you can find that footage if they did.

"Remember, the method means that if the culprit is a student then it's most likely from that faction, so tread carefully and don't oversell. But still, anything you can get for us would be good."

"And that leaves me with the skills students?" Dez asked, she was already at the door ready to go.

"I can't think why any of the Phooey crew would want to blow us up, but we can't ignore them." I ran a hand through my hair; I was missing something. *What—*? "Oh. Once you've done that, have a word with the staff at the spaceport. It's a longshot, but if you're right in suspecting the Bantus mob, see if any suspicious packages have come in from there.

"We'll reconvene this evening in my dorm room and see what we have."

I looked around. No objections. Avrim didn't look very keen, but even he wasn't trying to get out of it.

"Right. Let's get on with it. Come on Gadget Dude, we better get a hustle on."

I felt slightly guilty, Tom had asked us to stay put, but

they were right, I couldn't let this lie either.

# # #

Security at the Justice Academy was kind of feeble. Most of the things that security systems were designed to detect: energy spikes, explosive signatures, stealthy infiltrations and fisticuffs? That was just an average day at the Academy. And most of the stuff at the Academy was too cheap to be worth stealing, or already broken. Plus, who would actually try and break in here? It was the one place in the galaxy where you would definitely have to go up against superheroes if you did.

There were valuables here, of course, most of those powered suits, hot-, cold-, storm-, plasma- and onion-guns (don't ask) were unique, priceless items and some of the gadgets on the power suits were so far into the cutting edge that even asking "What's this button do?" could leave you bleeding (occasionally literally). But those tech heroes were also astonishingly good at supplying their own security. They were possessive of their inventions and were not characterised by their tendency to share.

Academy security basically consisted of a few cameras at strategic locations which were mostly used to harass persistent litterers or graffiti artists, assuming the perpetrators didn't have a power to block the cameras outright.

All of which meant that gaining access to the security footage was not going to be some amazing heist with laser-webs and motion sensors to dodge, finger-print and retina scanners to spoof, or hordes of guards to bypass. It was, essentially, a dusty cupboard at the end of an often-neglected corridor. The door was locked. But I'd acquired a duplicate of the key during my second week here. Just on principle. I didn't have powers to block cameras outright, after all.

Still, we would rather people didn't know that we'd taken a copy of the footage, so my job was to get Gadget Dude to the door without getting spotted. There wasn't much I could do about that last bit of corridor, but I could certainly get us to the general area unnoticed.

I led him along my second favourite unused by-ways, and the worst outcome was a fit of sneezing at the dust we kicked up. Otherwise, we made it to the fire escape closest to the security cupboard without difficulty. I eased open the door and peered into the corridor. "Okay Gadget Dude, coast is clear."

I looked around to find that somewhere along the way, the Zalex had put on a pair of goggles and had rigged up a safety harness and winch. "Avoid pressure sensors!" he proclaimed cheerfully.

"Sorry Gadget Dude, none to avoid."

He looked crestfallen but glumly followed me out into the corridor.

I unlocked the door and let him in, pushed the door closed enough that I could watch down the corridor without getting spotted.

Behind me, Gadget Dude chuntered away to himself while he set about his business.

"How long will this take?" I asked, kicking myself for not asking before.

"Not long," chirped Gadget Dude, and then, a beat later. "Done."

"Oh, right. Excellent. Let's get..."

There was someone coming down the corridor towards us. Of course, there was. Why wouldn't there be?

Whoever it was, they were somebody trying to be stealthy, but without any practical sense of how to do it. He was human, male, covered head to toe in black, wearing what appeared to be a balaclava and ski-mask, and he was actually creeping along the corridor. He couldn't have been more obvious if he'd worn a sign saying "Being sneaky".

No prizes for guessing where he was going.

I brought my mini-pad up and took a couple of photos for future reference. Fight or flight? No option really, there was nowhere to hide in the cupboard, and we couldn't leave without being seen. So.

I opened the door, looking back over my shoulder, deliberately not looking down the corridor. "Do you have it all, Dude? Tom will want everything backed up."

"Sure sure," replied Gadget Dude cheerfully.

I heard a startled gasp behind me, this guy would not have cut it in infiltration class. I listened for the sound of him opening a door to hide from us, rolled my eyes when I realised he'd tried a locked door and was now having to find another.

"Don't forget the triple-band wavelength scans," I said, desperately trying to come up with reasons to not look down the corridor while this idiot was hiding from me.

Gadget Dude looked confused. "One band only, just one."

"Oh, right, do we not have that... here?" Finally, I heard a door close behind me. "Quick, can you rig a camera to see who comes in here next? Keep it hidden."

Gadget Dude caught up quick. "Sure!" He dipped a hand into one of his pockets and placed what looked to me like a centimetre of black sticky tape over the security monitor. He grinned and shooed me out.

We left with our goal intact, and I resisted the urge to open the door our mystery man was hiding behind. I was trying to stop the school exploding into random fights, and I wouldn't do that by starting one.

# # #

We got back to my dorm room and plugged in the feed from Gadget Dude's camera, rewinding the recording to us leaving the security room. We fast forwarded the footage, but nobody came in. The room remained steadfastly empty.

"Where is he?"

Gadget Dude shrugged. "Arrives late maybe? Knows it?"

I nodded. It made sense. If he had come to delete the footage and saw us leave with a copy, he knew that ship had already launched.

"Or maybe not sneaking to there," Gadget Dude added.

"Maybe, but there's nothing else on that corridor worth sneaking to."

Annoyed, but unsure how I could have played it differently, we unplugged the camera feed, and instead uploaded the security footage we had copied.

"Oh. 2D." Gadget Dude sounded disappointed.

I was too. All we had was a single angle from a static camera, and the resolution was poor. I could already see we weren't going to get much from it.

Still, we found the explosion, fortunately, it was in shot, then stepped back frame by frame until we got a clear shot of the drone.

"Can we get a bigger look at it?"

Gadget Dude shrugged. "Resolution bad. Can try."

The resulting image was blurry as hell, badly pixelated and didn't tell us much. Academy security was shockingly antiquated. Where *did* it spend all its money?

Still. "It's definitely not one of the Winged Knight's, I can't see anything that looks like a blurry sword or wing motif on its casing."

"In disguise?"

"I guess it could be. But look at the propulsion system. You're the expert, not me, but all of the drones the Knight sent after me were steered by angling the main propulsion. But look there, what are they?"

Gadget Dude nodded. "Microjets."

"Yeah. And I can buy him not putting his logo on the damn thing, but why change your fundamental design?"

"Would not."

"So, that confirms something we basically already knew. Which is not a huge leap forward but is something. Okay, let's go back to full screen. Now we need to look to see if we can find anyone directing it."

But Gadget Dude tapped the screen pointing at another blurred section of the drone.

"What, Dude... oh, that's a camera isn't it? It could have been flown remotely from anywhere on the campus."

"Yes," but Gadget Dude shrugged, "worth try though."

We spent some time spinning backwards and forwards through the footage, looking for anyone paying undue attention to the drone, or who seemed to be controlling the device from minipads. We spotted a few likely candidates but look around any canteen at any university and you'll find a good percentage of the students glued to their pads. Looking down at screens could hardly be taken as a sign of guilt, but we saved a few images for later reference, in case we got anything to corroborate our findings. I created a new investigation board and pinned the pictures to that.

Somewhere along the way, Avrim and Seventhirtyfour joined us. Their survey of the powered students hadn't revealed much, except the distrust and suspicion levels were high. They were all adamant that it had been a drone that exploded, which was true, and that it was sent by one of the tech students, which was certainly our working hypothesis. But since nobody offered any fresh evidence, we couldn't really act on what could simply be prejudice.

Seventhirtyfour was taking it badly. "Since working with my psychic abilities, I've developed a... sensitivity to the minds and emotions of people around me. It's not telepathy, I can't read minds or anything. But this many people, angry, suspicious, scared, it's wearing."

Pilvi appeared next, looking flustered and frustrated. "Well thanks so much for sending me to the techies," she said. "They've closed ranks, nobody is talking least of all to a Skills like me."

I nodded. "Sure, I worried they might. Never mind."

"Oh, I still got stuff, I just had to be more creative. They may think they're stubborn, but they've got nothing on Marwick farmers believe me." She pulled out her datapad and read her notes. "I overheard two of them talking about a squawk of static at about the time of the explosion on 1.2 GHz, which Captain Turtle suspected was feedback on the control frequency when the drone's transmitter popped."

Gadget Dude's eyes lit up, and he immediately started digging components out of his pockets. We let him do his thing, as Pilvi continued.

"I simpered and cooed at Dynamite Lad about the explosion itself, eventually he told me what he thought about it. For bang-for-buck, he reckoned it wasn't a home-brew explosive. It's not impossible that someone's cooked up something new in the labs here, but considering the size of the payload and resulting explosion, that looked industrial grade to him, and would have been imported."

"Interesting, why go to that level of risk, when someone here could have made something as effective, although, bigger, I guess," asked Avrim.

"It's suggestive that the person who wants to actually blow me up is not local, I guess, which is a little reassuring."

"Though there are apparently people here happy to go along with it," Avrim pointed out.

"I was trying not to notice that. That does support the theory that this is a reprisal for Bantus. Maybe that's the story we should start telling anyway. We need to get everybody here to take a step back and a calming breath, and having it be known we're looking outside the Academy would help a lot."

"Would certainly help my nerves," said Seventhirtyfour.

"Great stuff, Pilvi, anything else?"

"Depends what you were able to get from the security camera. I heard that Cyberella had her camera running during lunch today, and I managed to persuade her to send me a shot of the drone. Any use?"

"Oh yeah, send it over, it must be a better resolution than the junk the Academy cam recorded."

She flicked the image over to my room console, and I put it up for us all to look at. It was much better resolution than the one we had, and this one we could zoom in on and still see details. The micro-jets were clear this time, it was definitely not the Winged Knight's work. The whole thing looked a good deal more robust than any of the lashed-together stuff that I'd seen Winged Knight send my way.

"I can't believe someone went to all that effort to make that to try and blow up Grey," said Seventhirtyfour.

"You can't?" asked Avrim. Pilvi punched him in the arm.

But I was staring at the photo. Something wasn't right about what I was looking at, and I couldn't quite... I reached forward to spin the image a little. It was only a two-dimensional image, but the console could extrapolate the basic shape... the more I turned it, the fuzzier the image got, as the extrapolation tool had less to work on. I spun it back and forth, watching it come in and out of focus as the front side presented itself... what was it that I was... wait... there.

"Is that a barcode? There on the casing of the drone?"

"I think... yeah," said Avrim. "Wait, does that mean we can look up something about it?"

"No, no the resolution's great, but not that good, and only part of the barcode is showing."

"Shame," said Pilvi "but we should copy it, in case we get a chance to cross reference."

"No, but don't you see? I've seen the students here decorate their gadgets with all sorts of logos and pictures? But a barcode? I mean we'd have to check if we have any tech students with a barcode theme... but I think this drone may be off-the-shelf bought. I don't think we're looking for a tech student after all."

Avrim gave a theatrical sigh. "So, after an afternoon's investigation, we have managed to at least triple the number of suspects."

"Well, maybe." I granted, slowly. "But it really does start to look like this is related to Bantus. Though I don't know, that still feels wrong to me."

Gadget Dude looked up from his project. "Done!" He bounced over to the console and plugged in his latest gizmo. A crude floor-plan of the Academy building popped up on screen. "Look for frequency! Find Transmitter."

We all turned our attention to the screen and watched as a dot appeared glowing on the third floor, and then one on the second floor to the south... and then, dozens more lit up in rapid order.

"Oh," said Gadget Dude, disappointed. "Popular frequency."

"Never mind Gadget Dude, it was a good thought."

We went around the information we had again, while Seventhirtyfour headed to the kitchen to make drinks and snacks. He came back in, trailed by Dez, returning from her mission at the spaceport.

"So, anything come in from Bantus?" Avrim asked.

Dez looked forlorn. "Sorry, no. There were a few packages that could have contained explosives, marked as chemicals or hazardous, but they were all above board and nothing from that end of the galaxy. I dug around a few likely suspects on the shipping manifests, but, no.

"There was one record of a drone being shipped in, the right kind of size as well, it arrived three days ago, but it didn't come from Bantus. I double-checked."

"Where did it come from then?"

Dez tapped her tail on the floor while she looked through her pad. "Here we go... a place called Nymanteles."

The others looked disappointed. Pilvi shrugged.

But I recognised that name. It had come up before. Where had... my Gravane searches! One of the things I was still trying to figure out was exactly where Gravane got kidnapped, there were conflicting reports on his last known whereabouts. The rankings changed from time to time, but the last time I'd looked, the front-runner for where Gravane disappeared? Nymanteles.

# # #

It took all of my self-control not to kick everyone out, there and then. Instead, I let the conversation wind down naturally, while I fidgeted in the corner. To have both of my ongoing investigations point towards Nymanteles was too big a coincidence. There had to be a connection, and each conclusion tended to reinforce the other.

It must have seemed odd to the others that I suddenly checked out. Even when Tom arrived to tell us off for leaving the Med Centre, and then going on to conduct an unauthorised investigation of our own—Avrim and Dez hadn't been so subtle. Still, we presented what we'd found out to him, and he listened to our thoughts and conclusions. He took it all in, then headed off to continue his own investigations.

Almost as soon as he'd gone, I began hinting it was time for people to leave. Eventually, even Seventhirtyfour got the hint and headed to his room.

Alone, at last, I fired up my Gravane searches to check if I had remembered correctly. I had of course. So, someone on the planet Nymanteles had kidnapped Gravane, possibly in the hopes of devastating the family and Corporation.

Neither of these things had happened though, in no small part because of me. I guess Skull-face was pissed at me. Enough to resurrect his original plan by killing off the stand-in for his original victim?

It did make sense, except, the same problem that I had with blaming Bantus mobsters. The timing was weird. The kidnappers had known about me for ages. They could have killed me on the beach. Why wait until now to come after me?

I was missing something.

But I had a big piece for two different puzzles, and it was time to tell Mrs. Gravane. I would have hoped that her own investigators were ahead of me, but she was paying me for my help, so she was going to get it.

I was a little disappointed to find out that she had known about the Nymanteles link. Her own investigators had followed a different set of leads but had reached the same conclusion. Moreover, she admitted, she had been in contact with the kidnappers again recently.

"Yes," she told me coldly. "They have made further demands. Which we will not meet. We are Gravane. When we make a deal, we abide by it. We do not change the deal, nor do we negotiate with those who do."

But I could see the mother's anguish in her eyes. The words were strong, defiant, but the body language on the comm screen was shouting her rage, frustration. A heartsick woman, with iron strength.

"I'm sorry," I said. But... "It does explain the timing of the attack here though. While the world sees your son as safe at the Academy, they can't apply full pressure on you, so now they need to get rid of me."

She nodded. "I fear you are right. I apologise. I had not thought that my rejecting their demands would affect you. I will, of course, authorise hazard pay."

I shook my head. "Not necessary."

"Ah," she looked down at her hands, didn't meet my eye. "You wish to resign. Well, I understand that. You will work your notice period, I presume?"

"You misunderstand, Mrs. Gravane. I may only be a pretend Gravane, but I don't break deals either. I'm staying on until we get your son back."

She nodded curtly, but I think that I'd impressed her.

"But," I continued. "I think for now I've stopped being useful at the Academy. Can you arrange a family mission like the Bantus one, but to Nymanteles this time?"

"Will you be wanting to take your little coterie with you?"

"I'm sure they would help, and be helpful, but I'm not sure I can drag them off into danger again. Let me think about that and get back to you."

"As you wish. You will, of course, be taking Martin... I apologise 'Sunbolt'."

"He wouldn't have been on my list."

"Perhaps not, but he is my agent at the Academy and he will be accompanying you. You may not like him, but if you discover and face the people who took my son you will need him. I will speak to him with some very particular instructions."

"Right. Sure." *I'm sorry, what*?

"I will also broach the subject of your true identity with him. I believe it is only fair he knows that."

"Yes. Of... course."

I promised to call her again in the morning once I knew my travel plans and bid her good night.

I'd kind of forgotten that she must have agents, other agents, here. I had always somehow assumed they would be a student, but, okay, I can see Sunbolt being a corporate sell-out. Ahem, don't look in the mirror. And now I thought, that was also probably why he ended up being assigned to the Bantus mission. Of course, if he was going to be briefed on who I was... I guess he'd be slightly less eager to protect a Gravane stand-in than Gravane himself. But fine, I could look after myself, I always had.

There was a knock at my door.

Odd. I checked the time, it was getting late, but not very late yet.

I opened it, without thinking, without checking, because I am a stupid idiot who deserves to be assassinated by a micro-drone. Or worse...

Seventhirtyfour and Pilvi were standing there. "Okay. Who the hell are you?"

CHAPTER 15
TRUTHS

Pilvi pushed me back into the room, and wordlessly, Seventhirtyfour followed. He closed the door behind them.

For my own part, I'd forgotten all words ever, unable to frame any kind of response.

"And before you start with the clever lies that you do so well," Pilvi said, "you should know we just listened to every word of your conversation with your mother. Except she isn't, is she?"

Against the vastness of the question of my identity, this one was a smaller, easier question. I found the word "No," and retreated further into the room.

"Stop, come on, Grey. Stop and talk to us. Help us understand why you've lied to us so long?"

I stumbled and all but fell into my chair.

"Talk to us, or I'll have Seventhirtyfour rip the truth from your mind."

Seventhirtyfour loomed over me, stone-faced, half cast in shadow. It had been a long time since I'd last seen the Brontom as scary, but in the right light, he was terrifying.

For a moment. Until he sagged in on himself. "Come on Grey, you know I wouldn't do that even if I could," he said. "You trust me, right, so, trust me, you know?"

I nodded. Held up one hand to ask for a moment to assemble my thoughts. I could tell them a half-truth, tell them that I'd always been an agent of the Gravane family, here as cover for Mirabor Gravane... but I was struck by the idea of how freeing it would be to be totally and truthfully honest.

And so... slowly at first, I told the story. Just like I'm telling it to you now. Well, perhaps a little less polished, that was the first time, after all.

They listened, kept reactions to a minimum, though I could see several points that Pilvi wanted to blow her top at, particularly during the Bantus field trip. When I finally caught up to their knock at the door, we all just kind of stopped, and looked at each other.

At long, long last, Seventhirtyfour was the first to break the silence. "So, all of this was just a joke to you, you were laughing at us and the Academy?"

I started to shake my head, but no, complete honesty. "For the first few hours. Yes. But hearing Pilvi talk about how she wanted to use what she knew to help people. I realised then I was being an ass. And okay, I may have lapsed on occasion... I mean, come on, the Avenging Spider? Lady Psion? Captain Turtle? You can't tell me there's not something just a little bit ludicrous about what goes on here. Some of what we do. But the heart, the soul of this place is amazing. The galaxy needs more space alien superheroes. Maybe I could be one, someday."

"Using your superpower of lying?" Pilvi's voice was hard.

"Do you know what? Yes. If that's what's needed. What's that line in the advert again, Seventhirtyfour?"

Grudgingly he quoted it. "'It's a big galaxy. Somewhere in it, whatever you can do, whatever you are, *is* special.'"

"Exactly. And tomorrow, I know where that place is for me. It's the planet Nymanteles because somewhere on it is a guy about my age, who's in trouble. He needs my help, and if lying my ass off helps him, that's what I'm going to do. It's what I have left, maybe it's all I ever had."

Pilvi ran her hands through her hair. "But you still

haven't said," she said, sounding anguished, "who are you? What's your name, even?"

I paused. Shook my head. "It doesn't matter. I'm nobody. Everybody here eventually has a new name they choose. I choose mine. Just call me 'Grey'. I've been more me as Grey than I have with any other name. So that is who I am."

I could see she wasn't happy, but she let it stand.

"Look, I'm sorry to let you down. Truly. There is a burning pit of shame and embarrassment in the middle of my chest that may never go away. But it's what happened. I can't unmake it. Before I leave tomorrow, and I can't imagine I'll be back, not now, but before I leave, I just want you both to know, I'm sorry. And it has been an honour to know you. I hope as friends, despite the pretence."

Seventhirtyfour's brow creased. "You sound like you're saying goodbye."

"Yes. I can't stay, I must go to Nymanteles, and I need to go tomorrow. My mo... Mrs. Gravane will be arranging it with Captain Hawk in the morning, and I have to go as soon as it's settled."

"Yes, of course, I understand that. But... we're coming with you, right?"

"I... what?"

Pilvi growled. "Well of course we are. Avrim probably wouldn't go, Dez still isn't ready for fieldwork, and Gadget Dude won't share a flight that long with Sunbolt, he never forgave him for killing that mechanical bird at the start of term. But you need me to keep you straight, and Seventhirtyfour to keep you honest. He saw through you."

I was stunned. Lost for words for the second time in the same conversation. I'd never imagined they would still be on my side.

"I told you," Seventhirtyfour explained, "I'd become sensitive to people's emotions, you know? And when Dez mentioned Nymanteles, your reaction was weird, I sensed a lot of excitement, quickly buttoned down. I knew you thought it was important, but I didn't know why. I told Pilvi."

"And I dropped one of Gadget Dude's bugs in here before we left," she said, positively daring me to call her on the breach of privacy.

I didn't. Couldn't. I was still amazed. "But after all this, you still want to help me?"

Pilvi rolled her eyes. "Of course, stupid. You may have lied about your name, convinced us to take on three mob families while still untrained and then stuck a target on our heads so big that some of us almost got blown up... but despite all that, you didn't lie about our friendship, did you? That wasn't an act?"

"No, of course not."

"Well then. We're your friends. We help each other. Right, Seventhirtyfour?"

"Right."

"Right," I echoed. I truly didn't deserve friends like these.

# # #

I don't know what Mrs. Gravane said to Captain Hawk this time but there was no private meeting or briefing. Just a note in my inbox that the *Metropolitan* was at my disposal. Fair enough. It's not like me and the headmaster were close or anything.

I packed my belongings; everything that I had bought with money I'd earned, not conned people out of. Everything which belonged to Gravane got left behind. I'd miss the top of the range kit and designer clothes... but I didn't think I'd be this way again, and besides, it didn't feel right to save a guy while wearing his jeans.

And I was going to save him.

This deal I'd cut with him had been a joke, a diversion, quick cash when it started out, but the Academy had taught me a lot, and not just about being a superhero. I owed Gravane. More than the money I'd taken in his name, more than that shirt of his I'd ruined in Parkour class, more than his education I'd co-opted, I owed him for finding me, even when I hadn't known I was lost.

My only regret was leaving the mystery of the bomber behind me. I sent what information we had to Avrim, Dez and Gadget Dude if they wanted to follow it up at this end they could, and maybe we'd turn something up on Nymanteles to help. I also sent them my confession, told them I wasn't Gravane after all, just a chancer nobody. I couldn't face the conversation again. But they deserved to know, too.

Pilvi, Seventhirtyfour, and Sunbolt joined me at the dock. Seventhirtyfour gave me an encouraging squeeze on the shoulder, Pilvi gave me a quick hug. It really felt like we were saying goodbye somehow, even though they were coming with me.

Sunbolt just sneered at me. "I knew you weren't anyone important."

We boarded, Sunbolt went straight to the back row. I took the corner at the front furthest from him. Pilvi and Seventhirtyfour sat on the front row, across the aisle from me. Close. But distant.

We passed the journey in awkward silence.

# # #

Nymanteles was a long way out, right on the very southern edge of explored (or at least inhabited) space. A good place to hide from your parents, I guess. It meant we'd have to change ships four times, and it would take us the better part of two weeks to get there. Of course, the first stop on the flight, and where we had to leave the *Metropolitan* behind, was Meanwhile Station. The place where Gravane struck his deal with me. It was odd to be back like I was unravelling the life I'd made this last year.

We had a few hours before our next flight. Sunbolt said he had stuff to do and would see us at the departure lounge. I was sure he was lying and just wanted to put some distance between us while he could. Technically he was still my bodyguard under Gravane's employ, there to make sure that I stayed safe while conducting my search. I didn't push the issue.

I remembered a suggestion Gravane had given me, a long time ago. "We have time for breakfast. I know a place, want to join me?"

Pilvi and Seventhirtyfour looked at each other and then, to my great pleasure, fell in behind me.

The station seemed smaller than I remembered, the corridors narrower and almost cramped after being used to the Academy. I still liked the yellowy-brown walls though, some things never go out of fashion. I took us up through the station to the nicer part of town, and the three of us stood looking out of the picture window at the planet. The clouds boiled for our pleasure.

"Those flashes is that a storm, or...?" Pilvi asked.

"I don't know, never found out."

She nodded.

We found a table at the restaurant and I ordered the continental breakfast. It was okay, but I needed something more filling, so I ordered a bacon sandwich to follow. Seventhirtyfour filled up too, his usual impressive order of cereal. Pilvi took coffee and toast.

In fits and starts, conversation began. Awkwardly at first, we were still finding the edges of our newly minted relationships, but slowly the remember-whens and the can't-believes wore away at the sharp corners. It was good to hear Pilvi laugh again, properly.

As the waiter cleared the plates away, the conversation hit a lull. Into the gap, Seventhirtyfour asked, "So, what happens when we get there? What's the plan?"

"I've been thinking about it, and I can't really offer anything except some old-fashioned detective work," I said. "I got some hits on this place for a Kayda Buchanan, she was an associate of Gravane's, possibly a girlfriend, who seemed to vanish from the social pages about the same time he did. We hit the streets, show some pictures, see if anyone knows or has seen Buchanan, Gravane or Hauberk."

Pilvi nodded. "Sky Diamond described it as a small outpost, right?"

"Lucy? Why would she...?"

"She's from there? She told us that night in the bar. Don't tell me you didn't remember?"

"I was very distracted, that was the night of the ransom call."

"Well luckily, I remembered and spoke to her before we left. You owe that girl an apology and a thank you." She flicked us some files from her wrist pad. "Her notes. Anything she thought might be useful. To sum up, there are no more than a couple of million residents on the entire planet, and most of them in a town around the spaceport.

"I was looking at the environment specs, looks like they'd have problems expanding, there's been no terraforming to speak of, and the soil samples don't suggest good farmland. It's the sort of place I could do a lot of good. I have some ideas..."

"One act of heroism at a time, Pilvi," I said, paging through Lucy's notes. "But, after we find Gravane, any help at all you need on the farming front, I'm there."

"Thanks."

Seventhirtyfour had his pad out checking maps of Nymanteles city. "Are you going to be okay here Grey? That's a lot of small, single-storey buildings and a lot of wide-open spaces."

I shrugged. "It will be what it is. I'm not looking forward

to it, but I'm not letting it put me off either."

"Do we know for sure where the last sightings of any of them were?" Seventhirtyfour offered up the map for me to look at.

"I don't have a last sighting for her, but Buchanan's old address was, let's see, yeah, over here on Library Street."

"So that gives us a starting point?" asked Pilvi.

"For one of us. We'll cover more ground more quickly if we split up."

"Not a good idea," she replied. "We don't know if we're on the right track, but if we are, there are some dangerous people around here. And it's not like Bantus where you're an unknown quantity and can talk your way out of anything. If the bad guys here were responsible for the attack on you, they know you and us. Splitting up just leaves us vulnerable."

"We can't just go around as a group though, we'll cover ground too slowly and besides, we won't be questioning people so much as mobbing them."

"Fine, so we split into pairs," she said, then paused. "I guess that would have to be... me and Sunbolt? Me and you, Grey?"

Seventhirtyfour said. "Dibs on not teaming up with Sunbolt. Plus, I don't want to get all powers snobby, but we should probably have one powered person in each pair."

"Fine," I said. "I see where this is going, I'll team up with Sunbolt, you two get to work together."

I tried not to feel too hurt that they high-fived at that point. I knew it was mostly about dodging working with Sunbolt. Mostly.

# # #

I could bore you with descriptions of space travel at this point, but we all know how it goes. The next two ships were fair size commercial liners, pleasant enough, particularly when you're taking them as a passenger and not cleaning toilets like I might have in the good old days. The next ship was a bit more run-down. Functional, but not comfortable.

The final leg was on a mail ship down to Nymanteles itself. The sort of thing held together with optimism and spot-welds. The pilot, the sole crew, met us at the airlock with a grin. "Four arms, glowing hair, a sweet girl and a cute but unreliable boy. You four must be the ones Lucy told me to look out for, surely? From the Academy? How's my little sky diamond doing?"

Now I remembered. Lucy said that her mother ran the postal service on Nymanteles.

"That's right, Mrs. McKenzie, I'm Pilvi, this is Seventhirtyfour, Sunbolt and... Grey. Nice to meet you."

"Please, everyone here calls me Lady Jane, no matter how often I tell them to stop. Might as well join in. And this is Grey, is it?" She looked me up and down. "Hmm."

"Very nice to meet you, Lady Jane," I said.

"*You* can call me Mrs. McKenzie."

"Right."

She turned back to Pilvi and Seventhirtyfour. "Welcome aboard The Beast. She may not look like much, but she's tough, and she's mine, and that's enough for me. We have a full load today, so it'll be a bit of a squeeze. You mind your head in there, big guy."

Seventhirtyfour bobbed his head. "Pardon me, ma'am, but this is an old Hyperflex Patrol Cruiser isn't it? We Brontom used to run a fleet of them as combat support vehicles."

"You have a good eye for quality machinery. You're right. Long since decommissioned, so no weapons or shields anymore, of course, but you could run her into an asteroid, and you'd need a new asteroid.

"But time we were pushing on, we have some post to

deliver. Make yourselves comfortable. As friends of Lucy, we'll take the special route into town."

The Beast rattled our bones on the descent, and Lady Jane skimmed us unnecessarily close to some satellites on the way down, spinning us as she whooped with glee. The ground came up terrifyingly quickly, and deceleration drove us deep into our seats, but touch down, when it blissfully arrived, was light as a feather.

Lady Jane laughed at our slightly grey expressions, but it was a joyful, not mocking, laugh. "You kids can fly with me any time," she said. "You think coming down is bad, wait until I take you back up!"

I didn't like to think, and the four of us grabbed our gear and made a hasty retreat.

# # #

My first ground-side view of Nymanteles was almost enough for me to turn back around and take up Lady Jane on her offer. The whole place was tinged with amber, a consequence of the orange hue to the local stone, reflecting a sky painted in shades of red.

I'd known, from the pictures and maps, that the world was under-developed, sparsely populated and had wide empty streets, but the reality was harder to deal with. The entire planet seemed to be made of open sky, with just a few ceilinged havens dotted hither and yon. I wasn't worried about Gravane's kidnappers, not really, perhaps I was being stupid, but I thought we could handle them. But all that empty air... how did anyone get anything done? I started to panic, just a little.

Pilvi reached out and took my hand, gave it a squeeze. "Come on Grey, let's get you inside."

Gratefully, I let her lead, over the road to a taxi rank, where we hired a car to take us to our hotel. Inside the car was much nicer, despite the smell and generally uncleaned and sticky feel of the back seat.

The hotel was a bland corporate thing. Clean, well-appointed and comfortable, if a little soulless. We took residence in a suite of rooms arranged around a central communal space aimed at the conferences market. The central room came well equipped with console and conferencing equipment, even its own small kitchen area. The roof, I particularly enjoyed.

Still, I couldn't cower undercover all day, much as I was tempted. We stowed our things and headed out.

The whole city was quiet. Not empty, you understand, there were plenty of people about, but there was no comparison to a world like Bantus, say. Roads were used by vehicles here because the pavements were plenty wide for the pedestrians. The place was designed to give you maximum access to the wide-open sky as if that was somehow a good thing.

And being paired up with Sunbolt wasn't helping. He was taking perverse delight in floating a few inches off the ground. I hissed at him to stop, partly because we were supposed to be keeping a low profile, but mostly because it was freaking me the hell out.

He was surly, but he complied.

Frankly, his whole attitude was starting to get on my nerves. "Look, I get that you're annoyed with me, that I'm not some golden ticket, after all, just a loser stand-in."

"Got that right."

"But seriously, of all the people to get pissed at me, you have the least right. Did you never once look at a picture of the guy you were supposed to be looking after, compare it to me and go 'hang on a second'?"

"It was an old photo."

"Sure, and it's nothing to do with you being gullible and lazy."

He let himself rise from the ground again, pantomiming

flailing arms. "Oh no, the gravity has stopped working again!"

Foolishly, I looked up at him and had to fight off a wave of the familiar reverse vertigo. "Get down here," I shouted.

He landed again but was looking very pleased with himself.

"Ass."

We decided that I should be the one to approach Buchanan's old residence. As the team's frontman, and with our strongest fighter to back me up, we were the logical pair. I braved the outside, again and again, going door to door, working our way along Library Street towards Buchanan's house. Seeing who was in, showing the photos we had of Gravane, Buchanan and Hauberk. Most of the people who would talk to me—and that wasn't everyone by any means—had no idea who the people in the pictures were. One of them did recognise the picture of Buchanan. I was told she was a planetary explorer by trade, though that seemed an odd fit for seeing her on the social pages of the news sheets. How did a woman like that cross paths with someone like Gravane anyway?

After the first dozen or so places, Sunbolt sidled up to me to whisper, "Have you seen we're being watched? "

"Yeah, I spotted him a couple of houses ago. He's not great at hiding, but he's definitely watching our progress." I paused. "Do you recognise the species?"

"No, I thought he was a Frantium, but..."

"Yeah, the nose is all wrong. Is it my imagination, or is he armed?"

Sunbolt looked over at our stalker. "I don't see... wait... yeah, I see it. Looks like a pulse pistol of some sort, though I don't recognise the make."

"Shall we go and talk to him? He might have seen the people we're looking for, after all."

For the first time in over two weeks, I saw Sunbolt give

a genuine smile. "It would be rude not to."

Our stalker backtracked when we turned towards him. For a moment, I thought he was going to run, but instead, as we crossed over the road, he pulled out his gun. He aimed for a beat at Sunbolt and pulled the trigger.

Sunbolt sidestepped at the last moment, judging it to perfection, just like he'd shown us dozens of times in class. He rolled his shoulders, leaning back, and the blast passed by harmlessly. "Idiot," he growled and leapt into the air, sunbolts blazing from his eyes.

The stalker tried to dodge, but he was too slow, taking a hit full bore to his chest. It lifted him off his feet, pushed him back down the road. But otherwise, it just seemed to annoy him. Now he fired continuously, and it was all Sunbolt could do to dodge and weave through the pulse fire, he managed a few return shots, but they were weak and unfocused.

Keeping my gaze firmly down, focused on our attackers' knees, I crossed over and ran forwards, I had no weapons to speak of, I'd trained in unarmed combat, and was good enough to impress Professor Red Ninja, but this guy was standing up to Sunbolt, I wasn't going to make a dent. I wished I had one of Gadget Dude's micro-grenades handy. Or a Power Ball stick, even. Still, perhaps a distraction would be enough. I lunged at his gun arm, letting my dead-weight drag at it... the gun barrel dipped, barely.

He pushed me away.

But the distraction was enough. As I was thrown clear, Sunbolt stared at the pistol, directing a precision strike at the gun. It exploded in a flare of sparks.

Our attacker yelped in surprise, and hopefully pain. With his off-hand, he grabbed my ankle and heaved. I felt the pain of my ankle breaking, and the terror as I was launched into the sky.

I'm not sure if I was thrown at Sunbolt, or if he

swooped to catch me and set me down safe, I'd like to think the latter. Either way, by the time we'd untangled ourselves and looked about for our attacker, he was long gone.

"Well," said Sunbolt, "I don't know about you, but I think that suggests we're on to something."

Tears of pain stinging at my eyes, I had to agree.

# # #

I tried to soldier on with my ankle, but in a show of uncharacteristic compassion, Sunbolt insisted we head to the med centre to get it looked at.

"Carrying on with you in this state would be idiotic," he said. "We need to get your idiot ankle to the emergency room, idiot." It may not have been compassion; he may just have enjoyed calling me an idiot.

We called Seventhirtyfour and Pilvi to let them know what had happened. They were going to come and join us at the med centre, but I told them to stay away. "Your work is more important. I'll be fine. But you should be careful. Keep an eye out for someone who looks like a Frantium but with a broader, flatter nose. If you see him, try and get a picture, but don't talk to him. Better if you just get the heck out of there."

Pilvi said, "Actually we saw someone like that earlier, a couple of them. Seventhirtyfour said he got a strange vibe off them, so we steered clear. We haven't seen them for an hour or so though."

"Great, so there's more than one? That's useful to know. Okay, keep us posted if you see them again. But keep them at a safe distance."

"Roger that."

We sat together in the treatment room, waiting for the med tech to arrive. Sunbolt fidgeted in his chair.

"Come on, out with it," I said, the pain in my ankle making me cranky. "You clearly have something to say."

"Yeah. Look, I... You did okay back there, in that fight."

"Sure, and now I have a broken ankle."

He shook his head. "You could have hidden from the fight, let me deal with it. Perhaps you should have. But you stood up beside me. He was bigger than you, tougher than you, it takes a special kind of idiocy to head into a fight like that. But it's a kind of idiocy... well I guess, I can respect that, or something.

"You did well. No shame in taking a hit. What we do is dangerous, nobody gets through unscathed forever. Take this pain, learn from it. Be better next time. But don't let it stop you. If you really want to be part of the Life, once all this is over? Come talk to me, Grey. I'll help you."

"Sunbolt, I... thank you."

"Idiot," he said, but with a smile.

The med tech came to have a look at my ankle at that point. Sunbolt wandered off to chat up some nurses, while the med tech scanned my foot.

"Well the good news is it isn't actually broken," she said "but you're going to have an impressive bruise, and it's going to pretty sore for a few days. How did it happen?"

"Door got slammed on it. How long before I can walk on it?"

"I'd stay off it as much as possible until the end of the week, at least. I can give you something to take down the swelling, ease the pain, but rest is the best healer for something like this."

"That's probably true, but I need to be mobile right now, I can't just sit still at the moment."

She stepped back, folding her arms. "Frankly, Mr. Grey, you should have thought about that before getting it caught in a door." She gave me a look. "What colour was the door?"

"Blue. Look I appreciate the concern, and I promise to get lots and lots of rest and recuperation, soon, but right now, is there nothing we can do?"

She gave a moue of disapproval. "We can strap it up. I can give you a shot, but I'll need you to sign a release form to say you're going against medical advice. And even then, it will get you walking, but don't go running any marathons or you can do serious and lasting damage."

"Thanks, right you are. Give me the thing to sign. I appreciate it."

Sunbolt nodded at me as I hobbled out. He passed his number to a nurse, and then floated over to me, his white-light hair shining. "Bet you wish you could fly about now."

"Thanks for that. Look it's too late in the day, let's go back to the hotel and meet up with the others. I think we know we're in the right place now. Something is happening here. We just need to figure out where and what and... do the superhero thing."

"An intricate and sophisticated plan. This is going to be Bantus all over again, isn't it?"

"Let's hope. That plan basically worked."

# # #

I spent a good hour fidgeting at the hotel waiting for the others to get back. The rendezvous time passed with no sign of them, and I began to fret even more. I tried calling Pilvi and Seventhirtyfour, and neither answered, which didn't help my calm.

When they did arrive, only fifteen minutes late, I felt like I'd waited a week. They both showed signs of having been in a scuffle, I leapt up to see if they were okay... and then I collapsed back into my chair again, as my ankle complained at the mistreatment.

My only consolation, despite their somewhat battered appearance, Seventhirtyfour was wearing a triumphant grin.

"You have news," I said. "Tell me you have news."

"We may have just broken this case wide open," said

Seventhirtyfour.

"We know who those people watching us were, and where they are based," added Pilvi.

"That's brilliant! How?"

Seventhirtyfour gestured to Pilvi. "You tell it, it was your idea."

Pilvi demurred. "Which wouldn't have worked without you, you should tell it."

Sunbolt growled. "We aren't very interested in the comedy routine. What did you find out?"

"Well," said Pilvi, "when you told us about your stalker, we started asking around about them, as well as Gravane and the others."

"That was Pilvi's idea," added Seventhirtyfour.

"Yeah, well people recognised the description. They're called the Vadram. And they've been a problem here for the last couple of years. A problem that's been growing. The first contact with them was... quite violent. Said first contact, so rumour has it, with a team of scouts led by one Kayda Buchanan."

"Really?"

"Yes. Thought you'd like that. What's less good news is there are at least a dozen Vadram on Nymanteles now, possibly more, they've set up a small colony in a cave system a hundred clicks north of here."

I shook my head in admiration. "That's really good work, guys. Though it doesn't explain why you look like you've been in a fight."

"Ah, yes, that," Pilvi looked embarrassed. "You know how you said if we saw a Vadram we were to steer clear."

"Distinctly."

"Well, we had another idea..."

"But it turned out to be a really good one," said Seventhirtyfour. "It's a little trick I've been developing in class, with my powers, you know? I can't read minds,

Professor Mindlord thinks I will never be able to, but I can project images into people's heads, and get a sense of how they react to them. When a Vadram showed up, we thought we'd try it."

"Honestly, the fight would optimistically be described as a draw," admitted Pilvi. "Neither side came out of it covered in glory... but..."

"He knew Gravane. He'd seen him recently," concluded Seventhirtyfour. "I don't know what sort of state he's in, but Gravane is definitely being kept in the Vadram base."

"About freaking time," said Sunbolt. "Let's go kick some alien butt!"

My first reaction was to counsel caution, to plan, to investigate further. But now the Vadram knew we were here. No telling what they'd do in response. They might move Gravane, or he might not live until the morning. There really was only one choice.

"So. Are we doing this?" I looked around the group. "No lies, this is going to be dangerous. We don't know how many of these things we're facing, but one of them held off Sunbolt. If we win this, it has to be together. Sunbolt, you ready for a rematch?"

"No question. They caught me by surprise last time. Not going to happen again."

I nodded. "Pilvi?"

"I'm not coming all this way to drop out now. We aren't going to leave Gravane there one day longer."

"And Seventhirtyfour?"

"This is why I came to Justice Academy, Grey, to help people in need. I am absolutely in."

"Okay then. Let's do this."

CHAPTER 16
RESCUE

"Can you see anything?" Sunbolt sounded tetchy. We couldn't risk people spotting the glow of his hair, so even with his hood up, he didn't get a turn at the binoculars.

"Yeah," I said "There's a couple of Vadram over by the main door. I don't think they're actual guards, but they might as well be. I don't see a way in except past them."

I shuffled back down below the ridge-line. "Looks like they've taken up housekeeping in a cave in that cliff face. They have their own shuttle, parked outside. The good news is unless they've been ferrying people in batches, their ship doesn't look big enough to carry more than about twenty Vadram. I guess that's also the bad news since even one of them was a pain in the ankle.

"The other bad news, though, between here and there, there's about half a kilometre of bare rock, no way we're getting over that without being spotted. Sunbolt could fly down the cliff, but for the rest of us, climbing down would be even slower than crossing the empty space."

"A direct frontal assault would be suicide," said Pilvi, though it's what we were all thinking. "And give them time to kill Gravane if they're inclined to it."

"So, we find another way in," said Seventhirtyfour. "It's a cave, there could be other caves that connect to it, they wouldn't expect us to come that way."

"It'd take too long," Sunbolt disagreed. "Even if there is another way it could take days to find it, and we agreed, this has to happen tonight."

I shook my head. "I'm afraid Sunbolt is right. So, if we must use that entrance, Rescueology 101 tells us, we need to get those Vadram away from the door. We need a distraction."

"Sabotage the shuttle?" said Pilvi, then before I could point out the flaw, "No, that might bring more of them out, not just distract the two of them."

"Hey, Numbers, can't you just daze them with your mind powers?"

"If he could do that, Sunbolt, he'd have done it to you long ago," Pilvi growled.

"Guys," I said, holding a hand up for quiet. "Look, we're all on edge, I get that, but sniping at each other isn't going to help. Keep all that focused that way." I waved vaguely towards the cave. "What we need is something curious, but not threatening to pull those two away without attracting more."

"Like a will o' the wisp," said Pilvi, and with a grin, she reached over and pulled down Sunbolt's hood.

"Ha!" said Seventhirtyfour.

Sunbolt angrily pulled his hood up. "That's idiotic. I'm your strongest, practically your only fighter, and you want me to move further away from the fight?"

"It's genius. She's right, a flyby from you is just the distraction we need. And you're right, you're the better fighter, once you get far enough away, take those two down and haul jets back. I expect we'll be in trouble enough by then."

I could see he wanted to disagree. But also, that he couldn't see a better plan in the time we had.

"Fine," he said. "But if you get yourself killed while I'm off being a wild goose chase, don't blame me!"

"You circle around to the left. We'll head right, the shuttle should provide us a little cover at least."

Sunbolt nodded. "You move as soon as I draw those two away. I don't know how long I'll be able to keep them on the hook, but I'll buy you what time I can. If they turn back, I can take them, I reckon, but it won't be subtle."

"Fair enough."

# # #

I watched Sunbolt work his way back down the ridge, veering away at the bottom, then Seventhirtyfour, Pilvi and I headed the other way. We moved in silence. I don't know what the others were preoccupied with, but for myself, I was wondering what to do once we got inside, because, obviously, I am an optimist, pining for a ceiling.

The key was going to be being quick and quiet. We couldn't afford a fight. The three of us together might be able to take a Vadram, if it came to it, or at any rate, Pilvi and I could help Seventhirtyfour, but not quickly, and not quietly. Which drastically increased the odds that we would be fighting more than one of them.

We got as close as we dared, then hunkered down behind some rocks. The bulk of the Vadram shuttle would do most of the concealing for us, but I needed to be able to see the front doors, so I knew when it was time to move. I gestured to Pilvi and Seventhirtyfour to stay down and edged sideways to open up the angle. I kept low and fell to my stomach when I caught my first glimpse of Vadram fur. I still needed a better view, needed to see both of them. I dragged myself forward on my elbows—a technique right out of Building Infiltration class. The Vadram weren't looking towards me. The bulk of the shuttle would keep them thinking this direction was "safe". In theory. As long as there were no cameras—I froze. *Cameras*. Why hadn't I—it was a cave, you don't think of caves having cameras. Right?

My mouth was dry, felt like it was coated with the reddish stone dust of the plateau. I moved my head, searching for any kind of cover. If there were cameras this whole thing might already be blown. But if I could find some cover, maybe I could still save this. Nothing. A wide flat open space.

My ankle throbbed. There was nothing to do but wait. And hope.

Time stretched. My heart beat against the rock of the plateau. Then, after an eternity, I saw a flash of light off on the far side. Sunbolt.

The Vadram saw it too; one pointed and there was a brief flurry of conversation.

When the flash happened again, the Vadram pointed more urgently, took a step in the direction of the light.

Almost.

Almost.

A *third* flash, and this time the Vadram moved, taking off at a jog, calling something over his shoulder. His buddy called after him, and for a second, I thought he was going to stay, but instead, he pulled out a comm and chased after him.

No reinforcements appeared, which was a relief, but I had to assume that the Vadram inside the caves would be on the alert. Not ideal but at least the way to the front door was clear.

In silence, we ran. No point trying to find cover, there was none, so we just covered the ground as quickly as we could.

We made it to and through the cave mouth. I felt the tingle of a heat shield as we crossed the threshold. On the other side, the temperature rose sharply, and the air was heavy, humid, and had an odd taste. If this was the kind of environment the Vadram preferred, I had to wonder what interest they had in a cold, dry world like Nymanteles.

Inside, I'd expected to find one large cave, but instead, a tunnel descended into the rock face. It was clear some effort had been made to increase its habitability; floor and walls bore signs of having been worked to make them smoother. Lighting and network cables were pinned to the wall. In fact, it had enough of a station-y feel, I felt positively at home. And if the ceilings were high, they were at least blissfully there, one less thing to stress about after being far too long outdoors.

The tunnel branched and without hesitation, I took the left path. On the general principle that if you have to make a decision based on no information, try to at least look like you know what you're doing.

It was becoming clear that the cave system was much bigger than we'd thought, with crisscrossing tunnels connecting wider spaces the Vadram were using as rooms. We caught occasional glimpses of one or more Vadram, but there was enough room we were able to keep out of their way. Which the optimist in me was trying hard to view positively, but it was starting to make me wonder.

I'd had visions of finding Gravane tied up in some dark corner of a cave, but this place... How were we going to even find him, let alone rescue him? We needed information, and I could only think of two ways to get it. Fortunately, we found an unattended console before we found a lone Vadram.

"Keep watch," I said. Hopefully, there would be a map, or schematics, or something useful to give us a clue.

I was a little surprised by the Gravane logo on the welcome screen; it's a common enough sight on consoles and pads, sure enough, but it felt weird finding it on the screen of his kidnappers.

I found the map, but my heart sank. "This place goes on for miles! Look there are barracks, kitchens, armouries, there's a room here annotated as the cinema!"

"That's great, Grey, but have you found the brig?" asked Pilvi.

"Not yet, I'm still looking. But what *is* this place? It looks more like a military base than the hideout of a group of kidnappers."

Seventhirtyfour loomed over my shoulder. "He's right Pilvi," he rumbled. "The scale... It's built for a lot more than twenty Vadram."

Then he gasped, grabbed me and Pilvi and pulled us into the corner behind the console.

Moments later, a Vadram came into the room. He didn't notice us, but there was no missing the fact that the console was open and running. He walked over and switched it off, looked around suspiciously.

Seventhirtyfour dipped a hand into his pocket and pulled out a strip of black cloth. I caught a glint of some wiring sewn into it. The Psionic Crown. The thing Gadget Dude had lashed together all those months ago. Seventhirtyfour wrapped the cloth around his head and stood up.

The Vadram spotted him instantly, and without even a surprised look, threw himself at the Brontom.

Seventhirtyfour swayed to his left.

The Vadram sailed by, but he gave a startled growl, twisted and jumped again. Once more Seventhirtyfour effortlessly avoided the blow.

"A friend made this for me, a long time ago," he said, continuing to avoid or block each of the Vadram's attacks. "He told me at the time it would enhance my powers, but I thought it hadn't worked, because I didn't understand back then what my powers actually were. Once I knew though, I found I could use the headband for all sorts of neat tricks. Though it gives me terrible headaches if I use it too much."

This time when he blocked, he twisted his shoulder, leaving the Vadram's throat exposed. He used a spare hand to punch it. "From the first day we're pulled from the pod, Brontom are trained and programmed for battle, but this is more instinctual. I call it 'Battle Precognition', I see exactly how you'll attack and how to avoid it before you even try. Cool, right?"

The Vadram staggered back, clutching at his throat. "I see your friends there," he croaked. "I have friends too; many, many, friends." He pulled out his comm.

Seventhirtyfour knocked it out of his hand before he could call anyone. "Yes, I saw that coming too. Still, even without calling for help, we only have ninety seconds before another one arrives, so I suppose we should get on with it. Grey, Pilvi, stay behind me. Let's see if the headband helps with one of my other abilities. Let's see... Where's Gravane?"

There was a visible rippling in the air, as Seventhirtyfour directed a blast of psychic energy at the Vadram. He sagged immediately afterwards. "Oh, there's the migraine."

The Vadram laughed. "Ha! I will tell you nothing."

Seventhirtyfour looked over his shoulder at me. "He's in the Control Centre. You know where it is."

"Yes."

"You and Pilvi get going. I can keep this guy occupied for 47 seconds after you leave, then I'll have to take the headband off. I can keep him busy a little longer after that, but I can't see if that's enough time. So, go!"

The Vadram pounced again, and this time connected. But I had faith in Seventhirtyfour; even if his Battle Precognition failed, he was still a Brontom clone, and they were born as warriors.

I looked at Pilvi. "Come on!"

As we ran from the room, alarms sounded.

# # #

Pilvi and I pressed on.

While there were similarities to a station, this was a cave system, and not all my instincts were right. We had to duck back around more than one corner that I had assumed would be helpful but turned out to be full of Vadram instead. And man, I missed service ducts. Still, I had a weird sense of déjà vu when a wrong turn sent the two of us into a Hydroponics bay.

Or that's what it looked like to me anyway. I didn't recognise the plants growing here, they certainly weren't the ones I'd seen on stations before, but the setup was the same; dozens of rows of planters, a complex lighting rig to provide plenty of light, and a network of irrigation tubes.

Pilvi gasped, amazed. "Grey, look at these!"

"I know, right, Hydroponics plants. I guess they're helping with the atmosphere mix?"

"Probably, a bit anyway, but no, look at these plants, have you ever seen them before?"

I shrugged. "I'm not really a plant guy, Pilvi. What is it you're seeing here that I'm not?"

She peered closely at them, not touching the plants, but she did rub some of the soil between her fingers, then sniffed it. "I've not seen them before either," she said. "I don't even recognise the genus. And I've studied plants, they're my superpower, remember?"

"Sure but, you can't recognise everything, right, it's a big galaxy, with a lot of plants."

"Shush, I'm thinking."

I shushed. But kept a nervous eye on the door.

She took a small toolkit from her utility belt, pulled out shears and a sample bag. She looked up and down the row. "This will take too long, Grey. I think you'll need to go on without me too. Can you get Gravane out alone?"

"I know I said I'd help with farming, but after the rescue."

"I'm not asking you to help, but if I'm right, this may be even more important than rescuing Gravane."

"These plants?"

"I think the Vadram may be new to this part of the

galaxy," she said. "I wondered when we didn't recognise them earlier, but it is a big galaxy, just like you said. I've studied hydroponic systems up, down and sideways, though, and I've never seen these arrangements before.

"This looks like a first contact situation to me, with a powerful, advanced species whose instincts involve kidnapping, thuggery and secrecy. We need to know about them, they could be dangerous. Well, we know they're dangerous, but I'm worried they might be *really* dangerous. And if they are, knowing things about their ecosystem could be really important."

I cast a glance back towards the door again. "Are you saying we need to abandon Gravane?"

She shook her head. "No. I'll take the samples I need, and then get out of here, but you still need to find Gravane. Will you be okay by yourself?"

I nodded. "Yeah, sure." My mouth was dry, there was a gnawing worry in the pit of my stomach, and it wasn't about the Vadram. "You be careful too, Pilvi. There's something off about this whole situation. Get what you need and get out. Don't take any unnecessary risks."

She grinned at me. "Right back at you, Grey." And then she set to taking her samples.

Alone, I carried on.

# # #

My problem was that the more I thought about it, the more that kidnapping seemed unlikely for the Vadram. The more we saw, the more convinced I was that the Vadram were not a bunch of space goons who had lucked onto the payday of a lifetime. They were organised, funded, well supplied. Pilvi was right, it was beginning to look to me as though the Vadram were properly dangerous and had a plan. And the idea that they had kicked off their plan by taking Gravane... No. I didn't believe it.

The software on their consoles, Gravane being 'kept' in the control room... The Vadram being discovered by Gravane's supposed girlfriend. There was a scam in the air, I could taste it, and I was fairly sure I knew who was behind it.

I slipped through an unguarded door to the control centre, ducked behind a console and had a look at who was doing the controlling here. And, yep. There we go. The person in charge of this group of hostile aliens:

Mirabor Gravane.

CHAPTER 17
ASCENSION

The guy I was there to rescue had been behind his own kidnapping all along. I should have known. I'm not sure how, but I'm sure I should have. I'd risked life, limb and friends to get to this point and it had all been a trick, a damned con game and I had fallen for it.

My first instinct was to go punch Gravane in the throat. But he wasn't alone. The Control Centre was an impressive space, decked out in monitors and consoles displaying a broad spread of data, I saw financials, shipping routes, security cameras showing various places around the caves, as well as the spaceport at Nymanteles. The consoles were staffed by Vadram, half a dozen in all, providing a constant background of chatter as they reported data to the man in the middle of it all.

Gravane for his part looked a little different than when I'd met him on Meanwhile Station. He held himself differently, seemed taller, certainly more confident, he was wearing a black pseudo-military uniform, the tunic looked to have a hood attached, though it was down at the moment.

One of the Vadram monitoring a security console spoke. "The Brontom has been subdued, sir, what do you want to be done with him?"

"Excellent. I am going to the Ascension Chamber, have him brought to me there. Where are the others?"

Another Vadram said, "The female was last seen in Hydroponics; a security detail has been dispatched to pick her up. No information on the other two."

Gravane nodded. "They will turn up, no doubt. Bring them all to the Chamber, once you have them. The boy must be kept alive, bring the others in whatever state they can be acquired."

"Yes, Doctor," the Vadram chimed.

Gravane strode out of the far door. I dithered for a moment, then ducked back out of the door on my side. I risked losing Gravane, but I could hardly cut across the crowded Control room.

Back out in the corridors, I ran, dull waves of pain rising up my leg each time I put weight on my bad ankle. If there had been Vadram there, I would have been caught instantly, I passed junctions and rooms without pausing to check, but I had to catch up with Gravane, there was a chance I could get to him while he was alone, and I had to take it.

I was hyper-aware of the sound of my footsteps, echoing off the bare stone walls. But what choice did I have?

I caught a glimpse of green out of the corner of my eye and skidded to a halt. Seventhirtyfour being carried by two Vadram, slumped, unconscious.

I hoped only unconscious.

I slowed my pace, soft-footed behind them. My chance to take Gravane alone was gone, but if they were taking Seventhirtyfour to Gravane, I could at least let them lead me.

A couple more twists and turns, deeper into the cave system. Less sign that this stone had been worked, but the tunnels were wider as they descended, and a mass of power cables was pinned to the wall. Whatever was in this Ascension Chamber drew an awful lot of power.

The Vadram stopped to readjust their hold on Seventhirtyfour and I heard him give a groan. He was still alive, thank the stars.

The corridor opened out. I dropped back a little, pressed myself against a fold in the rock of the tunnel wall. I could hear Gravane's voice from just up ahead, though I couldn't make out the words.

There were other sounds too, as I fought to steady my own breathing and heart rate, I could hear them better. A steady bass thrum of machinery ticking over, and occasionally a growling sound. An animal of some kind, it sounded big.

With a start, I realised there was another sound too. More footsteps, but these ones coming from behind me. And then I heard Pilvi, cursing loudly at, presumably, the Vadram that had captured her.

And I was stuck. There were no branches in the corridor here. The Chamber, Gravane and a pair of Vadram were at one end, and at least one Vadram was coming down the corridor from behind me. My hiding place was good enough to conceal me from ahead but would do nothing to hide me from the ones behind.

I checked the ceiling. Double-checked both walls. No hiding places. No choice. I squared my shoulders, and as casually as I could muster, I strolled into the Ascension Chamber.

"Nice cave," I said. "Like what you've done with it. That thing must have been a pain to get down the tunnel."

The thing in question was the source of the thrumming noise I'd heard. A rough cube of machinery about four meters to a side, most of what I could see was a twisted lattice of bronze-coloured tubes, intertwined and overlapping, buried into the ground, but shaped to form an alcove in one face large enough for a Vadram to stand in. A control panel covered in dials, buttons and lights stood out on another face of the machine. The lights reminded me of something, and it took a moment to realise what. Sky Diamond's headband. Whatever it was, it came from here, a fragment of this machine. There were other pieces missing too, components ripped out or damaged, replaced and jerry-rigged with much more familiar technology. Gravane technology.

Gravane himself sat at a trestle table, watching me take it in. Seventhirtyfour and his Vadram captors were closer to the machine. Seventhirtyfour's eyes were open, but he looked dazed and groggy, and they had him chained to the side of the machine. I couldn't see the far wall of the chamber, but I could hear what sounded like a waterfall in the darkness. That animal growl sounded from somewhere in the gloom.

Gravane smiled and gestured to the seat opposite him. "Come in, sit down. I am sure you have a lot of questions, and we have a few minutes before my men have collected the rest of your friends, I expect."

I approached, as casually as I could. "Well, I do have one or two things I'm curious about," I admitted. One of us was playing for time, and I had a horrible feeling it was me.

"Please, sit," he reiterated. "Can I pour you a coffee Mister... I'm sorry, I never did get your real name."

I sat. "Just call me Grey, everyone else does."

Gravane laughed. "Ah, very clever." He cocked his head. There was something different about him, I couldn't quite put my finger on it. "A contraction of 'Gravane' I guess? You were telling the world that you're not the real thing, but I bet nobody noticed, did they? You must have laughed your ass off at them."

"It wasn't like that."

"No? But I like it, you're caught between one extreme and the other. Yes." He poured me a coffee, though I hadn't asked. "Of course, it's a bit ironic. You've chosen a shorter name because you didn't feel up to the weight of being a Gravane, whereas I... ah, it seems our next guest has arrived."

Two more Vadram entered, flanking Pilvi. She looked

unhurt but furious. Her sample bag was bulging, so she had at least gotten her clippings before being captured.

"Sorry Grey, I didn't get as far out as I'd hoped," she said.

"No problem, glad to see you."

"Welcome," said Gravane, "could I ask you to take a seat over there by the Brontom? My men will need to tie you up, but I won't keep you long, there are a few things I need to tell your fake Gravane, and then we can get out of here. Thanks." He waited for Pilvi to sit, and for his Vadram to secure her to the chair, then he nodded and all four of the Vadram left.

Gravane studied me with a smile that slowly twisted into something else. I saw it now, the difference. The Gravane I'd met on Meanwhile was spoilt and out of touch, but this Gravane, there was a light in his eye, an intensity to his stare, his mannerisms were heightened, his energy wrong. He wasn't entirely sane. "Now you're wondering why I dismissed my Vadram, right? Thinking that I look like you could jump me, and take me prisoner? And yet, you're thinking, why would I leave myself vulnerable like that? I seem confident, there must be something you're missing."

"You're quite the mind reader."

"Not at all," he laughed. "But I do have certain resources of which you are unaware. And Mr. Hauberk is never far away."

That snarl sounded from the darkness again.

"So then, Grey. Yes, I do like that name, it suits you. A lot has happened since your help let me escape my mother. You don't know it, but you have helped me several times since. There is a lot I have to thank you for."

"Always happy to help..."

"Ha. But it seems for every time you've helped me, you have also found a way to block my plans or put me in fear of my life. Yes. I can't quite hate you, but I can't thank you either. You are somewhere between. Grey, yes."

"Look if you want to keep talking in cryptic allusions, that's fine, but I've had a long day, my ankle is killing me, and my patience is pretty much gone. So, either tell me what you want to or let us go."

Off in the distance, from back in the tunnels, did I hear a fight? Could Sunbolt be on his way?

Gravane stood up and moved over to the machine. "The Vadram call this their Ascension device. It, and others like it, was an important part of their culture, a rite of passage for each Vadram warrior to enter adulthood. A Vadram who passes through is... augmented. They leave it stronger, healthier, more fearsome warriors.

"It's quite a sight."

He flicked a few switches, tell-tales flashed blue to yellow, signifying... something.

"Its effects on humans are a little unpredictable. Kayda's transformation was... astonishing. But of course, you met her on the beach. She will be so sorry she missed you, but she is away at the moment.

"I was pretty excited to try it myself. But Mr. Hauberk insisted on going first, and I am very glad he did."

Behind the machine, I saw a figure loom. It had been human once, I recognised the face, twisted though it was, as Gravane's bodyguard Hauberk. He... it... had come at the sound of its name, but there was no intelligence there. A mass of melted flesh and muscle, it looked very wrong; powerful, but unnatural.

"He still protects me, that seems instinctual, but the rest of his mind is long gone," said Gravane, he looked up at the beast almost fondly.

That thing that had been Hauberk gave a rumbling growl.

"Obviously I couldn't risk it, once I knew what could happen."

"Obviously."

"But that was a problem. The Vadram find it difficult to follow the unascended. For as long as I had the money to buy them what their base needed, they followed grudgingly, but when the money began to run out, I started to lose them. I needed some more funds, more than my allowance covered. Building an army isn't cheap."

"So, you had the Vadram 'kidnap' you."

"Yes," he said. He pulled up his hood, to show the skull motif. He had been Skull face. He had been on the beach at the ransom payment. "But it wasn't enough. They had fallen out of the habit of following me."

"They seem to be back on your team again now." Realisation dawned. I was suddenly cold. He'd taken the risk. "You went through the machine."

"Yes. It was terrifying. Liberating. Agony and bliss. I left my family to become my own man. I am that now. That and so much more.

"The process changed me. In more ways than one." He turned a dial on the device's control panel, and the steady thrum rose to a higher, more urgent, pitch. "What do you say, Grey, do you want a turn? You want to be a superhero, right? This thing might get you there..."

"Or do what it did to Hauberk? I'll pass, thanks."

He stared at me a long moment.

Then he grinned. "Sure thing." He turned the dial back down and the machine returned to a purr. "Probably better that I don't give my nemesis superpowers anyway. Assuming the machine judged you worthy to receive them."

I breathed again. "Great. So... what did you bring us here for then, if it wasn't to feed us to your hell machine?"

"I would have thought that was obvious. I can't let you go having seen this. This place is supposed to be secret. The Vadram have gone to great lengths to convince people that there are only a handful of nomads here. We'll have to take

Nymanteles soon enough, but we're not ready yet. And you don't get to spoil the surprise."

A white light glimmered from the tunnel. There was a sound of rushing wind. I needed to hold Gravane's attention a little longer. I stood, moved towards him, making sure his focus was on me. I gestured to Pilvi and Seventhirtyfour to get ready, shielding the sign with my body. "You're planning to invade this place? What's the point? There's nothing here."

"Not an invasion, not here. A consolidation. We have big plans, the Vadram and I, and they all start here. I provide the funds for this place, and they..."

"What? What do you get from this deal?"

"Independence. Freedom. To be my own man, out of the shadow of my family. To be remembered for me, no mere footnote to the Gravane clan, not the sixth child that everyone —my parents included—forgets. I'm building something here, not in the Gravane name. In mine." He placed a hand on my chest to stop me advancing. "I wanted power, Grey, and I found it."

There was a flash of red light, and something kicked me in the chest with enough force to throw me back ten feet. I skidded across the floor, fighting to catch my breath.

Gravane's hands glowed ruby red, and he gestured towards me, a bolt of energy lashed out, and it was all I could do to throw myself to one side. The blast punched a smoking crater in the cave wall.

Now I was in trouble.

Sunbolt exploded out of the corridor in a blaze of white light, took one look at the situation and blasted Gravane. Gravane held up his hands, and his red light seemed to drink in Sunbolt's beam.

"Mr. Hauberk, kill this one," said Gravane, and the beast lumbered forwards.

Sunbolt blanched. "What is that thing?"

"Doesn't matter, just be careful of it," I gasped, still fighting for breath.

Pilvi was struggling against her restraints, but Seventhirtyfour was still dazed and out of the fight. For now, it was me and Sunbolt against Gravane and his monster. And right now, that meant Sunbolt against them both; he swooped and dodged, keeping out of Hauberk's reach while dodging Gravane's crimson energy blasts. He took shots back as he could, but focused on defence, the only blows he landed were glancing and ineffective.

All I had to help were words, but Gravane seemed the chatty sort, so maybe words were enough to keep him busy.

"Hey! Gravane!" I shouted, but Gravane kept blasting.

I continued anyway, shouting at Gravane's back. "You're pretty damn disappointing you know?" I staggered to my feet, my injured ankle burning in pain. "After all your mother has told me about being a Gravane, about it standing for something, honour, tradition, family first? You're a spoilt brat who didn't get his own way and has a major sulk on. Frankly, of the two of us, I am a better Gravane!"

That got his attention.

He spun, firing a wild burst at me. I stood my ground, partly in confidence, partly because I wasn't sure my ankle could take any more punishment.

More words. "You may have superpowers, but you're still weak, Gravane!"

"Don't call me that anymore," he spat at me. "Gravane died in that machine, and I Ascended in his place." His whole body began to radiate a blood-red energy, and he literally ascended, rising to hover two feet off the floor. "I was the death of the real Gravane, and now I shall destroy his feeble shadow. My name is Doctor Gravestone!"

Gravane... Doctor Gravestone... Gravestone, whatever you want to call him, seemed to be spiralling, the more he displayed his power, the more unhinged he seemed. He fired at me, again and again, roaring in wordless hate as he did. I did what I could to get out of the way, but that wasn't much. My injured ankle wasn't taking my weight, and all I could do was hop. If Gravane... Gravestone... had been a better shot, or just taken a moment to aim, I'd have been toast. As it was, it was only a matter of time before my luck ran out.

I was peripherally aware that Sunbolt was doing better against Hauberk. From what little I saw, the creature shied away from Sunbolt's light, the glare of Sunbolt's hair. His bolts were hurting it too, and Hauberk gradually retreated away from the machine and me. That was for the best, but I started to feel lonely and exposed.

"Hang in there Grey!" Pilvi shouted. "Almost free!"

Gravestone turned to look, and I took the chance to scoop up a rock from the floor and hurl it at the back of Gravestone's head. It turned to dust as it hit the red energy surrounding him, but at least it pulled his attention back to me.

"Hey Gravestone, anyone still in there? Anything you want us to tell your mum when we've kicked your ass?"

He just howled, abandoned shooting, and dove at me. We collided heavily, and he drove me into the wall.

All I could do was scream. Whatever that energy he was putting out was, it burned like acid, every inch of exposed skin stung. If he felt even a part of this when using his powers, I felt my sympathy rising, even as I punched him in the stomach. The hit seemed to hurt me as much as him.

If this went on much longer, his energy aura would do his work for him, even if he never landed another hit. I didn't have any of Gadget Dude's grenades, couldn't reach my grapnel gun. But Gravestone made a mistake bringing it to close range, he might have superpowers and a manic intensity, but I had months of training under Professor

Red Ninja and Sunbolt. I grabbed, put my shoulder to Gravestone's chest, twisted, heaved. Planted feet, balance and leverage would beat floating rage every time. Gravestone tumbled away from me, struck the ground with a solid thud.

I couldn't follow up my advantage, I was too busy slumping to my knees, even removed from Gravestone's energy field, I felt drained, every muscle spent.

I heard the pitch of the Ascension machine change.

Gravestone and I both turned to look.

Pilvi stood by the machine's controls, Seventhirtyfour sagged beside her; he looked to be in as bad a shape as me. Pilvi was turning every dial she could find to maximum, flicking every switch. All of the blue tell-tales had turned yellow, and one was burning violet.

"This thing is important to the Vadram right?" Pilvi shouted over her shoulder. "I don't know what happens when I switch everything to max with half a dozen flash grenades jammed into its workings. Maybe nothing, right? But I bet your pet army would be pretty annoyed if it blows up?" Another light switched to violet. "Is that a good sign?"

"Don't!" I'm not sure if I shouted it or Gravestone did.

"It's okay. I'm sure... Gravestone can fix this before anything really bad happens. But he'll be too busy to stop us leaving."

It was a fine plan or would have been, but Pilvi hadn't seen the look in Gravestone's eyes. There was no reasoning with him.

Gravestone erupted into motion, hurtling towards Pilvi...

Pilvi, shocked, turned to look, jostled a control...

All the lights on the Ascension Machine flickered to a virulent purple...

I saw Sunbolt, blazing white, flying back to the confrontation...

"No!" I couldn't stop it.

Gravestone roared again, crimson energy boiled from his hands, no need to aim, it formed a torrent of death washing towards Pilvi.

But then Sunbolt was there, shining like the sun. Just as Gravane had absorbed Sunbolt's energy, Sunbolt seemed able to counter Gravestone's. Sunbolt's light got brighter and brighter, it hurt to look.

For one moment...

One eye-blink of a moment...

I thought we were all going to get out of there in one piece.

CHAPTER 18
FALLOUT

Sunbolt could contain no more.

The moment broke in a burst of light.

Gravestone's beam reached him, struck him in the very centre of his chest, and Sunbolt screamed as he dissolved. Bright white light splintered from Sunbolt's body as it collapsed in on itself. Splinters struck the floor, the ceiling, Pilvi and Seventhirtyfour, the Ascension Machine.

And then Sunbolt was gone.

Just gone.

Nobody deserves...

Sorry.

Yes.

Sunbolt was dead.

# # #

Gravestone dropped to the ground, barely glowing a glimmer of red. "What are you doing, get away from the Ascension Machine!" he shouted, as though the last few minutes hadn't happened at all. He stumbled towards the machine. "Keep away from it!"

I hobbled towards my friends.

Pilvi had collapsed at Seventhirtyfour's feet. He was looking down at her with a confused expression, but he seemed more aware than before.

Gravestone fell to the controls, trying to undo Pilvi's tampering. He seemed to have forgotten we were there. "No, no, no. I can't... what have you done? Hauberk! Hauberk! I need you!"

I reached Seventhirtyfour and Pilvi. She was unconscious, the stray blast she'd caught when Sunbolt... died... it had knocked her out, though I could see she was still breathing. I turned to Seventhirtyfour. "I can't carry Pilvi out of here, not sure I can make it myself. Pilvi needs you." I grabbed him by shoulder, tried to give it a shake. The Brontom hardly moved. "Snap out of it. Come on. I promise, if you can get her out of here, that's all I ask."

A siren sounded all around us.

Gravestone was shouting, an edge of panic in his voice. "Hauberk! Hauberk! Come on! Where are you!"

I could see a light back in Seventhirtyfour's eyes, he frowned, looked at me for the first time. "Grey?" he croaked.

"Seventhirtyfour! We're in trouble. Pilvi's out, I can barely walk, let alone run, and I think this thing might be about to explode. We need to go. Now."

He shook his head to clear it, then stooped to pick up Pilvi. "I'd try to carry you too," he rumbled, "but I need you to lead. Don't know the way out."

"Okay, sure, but let's get moving."

We left, three survivors of a failed rescue attempt. Behind us, the monster that the man we came to rescue had become bellowed for his bodyguard.

We were in no shape to fight our way out of the caves, but for once luck broke our way. Half of the Vadram we saw were running towards the Ascension Chamber, the other half ran ahead of us towards the exit. Neither group seemed bothered by us. Not enough to try to stop us anyway.

Seventhirtyfour came back to his normal self with each step; which was a relief, because we hadn't made it to Hydroponics before my ankle finally and totally gave out. Seventhirtyfour slung me over his shoulder and ran. All I could do was call directions and try not to get jostled off.

Up the last corridor to the exit, we were running with Vadram. They were talking in their own language, and while I didn't get the words, I got the sense; they were in a panic. The siren still echoed through the tunnels, and a rumble from far behind us was building. Dust and grit rained down on us. Seventhirtyfour fought to keep his footing as the rock floor juddered.

"That machine is bringing the whole cave system down!" I yelled.

Seventhirtyfour just nodded and powered on.

There was an explosion, far behind us, down in the depths. The floor kicked us up, then vanished beneath us, sending us and the Vadram sprawling. I was thrown from Seventhirtyfour's shoulder, but he managed to keep Pilvi secure, his lower arms holding her into his body, while he broke his fall with his upper arms.

"Go!" I yelled and pulled myself forward with my hands. I could see daylight ahead, we were almost out, but I could feel the entire cliff we were under shifting and re-balancing, the air pressure from behind rose, pushed us onwards as tunnels and caves were crushed flat.

In a last desperate heave, I pulled, kicked, threw myself forward, rolling sideways as a great gout of rock-dust exploded above me.

We were out.

But so were a few dozen Vadram, and it wouldn't take them long to go from dazed and confused to looking for someone to blame, and we would be head of that queue.

Seventhirtyfour was there, covered in rock-dust, still cradling Pilvi to his chest. "Grey... Grey, where's Sunbolt?"

I shook my head. Later. No time for grief now. "We can't stay here. Can you carry me? We need to get to the car."

He knew what me dodging the question meant. I could see it in his face. He said nothing though, just nodded, shifted his grip on Pilvi, and dragged me up as well.

He set off at a stumbling run. I could tell that Seven-thirtyfour was exhausted. Already today he had taxed his psychic abilities to the limit, suffered migraines, a beating, and now I was pushing him again and again, draining his physical resources too. But I couldn't help. Could only be a burden, now.

We circled the ridge; the car was just ahead. His pace slowed, his breathing more laboured. What he was doing was superhuman, pushing the limits even for a Brontom. He was amazing. Pilvi was amazing. She'd faced off against Gravestone, afraid, but determined. What she did was downright clever, using the machine as a bargaining chip to get us out of there. Sunbolt had been amazing, beaten off one monster, then sacrificed himself to protect people that he didn't really like from another.

And I... had dragged my friends into danger, to rescue someone who not only didn't need rescuing but was, in fact, the biggest single danger there. And my greatest contribution to the ensuing confrontation was being extra weight for Seventhirtyfour to carry.

The last few steps to the car were torture. But we got there.

I slid behind the controls. Sunbolt had driven us out here. My piloting experience was limited to lifters in space docks, so it wasn't a smooth ride, but we made it back to town in one piece. I parked, badly, in the Med Centre car park, and Seventhirtyfour got me and Pilvi into the building.

# # #

The med tech was not happy to see me again.

This time she wanted to admit me, and restrain me, but I couldn't let her do that. We compromised on a cast and a wheelchair. I promised that I didn't want to walk anywhere right now. She told me in no uncertain terms that I wasn't to even try walking for a fortnight. There was only so much osteo-stim could do.

In the meantime, they were getting Pilvi settled. The med tech dealing with her was a little more forgiving than my sparring partner. He gave us a running commentary as he worked. Her vitals were good, though her temperature and pulse were a little high.

"No sign of any physical trauma. How did you say this happened?"

"An energy discharge," I told him, keeping the truth as simple as could be managed.

He hmm'ed. "I see some burning on the clothes, but there's no discolouration of the skin, no scarring or puckering. Skin temp is a little elevated, but not much. What type of energy discharge?"

"Honestly, I don't know." I kicked myself, I try never to say 'honestly' because it reminds people that the rest of what you said might not be true.

He hmm'ed again. "I need to check her neurological response." He took a pen light from his pocket and flicked it on. He pulled back Pilvi's left eyelid, then jumped back in surprise.

"Sorry, that was a shock. Her charts say she's human," he said, accusingly.

"She is!"

"Any cybernetics I should know about?"

"None," I said.

"In which case, I need a consult from a colleague." He pulled a curtain across Pilvi's cubicle and pressed a button on the panel on the wall. A low continuous hum started, and I could see a shimmer in the air. "Stay clear of your friend for the moment. Since you can't tell me what type of energy she was exposed to, I have to assume it was some kind of exo-tech. I can't say for sure if it's dangerous, but for your sake, better stay clear. Were either of you exposed?"

Seventhirtyfour and I shook our heads solemnly.

"Well, okay. But if you experience any odd symptoms at all, you let me or one of the nurses know immediately, understood? Okay, you'd better go back to the waiting room."

"What did you see? What's got you so worried?" I asked.

He shook his head. "Too early to make any kind of diagnosis. You boys go take a seat in the waiting room, we'll make sure your friend is okay."

I cast Seventhirtyfour a very quick glance. I caught a slight nod from him. "Thanks, Med Tech Naimon," I said. "Could I trouble you for a push in the right direction, I'm afraid I haven't mastered the chair yet."

"Let me call an orderly for you," he said and stepped out into the hall.

Seventhirtyfour quickly disengaged the quarantine lock, slipped through the curtain, and was back just in time to switch the quarantine on again before the Med Tech returned.

Seventhirtyfour was looking far too deliberately innocent; the med tech gave him a long look before saying, "So then, lads, the orderly is on the way, let me just move you to the hall."

"Thanks for your help," I replied.

He pushed me out into the corridor, Seventhirtyfour obediently followed.

Once the Med Tech left, I shuffled the chair around, so I could look straight up at Seventhirtyfour. "Okay, spill. What did you see, what was it that spooked the Med Tech so much?"

"Her eyes," said Seventhirtyfour, "they were glowing, with a bright white light... just like..."

"Sunbolt."

# # #

We retired to the waiting room. Seventhirtyfour folded himself into a chair, and I wheeled up beside him, intending to sit there and wait for news that Pilvi was okay. I sat, fidgeting, worried. Worried for Pilvi, but also worried about the wider situation.

I was trying to figure out what we had to do next. I needed to talk to Mrs. Gravane, but I was also worried about the Vadram. What would they do now that we'd taken down their leader, blown up their base and destroyed their Ascension Machine? I was all too sure that it was bad news for Nymanteles having a few dozen hostile, angry and abandoned alien warriors near to town. They might leave. If we were lucky. But their shuttle wasn't big enough to evac them all.

Seventhirtyfour broke me out of my spin with a subdued rumble. "Tell me what happened to Sunbolt, Grey."

I nodded. "In the fight he... how much did you get of what went down?"

"Not much," he admitted. "My migraine blotted out most of it, except loud noises, high emotions..."

"Yeah. Sunbolt died. He was saving Pilvi and you from Gravane who... No. It's too much. I need to start at the beginning to try and process it too. But in a moment. First. Yes. Sunbolt died a hero."

"And it was Gravane who killed him? How did the guy we came to rescue end up, you know, like that?"

"Yeah. The full story, near as I can figure it: Kayda Buchanan encountered the Vadram who were trying to infiltrate Nymanteles. For reasons I'm not so clear on, instead of reporting this to the authorities, she put the Vadram in touch with Gravane. Gravane for his part saw the Vadram as his own power base to let him cut ties to his family, so took some of the family wealth and helped the Vadram set up that base.

"The machine in there that we blew up was called

the Ascension Machine, and it gave Gravane, Hauberk, and I think Buchanan superpowers. The Vadram use it to augment themselves, the effects are less dramatic on them. On humans, it does something to the mind too... Hauberk was mentally... gone, and I think it affected Gravane too, although in a different way."

"You think he was working with the Vadram because their machine drove him insane?"

"No. That would be a nice out. But, no, I think he was already all in with the Vadram long before he used the machine. But it did something to him. The more he used his powers, the less of a grip he seemed to have. The stronger he got, the less coherent. When he... blasted Sunbolt, he was pretty much mindlessly raving. And calling himself 'Doctor Gravestone'."

Seventhirtyfour took a long moment to process it all. Eventually, he said, "We're out of our depth here, Grey. We need to talk to the authorities. We need to contact Captain Hawk."

I nodded. "And Mrs. Gravane. I hate to leave Pilvi here alone, can you…?"

"Of course, Grey. I'll call you immediately if there's any news."

I took the chair out of park and whirred away.

Time was of the essence, but I still didn't want to make the call out where anyone could listen in. The hotel was a better choice, it was nearby, and the route flat enough to navigate in the chair. There was the matter of the open sky, but I wasn't letting that stop me. I'd just survived a cave-in, if anything was going to cure me of the need to be under a roof, you'd think that would be it.

Sadly not. I still needed to close my eyes and push the control stick forward to get the chair through the front door. *One day, one day.*

It was full dark now. Late in the evening, but there

were a few people on the streets, heading home or heading out. Lady Jane's mail shuttle roared overhead, coming in for a hard landing, it all seemed so normal. I hoped it could stay that way, but if the Vadram decided to take out their frustrations here, then it could all change very quickly.

I had to decide what order to make my calls in. The most important was notifying the local police that there might be trouble, but on reflection, they'd have little reason to believe me. Oh, I could bring them around, a few choice words in the right places, but that would take time and I needed to get them mobilised fast. That required some proper heavyweight clout. Fortunately, I knew just where to find some, though it meant making the hardest call first.

I keyed in Mrs. Gravane's comm code.

I saw her greeting die on her face as she saw my expression. "You have news. And it isn't good," she said instead.

So, I told her everything. My first instinct had been to soften the blow, a few white lies to ease her mind, but I'd lied to her often enough, she would have known. And she deserved the truth.

She sat quietly like stone through my recap of events, and all that had happened to her son. When at last I had run out of story and breath, she nodded once, calmly to acknowledge the telling. Her expression was fixed, closed, but I could see a reddening of her eyes as she fought tears.

"You do not..." her voice cracked "... know if my son is dead for sure?"

"No, ma'am. I don't think it's false hope to suggest he could have survived the explosion and cave-in. I can't say what state he will be in mentally, he... was having problems, towards the end."

"Nevertheless, I must thank you, Mr. Grey, it is more information than my investigators brought me. Though many of them were associated with Mr. Hauberk, and I do wonder if there were divided loyalties fuelling their reports."

I said nothing. I'd wondered the same thing. Finding Gravane hadn't been *that* hard.

"We have more immediate concerns though?"

"I'm afraid so, Mrs. Gravane. The Vadram..."

"Quite so. I will speak to the Councillor for Nymanteles immediately and have him report to you."

"I... that's not what I was asking for. I need them to be warned, just in case..."

"Mr. Grey, if the threat is real, I need to know somebody capable is on hand to deal with it. With the greatest respect to the locals, they've done nothing about the Vadram before now. Whereas you have scored a victory."

"Not a victory. Not that. Sunbolt. Pilvi. Even your son. Not a victory, Mrs. Gravane."

"It was not a triumph, granted, but it was still a victory. You made it in and extracted your team with useful intelligence. You know more about the Vadram than anybody else on that world, it seems to me. You are a known quantity, Mr. Grey, and I have good reason to respect your competence. I can think of nobody better suited to lead in the event that tensions escalate. Stand proud. We are Gravane."

"I..."

"Still, it is probably best I arrange reinforcements for you. I have some mercenaries nearby. They won't be able to reach you for a few days, but if things do turn badly, you will no doubt need them."

My head spun. What must it be like to have the level of wealth that could conjure up a military resource at need? I still didn't think I was the right choice to lead, but with a bit of luck, the local police would refuse to defer to me anyway. "Thank you."

"Well then, we had both better get to our duties."

"Yes. Mrs. Gravane?"

She quirked an eyebrow.

"I... just want to say again how sorry I am about your son."

"It is not a situation of your making. There will be time to grieve later if grief is called for. But duty first. And... if you do see him again. Try to bring him home, if you can."

"I promise."

She ended the call.

What were *my duties*? The first thing I needed to know: were the Vadram coming to take their frustrations out on us? If they were just going to sit back and mourn their losses, problem solved. That would be nice. I needed intelligence, and I knew just the pilot to get it. I needed to get to Lady Jane at the spaceport and persuade her to do a flyby.

I backed the chair up to the hotel room door, leaned back to open it.

And standing on the other side were Gadget Dude, Dez and Avrim.

CHAPTER 19
REGROUP

"So, you're not the real Gravane, hey?" said Dez. "Well that's all fine and dandy I guess, and I guess that annoys us, but not half as much as telling us by bloody message and then leaving us to go off on another of your grand adventures. Without us! That's twice you've done it to me! I said to Gadget Dude, I said, serve him right if we don't come and rescue him, that would show him for lying to us and then abandoning us. But Gadget Dude said..."

"Grey in trouble."

"Yeah, like that, and I said, right, well we're going to go, and we're going to give him a piece of our minds and then we're going to pull him out of whatever mess he's gotten himself into. Sky Diamond said you were coming to Nymanteles, so we hopped on the next shuttle out of the Academy, and here we are. We've trekked across half the galaxy, had just about the most terrifying landing in shuttle history, so now, here we are. Sky Diamond's mother pointed us towards the right hotel."

"I came too," Avrim added.

"Right, yes, Avrim's here as well. He didn't really want to come but I told him he was being a winged ass, and that convinced him. You're not the only one with the powers of persuasion, see Grey?"

I was still busy being stunned at them being there. "Guys..." I said.

Dez frowned, her tail twitched. "Grey, what have you

done to your leg?"

I let out a noise, half laugh, half sob. "It's great to see you guys. Truly. It's... not been like Bantus. We really are in trouble, Pilvi's hurt, Seventhirtyfour is waiting at the hospital with her. Sunbolt is... Sunbolt died."

"Oh."

"But things aren't over, and I can really use your help. If you're still willing to give it. It will be dangerous."

I was surprised that it was Avrim who answered first. "If you need us, Grey, we're with you."

Dez nodded vigorously. "We didn't sign up to be space alien superheroes because it would be safe."

Gadget Dude just wandered up to my chair and started taking apart the motor. I took that to indicate his vote too.

"Thank you. All of you. I will catch you all up, very soon, but first, I need to speak to Lady Jane. Avrim, can you go fetch her?"

"I'll comm Sky Diamond," he said.

"Wait, Lucy's here too?"

"There's superhero work to be done on her homeworld, of course, she's here," Dez said, tail twitching. "She's just getting caught up with her mother."

Perhaps I'd get my chance at an apology and a thank you, after all. Although it made sending her mother into potential danger more difficult.

"Dez, comm Seventhirtyfour and see how Pilvi's doing. He will be glad to hear from you too."

"Right."

"Gadget Dude... I, uh, need to get back to the console to make some arrangements. Could you put enough of the motor back, so I can head there... or maybe give me a push?"

"Moment," he said, pocketed half of the workings from the chair's motor, then put something of his own crafting into the space he'd made. "Try?"

The chair moved smoothly, silently and notably

quicker when I pressed the control stick forward. "Nice. Thanks, Dude."

I retreated into the suite's communal area and fell to work on the console, documented everything we'd seen and found out about the Vadram, it wasn't much, but seeing it written down helped. I added in notes about the base, though the cave-in made most of the information I had about that redundant. Finally, notes about the Ascension Machine, and its effects on Hauberk and Gravane. I wrote the name Kayda Buchanan, and next to it 'Powers ????'. Maybe I could find something about that. If she was also unstable like Gravane, she might be finding it hard to keep a low profile. I set up a net search and left it running.

I was studying my notes, hoping to find some sort of answer, when Lady Jane and Lucy arrived.

"Hi," I said.

"Hi, Grey," she said, pushing her hair back away from her face. The jewelled headband sparkled; there was no mistaking it, that was Ascension tech.

Out of the corner of my eye, I saw Dez jab Gadget Dude with an elbow, nodding in my direction, flashing her grin.

"It's great to see you, Lucy, thank you for your help. For coming all the way here."

She folded her arms. "This is my home, I don't want you to break it," she said. Then she relented, somewhat. "I'm here to help, that's all. Tell us what the situation is."

I told them the full story, start to end, once more. They asked questions, and I answered what I could. At the end, I turned to Jane. "Sorry to ask this, but we need to know if the Vadram are moving. What the state of their shuttle is, what they're doing, basically. Can you do a flyby and report back? I can access Gravane funds, you'll be well compensated."

"Sure can," she said, "and I won't take your money, except perhaps refuelling costs. Their shuttle have weapons? Any sign of anti-aircraft tech at this base of theirs?"

"No to both, I think. They were trying to keep a low profile, and military tech would have drawn attention."

"Right. I'll get the Beast in the air, and let you know what I see."

"Thank you, Captain McKenzie."

"Pft," she said and left to find her ship. Without a word, Lucy followed her mother out.

Avrim volunteered to fly a quick circuit of the city to see if the Vadram were close already. An unpleasant thought, but I could see the sense in it, and he headed out.

My comm chimed, and I left Dez at the console while I took the call.

# # #

Chief Orinus Gult was the Frantium leader of the Nymanteles police and militia. Like the Vadram, he was solidly built, a little taller than me, but twice as wide at the shoulder, his broad face was encircled by wiry fur, starting to darken with age. He didn't like me much.

"*You're* the private security consultant that I've been told is in charge of me?" he said over the comm. "What are you, twelve?"

I didn't rise to it. Wouldn't have helped to respond. "I'm just asking for a little co-operation. The Vadram..."

"Have been causing trouble in town on and off for months, and we've handled them just fine. A night in the cells to sleep it off is all that's required. I'll tell my men to keep an eye out for trouble-makers."

"All due respect, Chief Gult..."

"If you were respecting me, you would have come to me, not pulled out a political hammer to hit me with."

"Chief. The Vadram are here in bigger numbers than you know and, I'm sorry to say, in no small part thanks to an investigation I was running, they're riled up. It may be nothing. I've asked Jane McKenzie to go take a look, I'll know more soon. But if it's not nothing, you'll need a pretty big cell to hold all these Vadram, and it's going to take more than sleeping it off to cool them down.

"I need to know what forces you have available, what sort of protective gear and weapons you can arm them with, and how quickly we can mobilise them."

"Ah, that's what you need, is it? Just that?"

I was off my game. I'm not saying I could have talked him around normally, but I'd be making better headway than this. I took a breath. "Guess what, I hadn't wanted to be in charge anyway. On one level, you're doing me a favour. Thanks. But I need you to at least believe the threat is real. You don't want me giving you orders, fine, I get that. But at least… it can't hurt to... consider the possibilities."

I hung up on him.

"Well, that could have gone better."

# # #

Gadget Dude had appropriated the desk for some project or another, it was already spilling onto the floor: cables, components and… was that Seventhirtyfour's Power Ball kit? I had to steer around it to get back to Dez at the console.

"I think I've found something," she said. "I'm not sure how much it helps, but I think I've figured out why the Vadram are here."

She hesitated, took a breath. "Look I don't talk about it much, but… before coming to the Academy I was… a librarian. I know you thought I was a rock star or something, but I used to spend my time buried in books. In a library."

She seemed to think I'd be shocked or disappointed. I wasn't sure why. "That's great Dez. Did you come across something useful there?"

"In the library?"

"Yes."

She shuffled in her seat. "Right, well, yes. Your

description of the Vadram reminded me of something I'd read, a kind of legend from thousands of years ago before you humans even made it out to the stars. The details aren't great. This really is the wrong end of the galaxy for good record keeping, but look, here."

She brought up an old text. "I can't be sure, but these aliens they're describing here, the 'Great Conquerors'? They sound a lot like the Vadram."

I skimmed the description. "Broad shouldered, powerful frame, skin tones in purple and grey. Well, it doesn't *not* match. Yes, it could be them."

"Right, and here," she brought up another book on screen, "it talks about the fall of their empire. They were run out of the civilised part of the galaxy, the last pitched battle was fought against them on a 'barren and cold world with crimson skies, the first the Conquerors took, and the last to be taken back'. There's no coordinates or anything, so, there's no way to be sure... but I think the Vadram are feeling conquery again. If I were some high muckety-muck Vadram and wanted to show people they were ready to take over the galaxy again, I'd start with the last place we lost. To make a point. I think that world was Nymanteles."

"Why not pitch up with fleets and assault craft then? Why sneak a hundred in for an infiltration, relying on funding from some human?"

Dez cocked her head, thinking. "Maybe not everyone back home is convinced, and one Vadram Warlord is hoping to show the way with a victory?"

"Maybe, but a victory with the help of a human?"

She shook her head. "Well, okay, they're not here to invade. But there's something here they need. Some relic of the last war? The Glorious Winged Hat of Glumthop III, or the like?"

"Ha! Or the Divine Laser Gun of Triumphant Glory?"

Dez laughed. "Yeah or... or..."

"Ascension Machine," said Gadget Dude right at my elbow.

"What about..." I stopped. *Oh no.* "I assumed they brought it with them, but what if it was why they were here? Gravane said its purpose was to augment their warriors. When would they need that most but in their last war? They didn't come to invade, but to reclaim a lost artefact and get it working again. They needed Buchanan and her surveying team to locate it and they needed Gravane's money to get the tech imported to get it repaired and working again. They came to this world because the Ascension Machine was here, an item of vast cultural importance.

"Which we blew up. And then dropped a cliff on."

Dez said, "They won't have liked that."

"No. And if we're right, it means we don't have a question of if the Vadram are coming here, so much as when."

# # #

We didn't have to wait long for the answer to that. I only got to stew over these new possibilities for about fifteen minutes, before Lady Jane commed me.

"Yeah, they're on the move," she said. "Put me on the console, I'll send you what I see."

I did so, toggling the console to record the call too, I might need this the next time I talked to Gult.

"I thought they were bugging out at first," she said and keyed up footage of the Vadram shuttle.

There was plenty of activity around it, but... "There were more than that survived the cave-in," I said.

"Yeah, figured that. Took me a while to spot them, they're using cover well and travelling faster than I thought, but, here they are." The console view changed, showed another group of Vadram sheltering under a rocky overhang. "They spotted me and took cover before I could get a proper head-count. Two dozen, I reckon. I'm following that group now, and they'll need to head out into the open sooner or later, so I can give you better numbers when they do."

"Thanks."

"If they push on through the night like it looks like they're planning, they'll be at the town by about midmorning."

"Midmorning?" Dez asked, disappointed. "Shouldn't they arrive at dawn? Or at the least, high noon?"

Lady Jane barked a laugh. "Looks like the Vadram haven't watched the same holos as you, kid."

"What about weapons?" I asked.

Lucy's voice joined the channel. "We've not spotted anything big yet, a few pulse pistols, maybe, but they could be keeping something larger on the shuttle. I did see one of the travelling group carrying something that looked like a large sack over his shoulder. It could have been a big bag of grenades, but otherwise, I don't think it was a weapon."

"Weird. Okay, thanks, I'll pass this on to Chief Gult, see if it convinces him to get the police out."

"Gult giving you some grief? Tell him from me to pull his finger out," said Lady Jane.

"Thanks, but I'm not sure that'll help calm him down."

"Ha. Maybe not. I..."

Suddenly the view of the travelling Vadram whip-panned upwards in a blur. The night sky swung into view, stars spiralling madly. Lady Jane swore viciously into the comm. Then an alarm sounded, another.

"Jane! Jane! Are you okay? What happened?"

The sharp retort of an energy discharge cut across the audio, and the comm screen dissolved into static.

"Jane! Lucy!"

"Dammit!" Lady Jane shouted. The comm screen was dead but the audio continued. The Beast's engines whined in the background. "Some kind of anti-aircraft laser. Lucy? Sweetie? Are you okay?"

"I'm fine, mum," Lucy sounded strained. She was using her powers to pilot the Beast. "I have us."

"Good girl. Get us out of here. Sorry, Grey, I know you need eyes on, but we can't stay. The Beast is tough, but not designed to take hits like that. One blast fried half the control console. I hate to think what another would do."

"Understood Captain, thanks for the help. Get the both of you back here."

"That's in my daughter's hands now, but I know she can do it."

"Thanks, mum. I've never tried controlling a ship this damaged, it's taking a lot of concentration. The Beast is hurting."

I nodded, though they likely couldn't see. "Understood, Lucy. Sky Diamond. Get home safe."

Lucy answered. "We're on our way. But, Grey, you should know: I saw the beam that hit us. It wasn't coalescing properly, it was kind of ragged and angry looking. Red and black. Just like you said."

I turned back to Dez and Gadget Dude. "Gravestone is still alive."

CHAPTER 20
ILLUMINATION

I commed Chief Gult. In fairness, it didn't take much to convince him once I showed him Lady Jane's footage.

"Seems you're not making it up. I'm still not giving you control over my men, but I'll pull them together, and consult on defence plans. I assume you have something to contribute other than a busted-up leg and a wheelchair?"

"I have, sir, my team has taken a beating, but we're still up for the fight. We can offer technical support, aerial reconnaissance, and Battle Precognition." I didn't know what use Seventhirtyfour's ability could contribute to a pitched battle, but hey, Gult didn't need to know that.

"We'll take what we can get. Listen. It'll take a couple of hours to pull my team together, longer to bring them up to speed. You look like death. I suggest you get some bunk time. I won't leave you out of the fight. You brought it to our door after all."

I shrugged, embarrassed. "We brought it sooner, but from what we know about the Vadram, I think it was always going to come to this."

"You're the expert. Gult out." He cut the call.

We weren't on chatting terms yet, clearly, but at least there was a sign of co-operation. And man, he was right, I was absolutely shattered, in just about every sense. Dez and Gadget Dude were on the wrong time zone to sleep now, so I left them to what preparations they could come up with between themselves.

I wheeled my way to my bedroom. Looked at the shower but was too tired to faff around with my cast. I levered myself out of the chair, collapsed onto the bed, still dressed, and was asleep before I could think.

I was woken by my comm. It was still full dark outside, and I hadn't slept long, but when I saw the call was from Seventhirtyfour, I did my best to assemble the shreds of my brain to be able to answer.

"Seventhirtyfour! What news?"

"She's awake, Grey! She seems to be okay, I explained what's going on, and she's asking for you."

"That's fantastic, I'll be right there." I hauled myself out of bed, forgetting my injuries in that moment, found I couldn't stand up, and toppled sideways with a thump.

"Ow. I'll be there as soon as I can, anyway. Hold tight."

"Will do."

Dez tentatively opened my bedroom door. "You okay in here?"

"Ah! Dez, excellent, just the person I was looking for, I don't suppose you could arrange to get me to my chair? Pilvi is awake and I need to see her."

Dez bounced over to me. "That's great, Grey, any side effects from her glowing eyes?"

What was she... oh, right. "I didn't ask." My brain *was* fried.

Dez heaved, and I grabbed the side of the bed to assist. We got me sat on the edge of it again.

"No offence, but, you need a shower," said Dez, "and not just because it'll help wake you up. We need you fresh and thinking straight tomorrow. Well, today."

Grudgingly, I had to admit she was right.

The shower was nirvana. A lot had happened in the couple of days since we had arrived on Nymanteles, and it felt like it had all beaten itself into my muscles. The shower let them loose again, let my mind focus, and while it was not as good as another four hours sleep would have been, it got me functioning again.

Fresh clothes did the rest of the job. I had to choose the loosest fitting jogging bottoms I had to fit over the cast, but that and a clean Academy t-shirt, I was feeling presentable again.

The three of us decamped and headed across to the hospital.

# # #

Seventhirtyfour met us in the lobby and took us up to see her. "Pilvi woke up about an hour ago," he rumbled, "she says she feels fine, but, she's changed. I think, maybe, some of Sunbolt's power passed to her, when he died."

"You mean…?"

"I'm not sure that I mean anything, you know. We don't know how it happened, if it's permanent, or even how much of his power she has."

"But she's okay, otherwise?"

"She says so. The doctors don't know what to make of it."

"I bet!" said Dez. "I could see if I can get hold of Sunbolt's medical files if it'll help? I have an in at the Med Centre at the Academy."

"Thanks, Dez, good idea. I'm going to have to talk to Captain Hawk about what happened. I meant to do it last night, but it got lost in the shuffle."

The lift door opened, and I followed Seventhirtyfour down the hall to an isolation room. A nurse sat outside, and she didn't look pleased to see us.

In a hushed voice she said, "I already told Mr. 4,923,016,734 that it was too late for visitors, there are other patients on the ward who can't be disturbed."

Pilvi was awake and waving at us through the window of the room. Her eyes had returned to normal, but her hair, normally a rich golden blond... was it glowing, just a little?

I gave the nurse my best smile. In a low, friendly, voice I said, "Look, I really appreciate your position, my friends and I will be really quiet and well behaved, I promise." As I spoke, I watched over the nurse's shoulder as Pilvi slipped out of bed and started gathering her possessions. "Is there no form we can fill in, no special procedure that could be applied in this one case. We can all be super quiet, right guys?"

They all nodded silently.

"Perhaps there's somebody we could talk to? Is there a med tech on call? A doctor? I appreciate your position, really, I do, it must be difficult dealing with demanding friends and relatives all the time. Always trying to make just this one exception, and yes, I'm guilty of that too. But as you can see, my injuries are extensive, I'm going to need surgery, first thing tomorrow, and I was kind of hoping, before I go under the knife, I know it's ridiculous, but I was hoping, I'd just feel better if I could talk to..."

Pilvi tried the door from her side, but it wouldn't open. She frowned staring at the lock... a beam of searing white light burst from her eyes and burnt right through the lock.

The nurse turned, as Pilvi stepped through.

"I'm checking out," said Pilvi, "thanks for all your help, but I can't stay right now."

"Ms. Rissanen, please go back to bed, the Doctor hasn't cleared you to leave isolation yet, let alone leave the building. Your symptoms are..."

"Not symptoms, powers," said Pilvi. The dim glow from her hair flared up, and she, quite literally, flew down the corridor.

I gave an apologetic shrug, and as quietly as we could, we followed Pilvi.

# # #

We caught up with her just outside the hospital, well the others did, I sensibly stayed under the porch and watched Pilvi flit back and forth, a few feet off the ground.

"This feels amazing guys!" Pilvi grinned and seemed to glow brighter still. "How could Sunbolt be so grumpy if he felt like this all the time?"

"A bit soon, don't you think?" said Seventhirtyfour.

"Yes, sorry," she said, but spoilt it somewhat by flying a spiralling loop, laughing all the time.

Dez sidled up to me. "So... the Ascension Machine drove her crazy too?"

"I... don't think so. Maybe, but I think this is different, this is more like..."

Pilvi hurtled past. "Wheeeeeeeeeeeeeeeeeeeeeeeee!"

"... like she's drunk," I concluded. "I think she's having trouble adjusting. Maybe if we can get her to burn off some energy, that might level her off a bit."

"I don't know, she's burning off quite a bit as it is."

"Yeah, but, it's worth a go. Hey Pilvi!"

Pilvi looped around and hovered above us. "Hey Grey. You really messed up trying to rescue Gravane, you know? I wasn't going to tell you, but maybe it's better you know, you know? You know?"

"I know, Pilvi," I said, and swallowed hard. "Listen, I need you to do something, the Vadram are coming, they'll be here soon."

"And we're ready, Grey. They won't get past us."

"That's great, but we can slow them down. Can your sunbolts dig a trench?"

"I expect so, sure... though I don't know I like the name 'sunbolts'. Dez, you're good with words, what should I call them?"

Dez thought for a moment. "Crepuscular rays?"

"Grey, you're good with words, what should I call them?"

"I don't think that's a decision to be taken in haste, Pilvi. Think it over. But in the meantime, dig me a trench?"

"Sure Grey, where do you need it?"

I paused a moment to get my bearings. The idea of a trench wasn't a bad one, in fact. The Vadram could circle around it, but anything we did to limit the angles they could approach us from gave us less ground to defend. "In the V between the river and the main street? About half a mile outside of town."

"You got it, boss man," she took off at top speed in that direction, passing a startled looking Avrim on the way.

Avrim landed and furled his wings. "Was that...? What...?"

"That's about where we're all at, yeah," I replied.

# # #

I sent Dez and Gadget Dude back to the hotel to continue on their work, while Seventhirtyfour and I called a cab to follow Pilvi. We found her, sitting by a still-smoking trench, head in hands, surrounded by Chief Gult's militia. They stood in a semi-circle around her, guns up, shouting for her to not move.

"Chief!" I called from our cab. "She's on our side!"

"She may be on *your* side," Gult said, stomping over to us, flanked by two of his officers. "But I'm still only half convinced that *we* have a side." Still, he gestured, and the militia parted to let Pilvi join us.

I swung myself out of the taxi, kept a grip on the door as I balanced on my one good leg. "How are you feeling?" I asked her.

"More myself," she said with a shrug, "which means, worse. But still... Sunbolt-y."

Gult interrupted, "Is this trench part of your defensive plan?"

"Yeah."

"It's not a bad start. We'll get an excavator and widen it a bit, the Vadram aren't great jumpers, but they have the upper body strength to climb. We probably need something in the trench to stop 'em climbing down and back up again."

"My cousin has some trembler wire left over from securing his paddock," one of Gult's officers suggested.

"Perfect. If we can secure the bridge at Wolldorb's farm, that should funnel the Vadram into the area between here and... Carven Rock? Yes. That's a fair distance still, but more containable. We'd need to watch they weren't flanking around the Rock though. Kid, you said you had some aerial reconnaissance available? Is this girl it?"

"No, sir, one of the team is a Polifan, called Avrim. I have him flying circuits to avoid surprises."

Gult grunted. "You make sure he gets some rest before the Vadram get here. When they do, I need him watching west of Carven Rock to make sure they don't go that way without us knowing. The Vadram are head-on sorts, and it would mean them going out of their way, but still best not to get caught napping."

"Will do."

With that Gult dismissed us and stomped off. He and his officers continued the planning without our input. It was fair enough really, he knew the land, and his men, far better than I did. It wasn't what Mrs. Gravane had told him to do, but I was content for now. I had other concerns.

"Pilvi," I said.

"Grey, I'm so sorry," she blurted out. "What I said before, about rescuing Gravane..."

"Forget about it, it wasn't anything I hadn't thought myself."

Seventhirtyfour reached over, patted me on the shoulder. "That's not being fair to yourself, Grey. You did the right thing, coming here to rescue Gravane, and we all came along willingly. There was no way to know this would happen."

"Thanks, Seventhirtyfour, thanks Pilvi. But, whatever, we need to put that to one side, and focus on what's happening now."

Pilvi squared her shoulders and her hair glowed a little brighter. "Of course, Grey. I assume you'll want me on the front line? I'm feeling steadier, and I know I can still fire sunbolts. By the time the Vadram are here, hopefully I can be flying again too."

I shook my head. "It may come to that. But I need you to learn what you can from the samples that you took from the Vadram Hydroponics. I know it's a lot to ask, but if you can determine anything about them that might be useful... it could be a lot more important than flying around blasting."

"Of course, I can work on that. But, are you sure, Grey, I... it feels weird to say this, but I'm one of your big guns now."

"I'm sure. Besides, I'm not talking about keeping you out of the action completely; I want to hold you in reserve until the right moment. You will be a nasty surprise for the Vadram I'm sure. And if 'Gravestone' shows up, we may need you for that, Sunbolt was able to protect against him, a little."

"Okay."

"And Seventhirtyfour?"

"Yes boss?" he grinned.

"You, I do want front rank. Try not to use the crown unless you have to, we need you for the long haul this fight, I expect, not a short burst."

"Makes sense." His hand went to the pocket where he kept the crown. "I need to speak to Dez about a better name for it, I was thinking 'The Quantum Brow'?"

I laughed. "I think we can do better. In the meantime, check the terrain between here and this Carven Rock. Decide where best to put yourself."

They both nodded. Seventhirtyfour set off at a jog to check the terrain, and Pilvi, after a moment's thought, rose gently into the air, before flying back to the hotel and her samples, much more sedately than earlier.

As for me... I sat and stewed for a moment, trying to think what I was going to contribute to the fight ahead. Everybody seemed to have a role but me. And I couldn't even jump in and punch people, I couldn't even stand without support. Eventually, I had the taxi take me back to the hotel, for want of anything else to do. I felt kind of useless.

# # #

I tried to get some more sleep, but it was pointless, I felt completely strung out, stretched to breaking point, but I couldn't bring myself to close my eyes, let alone doze off. Instead, I stared at the ceiling for an hour, trying to guess how the fight was going to go, but there were too many variables.

Dez was right. Midmorning was a weird time to wait for.

I got back out of bed and hauled myself into my chair. The light in the living room was on, I wasn't the only one awake. Dez was intent at the console, singing under her breath, I didn't recognise the song, or the language, but she sounded good. Meanwhile Gadget Dude had turned the floor of the room into an obstacle course of pipes, cables and components, whatever he was building was bigger and sturdier than I'd seen him make before.

Not wanting to disturb them, I tried to navigate my way to the kitchenette. I was stymied by a heavy-duty power cable that Gadget Dude had plugged in when he had run out of sockets in the living room. He stood up to come help me, but I waved him to his seat again.

"Don't worry about it, Dude, I can go over... oh!"

For a guy who had lived his life on space stations

and space ships, I was being idiotic. We'd spent so long worrying about ground defences, I'd completely forgotten that the Vadram had a shuttle. There was nothing to stop them sending a cadre of troops into the city whenever they wanted, to wherever they wanted. We needed to defend...

"What are they after, guys? I mean, we know they're coming, but what do they want when they get here? It can't just be to cause havoc, can it?"

Gadget Dude paused, weighing a piece of a domestic cleaner bot in his hand. "Not spaceport. Not communications. Not government," he ticked off possibilities, then he shrugged, and inserted the module into the tangle at his feet. "Grey?"

"I can see Gravane coming after me, I guess. I don't see the Vadram following him so blindly to go all out for me, even if Gravane's Ascension gave him super-leadership powers."

Pilvi joined us from her room. It was clear she hadn't been asleep either, she had an old lab coat on and safety goggles hanging around her neck. She yawned mightily. "The samples need to bake in the Chem Splicer for a bit. What are we talking about?"

"What we think the Vadram plan to get out of this attack. I think they're going to pull our forces to defending the edge of town, then drop their shuttle on their main objective, but we can't figure out what their main objective actually is."

Dez looked up from her console. "We still don't know for sure that the Vadram are these ancient conqueror-types I read about, and even if they are, they've had thousands of years to get their collective acts together... but, I found this reference in a novel set at the time, that made me think of a documentary I saw as a squib, and I looked that up. The conquerors were far more dangerous in defeat than victory. Any resistance to their rule was met with, like, major consequences. One of their minor lordlings was pushed from a balcony, broke his arm; the conquerors burnt down the entire town. Thousands dead for one tiny act of rebellion. From what I can tell, it's how they were eventually beaten, minor defeats leading to them overextending leading to major defeats."

"So, you're saying they *could* just be here to cause as much damage as possible, to repay us for blowing up their cave?"

"Sorry. Not helpful, I know. Well, but, if Gravestone was able to tell them how the machine was damaged, their primary focus would be the ones most to blame."

"Me," said Pilvi.

Dez shrugged. "Sorry. But yeah, that's my guess."

Pilvi ran a hand through her shining hair. "So, I head to the front-line after all. We can put all the bad guys in one place."

"Maybe," I said. "But if you're up for it, I think I have a better idea. We're going to need transport for it. Gadget Dude, I have a job for you."

"Yes, boss."

"Anything that you've put together to help the defences, get that to Gult, then I want you to go check out the Beast. See if she's air-worthy and see what you can do to secure it against more Gravestone blasts. We can't concede the skies to the Vadram shuttle."

"Yes, boss."

He and Dez ducked out of the door, reappeared moments later with a hotel cleaning cart. They dumped its contents in a corner and loaded it up with the devices he'd lashed together since he'd arrived. As an after-thought, he added Seventhirtyfour's Power Ball drone to the cart. They left to find Gult, and Pilvi returned to her Chem splicer.

I sat alone and stewed, trying to find another angle, something else we could do to help with the defence. At some point I must have drifted off again.

# # #

My comm woke me in the morning with a chime.

"Grey," said Lucy, "I just came to start repairs to the Beast."

"How bad is it?"

"Let's table that discussion until after you tell me why Gadget Dude is here and has disassembled three of the ancillary consoles?"

"Ah, that."

"I could understand if he'd been trying to fix the main controls, I get that you might need us in the air again. But he's not touched those and is plugging something else in instead. When I asked him what the hell he was doing, he said to ask you."

"Wait there, we'll be right over."

# # #

We found Gadget Dude sitting in the belly of the Beast, most of the consoles open, cables snaking everywhere. I'd never seen Gadget Dude looking happier.

Lady Jane had joined her daughter by the time we arrived. She caught me, and took me aside, before I had a chance to speak with Lucy. "What is he doing to my ship? Hasn't it suffered enough?"

"It has, Mrs. McKenzie. That's why Gadget Dude is here. I asked him to find a way to protect the Beast from Gravestone. It looks like he's connected a Power Ball drone to your ship. If I had to guess, and with Gadget Dude I usually do, he's rigged an amplifier to the drone's shield, to protect the Beast."

"You sure this boy knows what he's doing?"

"Absolutely," I said, and was confident I wasn't spinning her a line.

Gadget Dude extended an arm from under the console and gave an enthusiastic thumbs-up. "Ball go here, where old shields were."

Jane crossed her arms, shook her head. "You kids have made one royal mess of the place."

"Sorry."

"He's not even touched the main flight console. That will need a good couple of days to fix, assuming your Zalex friend isn't planning some other technical wizardry..."

"Sorry, again, no."

"I know what that means. You're planning to send my girl into the fight without me," she said, grim-faced.

"I haven't asked her yet, but, yes. It was a time thing. Gadget Dude could fix the controls or rig the shield. This is the safer option." I took a deep breath. I had to convince her to send her daughter into danger. "Lucy signed up to be a superhero..."

Lady Jane held up her hands. "Oh, I'm not planning to stop her, son. Girl needs to fly, and I know the Beast will look after her. But. I know my little sky diamond took a shine to you. You've had a falling out over something trivial or other, but I know it's true. I don't want you doing anything reckless to try and impress her. I know how young boys are."

"Mrs. McKenzie, maybe six months ago... I'm sure you're... that is, I don't think any more... we're just..."

"That's what I thought. Promise me."

"I promise."

"Hmmm. We'll see. I shall leave you to your battle plans. I won't tell you to keep my girl safe, that's her job, not yours."

She walked back down the ramp, to where Lucy stood with Pilvi and Dez. She patted her daughter on the shoulder. "Fly right, my sky diamond," she said.

"Don't worry, mum, I will."

Well that was that settled, it seemed.

Dez, Lucy and Pilvi carried Pilvi's Chem Splicer aboard. Pilvi could continue to work with it until we were ready for her to go into the field, and I still thought it could be the thing that made the difference.

Lucy nodded to me and headed to the cockpit. She didn't need to be there to use her powers, but it had the best view out.

"All set?" I asked Pilvi.

"The Splicer will need recalibrating, but yes," she said.

"I'm going to go join Seventhirtyfour," said Dez. "I can't do any more good here, and if all I can do is run messages and bite the occasional Vadram knee down there, well, those are still both useful things to be doing."

"Dez, if what your research has given us pays off, you may well have won us the battle. Don't belittle your own contributions. The whole point of the Justice Academy is to find the way for you to do the most good, right, whoever you are, whatever you do, and all that? Your librarian research skills have done us proud."

She shot a worried look at Lucy's back. "Keep it down, Grey! I told you that in confidence!" Then she laughed. "I really have to get used to that not being a big deal around people out in the galaxy. Good luck, Grey. See you on the other side. Maybe next term I won't pretend I was asleep at the back of classes."

I grinned. "Good luck, Dez. Go do your biting, if that's what you want."

She waved, and bounded down the exit ramp, off to join the fight.

"Okay, Lucy," I called. "Let's go hunting!"

I slapped the ramp control, and as it whirred shut behind us, I watched the ground fall away. We were heading into battle.

CHAPTER 21
BATTLE

Lucy gave us a pass over the defensive line. Gult and his men had worked through the night, setting up defences, limiting the options for the Vadram's approach. The bridge at Wolldorb's farm had been blocked with as much junk as they could lay their hands on, a few wrecked vehicles and white goods that even the Vadram couldn't just push aside. They could climb over, but if they tried, Gadget Dude had provided a few little tricks in the barricade to dissuade them. Gult stationed a few men there to keep an eye on it, but we hoped the Vadram would take the easier route into town.

Pilvi's trench had been expanded and deepened, with some trembler wire lining the bottom on our side, any Vadram climbing in would regret it, and climbing out would be unpleasant too unless they retreated.

That still left a mile for us to cover, and Gult's men looked lonely, dotted along that mile. Seventhirtyfour stood in the centre of the line, and I think his presence bolstered the men there. Here was a Brontom clone warrior, fighting on their side.

We backed off a bit, the idea being to act as reserves, after all, and so watched the start of the battle over a monitor.

Avrim spotted the approaching Vadram first. He commed, "They're here!"

I heard Gult's commed orders in response, the militia

drew themselves up, nervously, perhaps, but standing.

And then we could see them too, a ragged line of a dozen Vadram, jogging over the ridgeline, at the top of a gentle slope down into town. They broke step for a moment when they noticed the defenders, but when they moved out again it was at a full run down the slope, shouting and roaring, making as much noise as possible. They didn't seem to be armed, beyond a few knives and improvised clubs, but the sheer size of them, the aggression, it was... well, frankly, it was scary as hell.

Our defensive line took a half step backwards, even over the monitor, I could see the moment their courage wobbled. But then Seventhirtyfour roared something and ran to position himself to meet the charge, and a group of militia went with him. The line steadied, braced.

"There were more than that before," Lucy muttered.

"There!" I pointed to a hill further back, another group of Vadram hadn't joined the charge, instead, they took up sniping positions with their supply of guns.

Before we could warn Gult and his men, laser light cut across the battlefield, two militia fell immediately, and I saw Seventhirtyfour stagger as a shot grazed his upper left arm.

It was earlier than we had planned for Pilvi to do her thing, but I couldn't let those snipers go untroubled. I scooted back into the cargo area. "Pilvi, how's the science coming?"

She had her goggles on and was holding a test tube over the Splicer. She shook her head. "It's one night, not even that, I've identified a few of the plants' traits, but nothing useful. I've barely started. I really think I'd be more help on the battlefield..."

I was starting to think she might be right. "You've not found anything?"

"This sort of research takes months, Grey, and a fully

stocked lab. I'm trying to do this with a handful of samples, the most basic equipment, in the back of a moving shuttle. The only thing I've found is a similarity to a few species on the planet Torristacam. And the only thing that would help with is... huh."

"What?"

"No, nothing. You need me out there or you wouldn't have asked. I'm on my way."

"No," I said. "Don't kid a kidder Pilvi. You've thought of something, and I don't care how eager you are to test those new powers of yours, if this is something that could help, we need it. Now, is it something?"

She paused a long moment. "Yes. Or, well, it could be.

"The plants we found have some similarities with some found on Torristacam. Plants which are used by the locals there as a narcotic, and as a basis for anaesthesia... there's a chance that the same biological principles might, just, apply to the Vadram. I could try to synthesise a gas that will, or at any rate could knock them out briefly. I need half an hour to synthesise it, and even then, we won't be sure it works until we try it. They'll all be dead if I wait that long."

"No, they won't. Stop wasting time with me, shout when you know if this is something or not."

I commed Avrim. "Anything doing at Carven Rock?"

"Nothing so far, Grey."

"Good. I need you to break station, give me a flyby and drop something heavy on some snipers. But head right back, don't engage, we still need eyes on that flank. And Avrim, Gravestone is out there somewhere, so watch for his blasts too."

"Roger."

I let Avrim deal with that. Pilvi's sunbolts would have been quicker and surer, but my gut told me we needed more than brute force from her right now.

Out of the window, I could see Seventhirtyfour in the

thick of it, two Vadram had ganged up on him, and even that wasn't slowing him down. The militia around him were fighting hard too, though it took three of them to tackle a single Vadram. I caught a flash of green further down the line. Dez was in the thick of it too, she'd managed to climb a Vadram and was sitting on his shoulders, beating out a rhythm on his head with a stick.

Avrim shot past at top speed, a line of flash-bangs exploded on the hill in his wake. That should help keep the snipers' heads down for a bit at least.

Avrim slowed to turn, and as he did, a bolt of red/black energy pierced the sky, clipping his right wing. My heart leapt into my mouth as Avrim plummeted, but I breathed again as he stabilised and with two mighty wing-beats got himself moving again. Twice more Gravestone's blasts followed him, but Avrim was more careful now, and he was out of sight and back to his station moments later.

"Interesting," said Gadget Dude, at my elbow.

"What is, Gadget Dude?"

He waved a hand-held energy monitor at me. I could see he'd done some work on it, and it was probably out of warranty now. "This. Interesting energy."

I checked the display, but it told me nothing I could interpret. "Is that Gravestone's energy signature?"

He nodded.

"Can you... adjust the shields to further boost the protection against it?"

He considered it, then grinned. "Yes, boss!" he said and dived under the console again.

I checked the monitor. Our line was holding, but suffering, some of the militia were being dragged back away from the fight, and while there were a couple of Vadram down, we weren't going to last Pilvi's half hour in a flat-out brawl. Well, we'd known that. I commed Gult. "Chief, I think we have their attention where we want it, now."

"Agreed. Any sign of that Vadram shuttle?"

"Not yet, but you better believe we're keeping an eye out. Pilvi tells me she may have something but needs us to buy her time. I think we should fall back to second positions."

"Thank you for thinking of us. I can't run this fight on your maybes." He cut me off.

Dammit.

We had a plan.

Second positions meant falling back into town, drawing the Vadram in to an area that the militia had evacuated for this very contingency. Then the militia would split up, dividing the Vadram forces. If we could hit and fade among the buildings, we could keep the fight running longer. It wouldn't be easy in the open layout of the town, but the point was, it would be harder to lose fighting guerrilla style. The only problem was that it was harder to win that way too. It was only supposed to be for if we were actively losing, and we weren't there yet, but if Pilvi was right...

"Seventhirtyfour," I commed.

"Here, Grey."

"Pilvi thinks she has something, but it's going to take time to brew up."

There were muffled sounds of fighting for a moment, then, "You want us to fall back?"

"I think it's best. Gult didn't go for it, but dammit, Mrs. Gravane put me in charge, and this feels right."

"It's a gamble."

"Yes."

I waited for his response, didn't want to distract him. Bless Seventhirtyfour, he didn't waver for a second. He trusted me, and he trusted Pilvi.

"Okay, Grey." Before he cut the comm, I heard him roar to the troops around him. "Second positions!"

My comm chimed almost instantly. Gult, of course. I

didn't let him talk. "This isn't us admitting defeat, this is us buying time for another option. If we stay in the open, the snipers cut us down. I can't run this fight on your bullheaded pride."

He may have answered, but that was the moment the Vadram shuttle arrived in the fight.

# # #

Lucy threw the Beast into a hard bank, accelerating as she did, laser fire painted the air around us. "She's armed!"

"Don't worry, Gadget Dude's shields can take it."

A shower of sparks erupted from the console. Gadget Dude laughed from within.

The world danced outside the window as Lucy led the Beast through an upward barrel roll. I grabbed the door frame as the Beast's minimal anti-gravity gave up.

"Dammit, Grey!" shouted Pilvi. She swam through the door, hair blazing. "I almost lost the samples! I got them in the splicer just in time."

My chair crashed to the ground as the anti-grav fizzed back to life. "Pilvi! Is it ready?"

"I told you it would take half an hour. It needs to bake in the splicer. But I can leave it now, for a bit at least. Where do you want me?"

"Perfect timing. Let's find out if it's really you they're after."

Pilvi and I headed to the back of the Beast, as Lucy pulled out a short lead on the Vadram shuttle, pulling them away from town again. I braced myself and hit the ramp control.

I had to shout over the sound of the engines and the sky roaring past us. "Pilvi! Blast them hard, and make sure they see it's you. Lucy! If we're right, this is really going to focus their attention on us, get ready to dodge like you've never dodged before. Gadget Dude! Try and keep the shields working. Everybody ready? Go!"

Pilvi lifted off the deck, let herself drift out of the back of the hatch, once she was sure any Vadram watching had spotted her, she unleashed a sunbolt directly at them. They weren't expecting it, so she scored a direct hit, but the shuttle had shields too, and they soaked up most of the blast. I saw Pilvi lining up for a second shot.

"I can take them," she yelled over her shoulder.

"Not here! Get back inside!"

Reluctantly she turned, just as the Vadram returned fire. There was a flash of bright white light and Pilvi was propelled back into the Beast. "Ow ow ow ow ow."

I hit the ramp controls again, as the Beast began evasive manoeuvres.

"We definitely have their attention now," Lucy called from the cockpit.

"Keep us alive, and get us away from the city, we'll see if we can annoy them some more!" I replied.

"Roger!"

"Pilvi, are you okay?"

"Just embarrassed," she said. "You'd think after all I got from Sunbolt, I'd remember his lesson about dodging."

I grinned. "As I recall we skipped out on that lesson."

She picked herself up and made a quick check on her splicer. "It's still not finished. When all three of these lights go green, we're in business," she said.

The second light flickered on as we looked. "In the meantime, are you still up for phase two of the plan?" I said.

"I had better be."

The Beast lurched sharply downwards. "We're coming up on Thunder Road!" shouted Lucy. "Do what you're going to do!"

Thunder Road was a tunnel that Lady Jane had told us about, wide enough, just, for the Beast, but probably too narrow for the Vadram shuttle. We knew it was a tunnel, with two ends, but we were betting the Vadram didn't. It would look like we were going to ground. Lucy aimed the Beast at the tunnel mouth and we dived.

The roar of the Beast's engines echoed around us, as Lucy brought us in to land. The Vadram knew where we were, probably thought they had us trapped. They could just try and wait us out, which would be fine by me, it was time we needed, but if our take on the Vadram was right, they would follow us in, on foot if they had to.

We didn't have to wait long. The Vadram had a mad on for Pilvi, that was clear. The Vadram shuttle landed by the tunnel mouth and spilled out Vadram warriors. They came hustling down the tunnel, weapons out, ready to take us on.

Pilvi gave me a thumbs-up. "See you on the other side, Grey." She opened the ramp, and stepped out into the air, glowing her brightest, to make sure the Vadram knew where we were. Pilvi flew to meet them, eyes on fire.

Considering she had only had these powers since the day before, she was... amazing. She was always in motion, flight path unpredictable, sudden dives, stops, accelerating upwards... at one point she swooped down, ran four or five steps before taking off again. I'd never seen Sunbolt move like this, he was always 'blast forward and fire', but Pilvi was graceful. The Vadram couldn't touch her, couldn't advance on the Beast without dealing with her. They filled the air with pulse fire, but she danced around the beams, pirouetting, leaping, her hair ablaze. She didn't attack often, concentrating on evasion, but when she did, each beam found its target. She wasn't hitting as hard as Sunbolt, but I couldn't tell if that was her energy levels, inexperience, or simply a choice. All the same, one Vadram was down.

She couldn't keep it up forever, and the Vadram were expending much less energy, just standing and shooting. A stray Vadram shot dislodged something from the tunnel ceiling, Pilvi saw too late and a chunk of rock caught her on the hip. She cried out, plummeted to the ground, and the Vadram charged in for the kill.

"Pilvi!" I shouted.

"Stay there!" Pilvi blasted upwards again, her trajectory had a bit of a wobble, but it was enough to get her out of the way.

From the corner of my eye, I saw the third light on the splicer blink on.

I manhandled the thing open. Two canisters of a gas which might knock out Vadram. It was obvious how to use the first at least, but the wheelchair ruled me out from using it. "Gadget Dude!"

"Yes, boss!" He extracted himself from the console, one end of a sparking power cable in his hand.

I tossed him a cannister, he caught it one-handed. "Can you get to the Vadram shuttle and add this to the mix on their air supply?"

Gadget Dude bobbed his head, then passed me the power cable.

"Back soon," he said, and jumped out of the back of the Beast.

I held the power cable away from my body at arm's length and let it spark.

Long minutes passed. I could see Pilvi was flagging. She had stopped firing at the Vadram, concentrating purely on keeping their attention. That much was working, but I could see their blasts were getting closer, and Pilvi was slowing down. I itched for something to do that would help, but all I could do was wait for Gadget Dude's return.

Pilvi fell. She managed to control her fall enough to land on the ground near the Beast, but I could see she was too tired to fly again. She staggered to her feet, letting out a wide but weak burst of sunbolts as she did, to keep the Vadram off her, then staggered towards us.

"Sky Diamond!" I shouted back at the cockpit. "We're

going to need to go, quickly, soon."

"All primed and ready, Grey. Say the word," she called back.

The Vadram were firing again, they fired at Pilvi, at us, at everything. They must have been dazzled by Pilvi's sunbolts because their shots were wild, but getting closer.

Pilvi sagged, a few feet from the entry ramp, and I was going to try and get out there and pull her back when Gadget Dude appeared beside her. The two of them helped each other to the ramp.

"Now!" I roared at Lucy.

The Beast surged forward again, laser fire lighting up the tunnel around it. The sound was deafening, I fumbled for the ramp toggle, and even as the ramp closed, the thunder still rang in our ears.

"Pilvi! Are you okay?!" I shouted.

She lay on her back, panting hard, but gave a half wave that I took as encouraging.

Gadget Dude reclaimed his power cable and dived under the console again, freeing me to wheel back to the cockpit. The walls of the tunnel blurred past, but I could see the far end of Thunder Road, a circle of sky coming up on us fast.

"We'll have bought some time if those Vadram need to go back to their shuttle," Lucy said, her eyes locked on the horizon. "I hope Pilvi's gas does the trick, or this is going to be a really short escape."

"If they keep their shuttle air pressure up like they did their cave, the effects of the gas should be pretty quick," I reassured her. Assuming there would be any effects at all, of course.

The Beast erupted from the tunnel, and Lucy whooped, guiding the Beast into a lazy roll. "Woo! I always wanted to do that run. Where to now, Grey?"

"We need to get back to the fight in town, a sweep back

that way, not direct, we need to give the gas time to work."

"Roger."

She levelled the Beast out and began a wide curve back to town.

# # #

I commed Seventhirtyfour. "How are things?"

He replied in his rumbling whisper. "We're holding our own. Taken down a few more. I think we're down to six Vadram in town now, but we've lost people too. We don't have the numbers to finish them anymore. We're just playing hide and seek now."

"Right, I won't keep you. We're on our way back, and I'm hoping we have good news. Either way, start pulling the Vadram together, it's time to finish this."

"Okay."

"Good luck. We'll be there soon."

Then I commed Avrim. "We're in the endgame. I think we need you on the ground now. Go reinforce Seventhirtyfour."

"On my way."

Lucy tapped me on the shoulder, then pointed out the window. "There's the Vadram shuttle, it's heading right for us again. I don't think your plan worked."

My heart sank. "Okay. Okay. Well. Plan B then." What the hell was plan B? "Keep them off us a little longer."

She nodded. "They'll be in firing range in 30 seconds."

"Right."

I spun the chair back to the cargo area. "Gadget Dude, everything we can in the shields. Pilvi, do you have any more in the tank?"

She was standing again, a faint glow to her hair, but she was leaning heavily on the back of a chair. "I've got a bit more in me," she said, but I wasn't convinced. "Just need a little more time to catch my breath."

We didn't have it. "Sure thing. Let me know."

"Brace yourselves!" shouted Lucy.

"Shields up!" replied Gadget Dude.

We tensed, ready for the hit.

"They're still closing! I think they're planning a kill shot."

"Can we lose them?"

"Terrain's too open here... we can try... hold on!" Lucy fired her retros full, the Beast groaned in protest, metal grinding, as we decelerated and twisted right. I fell from my chair and hit the deck hard.

"They've overshot!" shouted Lucy, and I could feel the roar of the shuttle as it passed.

"Wait... they... they aren't turning! They're slowing!"

Dammit, I needed to see this, and here I was an idiot lying on the floor. I abandoned my attempts to get back in the chair, and instead pull-crawled my way back to the cockpit. "What's happening, Lucy?"

"I think your plan actually worked. The shuttle's slowing, descending. It looks like the pilot was able to keep it together long enough to activate an auto-landing."

I hauled myself up into the navigator's seat. She was right, the Vadram shuttle was already on the ground, but there was no sign of movement from within it. I grinned at Lucy. "We might actually win this after all. Take us back to the city, quick as you can!"

"Right you are, boss."

# # #

Lucy took us back to the fight, banking over the city until we spotted our last stand. It was not a great picture; the militia had fallen, couldn't tell from here how many dead, but none were up and fighting still. Most of the Vadram were down too though, the fight had been more balanced than I'd calculated. Four remaining Vadram surrounded

Seventhirtyfour, Dez and Avrim. Avrim was on the ground now, he looked exhausted, and his wings were furled, but he had acquired a Vadram gun along the way and was guarding Seventhirtyfour's back, taking shots at anybody who tried to flank him. Dez slithered between Vadram legs, not stopping to attack or be attacked, just trying to upset their balance and distract them.

Seventhirtyfour was injured, his upper left arm hung by his side, but he was wearing the crown and doing his battle precognition, it was magnificent to watch. Despite his injury, he was untouchable in this mode, dealing out strikes at the Vadram with impunity. But even from the shuttle, I could see he was beginning to fade. We didn't have long.

"Pilvi, are you recovered?"

She looked tired but was glowing again. "One last push, right?"

"Right. Can we just empty the other cannister on the troops? Will it affect Seventhirtyfour?"

"It shouldn't. Air dispersed it probably won't affect the Vadram so much either, but it might slow them down at least."

"That might be all we need." I passed her the cannister. "Meantime, we'll find Gravestone. Get back as soon as you can. I'll need you to run interference on the Vadram with Gravestone, if you're up to it?"

She nodded and dropped out of the back of the Beast, canister in hand.

We turned back towards the hill the snipers used earlier.

"There!" I said, pointing at the edge of the ridge. Gravane was floating on the brow of the hill, red-black energy crackling around him. He was accompanied by the misshapen twisted form of Hauberk and two last Vadram. "Okay, when we hit the ground, let me go first. I think I can keep Gravane's attention on me, for a bit. Hopefully Pilvi will get back in time to keep the Vadram off me. Gadget Dude, got anything in your bag of tricks that could keep Hauberk busy?"

He peeked out of the window, nodded, and started plucking items from the pouches on his belt.

"Good. Once you've taken down your guys, all attention on Gravane. I don't know how long I can keep him distracted so..."

"Gadget Dude, ready."

Gravane fired bolt after bolt at us, as we approached. The Beast shuddered, but the shields held.

Lucy put us down close, but not on top of, Gravane's command group, and opened the hatch.

And I froze.

Right there at the top of the exit ramp, I took one look at the sky, and that little voice I'd managed to push down the entire battle, too busy worrying about all the different things going on, but now, I only had one thing to distract me, and suddenly it wasn't enough. I just couldn't bring myself to push forward on the chair's control stick.

"Guys," I hissed. "I... help..."

"Ah! Sorry!" chimed Gadget Dude. He shimmied back under the console he'd been playing with earlier. He came back out again with the Beast's main shield emitter in hand, a power cable as thick as my arm connected it back to the console. He hung the emitter on the back of my chair.

"Protect against Gravestone," he said, then paused, adding, "Some." He flicked a few toggles on it. "Also..." He disappeared behind the chair tinkered with something, I heard a click, a whirr, and the shield, little more than a shimmer in normal operation, grew faintly opaquer above me. Not enough to make a difference, you'd have to be looking for it to even notice it. But I was looking.

"Shield phase: umbrella!" said Gadget Dude, proudly.

"Dude!"

"*Gadget* Dude," he grinned.

# # #

I pushed forward, and the wheelchair obliged, taking me down the ramp, towards Gravane. "Sorry Mirabor," I said. "Afraid that your attack team were no match for us." Gadget Dude strode proudly behind me, I glimpsed Pilvi's light streaking back towards us.

"Grey." Gravane drifted towards me, a little, that red-black energy crackled around his hands. "You really are beginning to piss me off."

"The feeling is entirely mutual."

Pilvi struck to my left, firing at the two Vadram, they threw themselves sideways, rolling into firing positions, pulse pistols braced. I put them out of my mind, Pilvi could handle it. Gadget Dude hopped off the ramp to the right and fired something at Hauberk. I put that aside too. Gadget Dude was a miracle worker.

Gravane looked around. "Just you and me then? Fine." His energy field whirled around him. "I took a few bruises from that cave-in you caused, but it looks like you came off worse. Have you brought a wheelchair to this fight? I brought... ultimate power!" He reached out a hand and a thunderous torrent of energy washed over me; the world turned red, I could feel the heat, hear the roar of Gravane's blast... but Gadget Dude's upgrade to the chair held... held... held...

Gravane's blast stopped. He hung there, two meters above me, looking down in astonishment.

A circle of stone glowed around the chair, smoking slightly. I cocked my head and quirked an eyebrow at him. "Ultimate power? I see."

"Impossible! How...? Impossible!"

"I noticed something, the last time we fought," I said, as casually as I could manage. "The more energy you expend, the more... feral you become. That was quite a blast. You still in there Mirabor?"

"I am Doctor Gravestone!"

"Sure, you are."

This time he levelled both hands at me, and the blast was much more intense. Instantly I was drenched in sweat; even the fraction of heat that penetrated my shield was too much. I breathed in a lungful of superheated air, my throat, my chest felt like they were on fire.

This blast ended much more quickly.

I heard some discouraging popping sounds from the shield. Oh well, nice while it lasted. It was down to me now. I put my good foot down on the warm bare earth, pushed myself upright, all my weight on one leg. There was a distinct rasp to my voice. "I wasn't injured in the cave-in, Gravestone. It was the explosion from the Ascension Machine that did for me. Hopefully, the leg will heal, but the power it has granted me, Gravestone, oh the power."

"You're lying."

"If you say so. The temptation of power, to rely on it, revel in it? So pure, so joyful. But you've seen the cost, haven't you? It eats away at your mind, burns to be used? Oh, the temptation is strong. I feel it. I could atomise you with a blink of an eye, but I don't want to end up like you. You were a very clever man once, but you burned too bright, and now you're just hanging there, listening to me talk, too scared that the next time you use your power will be the time your mind doesn't come back, right?"

He actually growled at me, and his aura flared again. I'd over-played it, or maybe he had. Either way...

I braced for death.

"My Vadram... will... kill you," his voice was thick, his words slurred, it was taking him intense concentration to keep it together, to resist blasting me again. I felt sorry for him.

His energy field faded, and he drifted towards the ground.

I snatched the grapnel gun from my belt, pulled it up, fired. The claw sailed over Gravestone's shoulder, the cable fell across him, and I hit the retract button before he could power back up again. The catch was glancing at best, but enough to propel Gravestone towards me, and my fist. I caught him full in the stomach, and as he folded over the blow, I brought the other hand, with the grapnel gun, down on the back of his head.

Gravestone fell.

CHAPTER 22
EXAMINATIONS

Two days later, Mrs. Gravane's mercenaries landed at the Nymanteles spaceport. I sent Dez to greet them, I was too busy being strapped in place with Doctor's orders to sedate me if I tried to move. I wasn't planning to test that order. My lungs had taken a beating to join my leg, and I was still on a respirator, on and off. Seventhirtyfour was in the room next door to me, getting his injuries tended to, much more gently than mine, I suspected. He was, quite rightly, being feted as the true hero of the Battle of Nymanteles. Pilvi was readmitted to the Med Centre too, not because she felt unwell, but because there were tests she had skipped out on, and now we had time for them.

It wasn't just us filling the Med Centre, though, the wards were packed with injured militia and police, and they came first. I made sure that as much of the Gravane money I had influence over trickled down to pay those bills.

Three of them hadn't made it to the Med Centre. That hurt.

My team at least had all survived. Seventhirtyfour had taken the worst beating, but none of us had walked away completely unscathed. Even Dez turned up with a black eye.

Clean-up hadn't taken long. The Vadram had been stripped of weapons and thrown into an old silo until the galactic police could collect them. There was going to be a diplomatic stink over this, and the Vadram government sent messages greeting the galaxy at large and apologising for this 'rogue element'. This was, they said, not how they wanted to return to the galactic stage. Or so they told it.

Gadget Dude had been able to provide something to keep Gravane's Gravestone powers in check. It was probably the best thing for him. Gult was more than happy to hand Gravane over to the mercenaries. There had been some backroom deals done there, I could tell, but I was glad to be left out of them.

I had a very brief conversation with Mrs. Gravane. She thanked me and the team for our efforts, promised a suitable reward, but said she would wait for a full briefing when I got back to the Academy. She was going to be busy in the short term, seeing to her son.

I entirely understood.

# # #

A week later, we were all fit enough to travel, and Lady Jane transported us on the first leg of the journey back to the Academy. I'd never seen her fly so sedately, the newly repaired Beast practically purred. "You guys earned it," she shouted over her shoulder, "Heroes of Nymanteles."

Everybody laughed, and Dez regaled her with war stories; if you believed half of what she said, you'd have to assume she won the battle for us.

"If you think that was cool," said Seventhirtyfour, "you should have seen Avrim at the end there. I was struggling to find a free hand to get my headband out, and I don't know if you've noticed, but I have four hands, so let's just say, I was kind of busy! Then, out of nowhere, Avrim is there, divebombing this one guy, hit him full speed in the chest, I swear I heard a rib break!"

"Or Avrim's skull!"

"Hey!"

"But, the two of them roll over each other, and Avrim's beating on him, fist, knee, slapped him with a wing at one point, and then... he's in the air again, but this time, he's got the Vadram's own gun, and he's all like, 'My turn!' So awesome."

"So that's when you got your headband out?"

"Ah, no. I was so busy watching Avrim being cool, I kind of forgot to. But it was *very* cool, you know?"

Dez snorted. "I mean, sure, if you like your avenging angel motif. Hey, that's a name... Avrim, the Avenger? The Angel?"

"No. And no."

"Suit yourself. No, but, yes, like I was saying, avenging angels are all well and good, but just a bit, I don't know, one note? Now if you want the complete package? She's got the origin! She's got the powers! She's got sciencey type stuff! Ladies and gentlemen, I give you: Pilvi!"

"Not trying to name me, Dez?"

"I wouldn't dare unless you're willing to reconsider 'Captain Crepuscular'?"

"Absolutely not!" she laughed.

They were all a bit giddy. It was over, we'd survived, more, we'd won. I felt a little disconnected from it all. I couldn't quite bring myself to celebrate. I couldn't help but wonder, what would have happened if I hadn't come chasing after Gravane? Maybe the Vadram would have finished their business on Nymanteles and just left? Nobody hurt, nobody dead. Maybe?

I don't know.

You tell me.

Anyway, we spent most of the rest of the journey cramming. We'd missed rather more of the academic year than was good for us, and while Captain Hawk arranged for us to get the textbooks and vids of the lectures we'd missed, we had all been a bit distracted on the way out to Nymanteles. So, we had a little under two weeks to get through a little more than six weeks of material. Dez was the real hero of that hour. Now she'd confessed her librarian background (which apparently was a big deal, though none of us really understood why) she really showed off: she created study plans for each of us, helped categorise and organise and was a wizard with research.

By the time we had transferred to the *Metropolitan*, my head was swimming with new facts, didn't know how long I'd retain them, but if I could keep them in my skull until after the exams...

And I was back to myself. My leg was healed, I'd put Nymanteles aside for now. I will probably still wonder about it for a long time to come, but, you know, I did my best, and I'm not going to start second guessing myself now. It was what it was. And I wouldn't for a second want to take away from the others. Seventhirtyfour, Pilvi, Avrim, Dez, Sky Diamond, the miracle worker that is Gadget Dude.

Sunbolt.

Each and every one of them were real, honest to goodness, bona fide space alien superheroes. And if you've any doubt, ask Lady Jane, ask Chief Gult, ask the people of Nymanteles they saved. That team, my team, were exactly the heroes that world needed.

Even if I did bring down the crisis on their heads in the first place.

# # #

It was almost midnight when we finally made it home to the Academy. Despite the late hour, a small crowd of about thirty students and staff were there to welcome us back. I guess saving a city from rampaging aliens was more newsworthy than Bantus had been. Still, I hadn't expected anyone, and was too exhausted and hungry to shine. Dez danced over enthusiastically to meet "her fans".

I noticed a flash of feathers approaching across the quad and for a moment I froze. *Veritas*. But then my tired brain caught up. I had no lies left to hide from her. Well... not many anyway. None that might get me thrown out of school, at least.

She ignored me completely and pushed through the crowd to give Avrim a hug. "It's good to see you safe," she said.

"Nymanteles *was* more dangerous than here," Avrim replied. I'm sure that's not what he'd wanted to say, but even he wasn't immune to her ability.

She took a step back. "I will leave you to your party, I doubt you want me here, cramping your style."

"No, I don't."

Veritas laughed; the scent of cinnamon surrounded her. "Come visit me in the morning, Avrim. It's good to see you too, Grey," she said. With a mighty beat of her wings she launched herself into the night.

I didn't raise my eyes to follow her skywards.

"Who was that?" asked a Welatak student I didn't recognise.

"That was Veritas, she teaches ethics classes. She's Avrim's aunt," I said.

The Welatak nodded. "Wow, it must be weird for her."

"Weird how?"

"To have a really famous nephew, like Avrim."

Avrim grinned so widely, I though his face might split in half.

"Yeah," I said. "It must be really weird."

# # #

I passed a restless night back in my dorm room. I got up the next morning, showered and dressed, and was outside Captain Hawk's office twenty minutes before my appointment.

He flew in through the open window, landed across the hall from me, and let his yellow cape flutter artfully in the breeze, while he studied me, arms crossed across his chest.

"Mr. Grey. You had better come in," he said at length.

"Yes, sir."

He hung his cape on the coat stand by the door, paced around his desk, and took a seat behind it. "I run a school for superheroes. A lot of big personalities have come through the doors of the Justice Academy over the years, for better or worse. I've seen a lot of champions and troublemakers both. And a few, like you, who fall under both headings. You have disrupted the academic studies of two of my brightest students and put the lives of many at risk.

"You came here under false pretences, you never passed the entrance examination for the Academy, and if you had sat it on your arrival, I am confident you would have failed. You arrived treating the institution as a joke, something to play with until the next shiny thing came along to distract you."

"Sir, that's not..."

"And yet, the Avenging Spider and Professor Red Ninja speak very highly of you, and I am fully aware that you helped defuse the tensions around the bomb in the cafeteria. But it can hardly be ignored that the bomb was aimed at you."

"No, sir."

"Oh, sit down, Grey, we fliers hate looking up at people, our necks don't bend that way."

I sat.

He drummed his fingers on the table. "You got Sunbolt killed. How do I overlook that?"

"You don't. I don't." I had volumes to speak on that matter, but it wouldn't help any of us, Sunbolt included, to open that up.

"Your actions on Bantus and Nymanteles were unorthodox. But the aim of this Academy is not to find the orthodox solution, instead we find the right hero for the right situation. We are about providing people with the chance to be who they are as hard as they can be and using that to make people's lives better.

"Who are you, Mr. Grey?"

It was not a question I liked to examine too closely. For most of my life that I care to think about, I've been a homeless drifter, a liar, a petty criminal, and I'd been a lot of people in a lot of situations. And being all of that, it all brought me to the Academy. But sitting there, in Captain Hawk's office I realised something. Since leaving for Nymanteles, since coming clean with my friends, being honest with them, I'd been nobody but me. No pretence. No lies. I had been me. I had found me.

"I'm Grey," I said. "That's it. That's who I am. And I want to stay here and keep being Grey if you'll let me."

He stared at me a long time, with that piercing stare of his. "You have a lot of potential, Grey. I think you could be a true asset to this school, and I think you have even come to appreciate its principles. I think if we sat you down to the entrance exam now, you would pass. And I think we can help you avoid repeating some of the mistakes you've made. Are you committed to this school?"

"Yes, sir."

He nodded. "Very well, Grey. You may stay at the school, pending the results of your final examinations of course. I gather the Avenging Spider has confidence that you will ace Grapnel Gun Maintenance."

"Perhaps. I've mistreated mine."

He laughed, more than the joke deserved. Then he leaned to his console to call his secretary. "Has our guest arrived yet?"

"Yes, Captain. She is... eager to join you."

"Very well, send her in."

He hadn't finished his sentence when Mrs. Gravane

swept in, flanked by her two bodyguards. "Gravanes are not accustomed to being kept waiting," she said and sat in the chair next to mine. She cast me a look, a little twinkle in her eye. "Now, Henry, tell me you have been sensible and agreed to let Grey continue his studies?"

"I have weighed up the choices, and believe that he is fully committed to the opportunity of the Academy..."

"Yes, yes, very good. Well, I shall ensure that the Gravane Education Charity is suitably grateful."

Money. And Hawk had been so about the ideals moments before. But still... I was reminded of that odd question of where the Academy's funds actually went. I suppose it wasn't really my job to question it... but... hmm.

"And now that that is settled, I think we would both like to hear first-hand about the events that led up to this 'Battle of Nymanteles' and my son's part in it."

"Of course, Mrs. Gravane." And not for the last time, I began to tell the tale.

# # #

Exams were hell.

Even with Dez's help. I'd never really studied for... well, anything. And the whole formal exams thing? Nobody gets to talk. I mean, nobody. What other part of life are people not allowed to talk in? I didn't do the course, but Seventhirtyfour told me that even the exam for Combat Banter 101 was written in silence.

It's unnatural, and I don't approve.

I gave the best accounting that I could. I know I flunked the B part in the Clue Analysis paper, I realised twenty minutes after I left that I'd misinterpreted the question, in all the stress. But Prof Craft must have liked the stuff enough in the A part to give me a pass.

The final practical exam was something else though. As a group, we'd missed the prep for it, and hadn't been allocated project groups, so we ended up being grouped together. Avrim grumbled because it's what he does, but I think the rest of us were happy enough.

"Okay," said Dez, as we hunkered down behind one of the barricades. "Near as I can figure, we have the Power League over to our left, led by Lady Psion, and we all know what a pain she is. Over on the right, we have the Technauts led by Cyberella; she's okay, but her power suit has gotten some serious upgrades while we've been away. I don't think that even I could handle it..."

Pilvi's hair glowed brightly as she grinned. "Don't worry, I can take Cyberella."

Gadget Dude pulled a black box from his belt. "Give Lady Psion headache."

Avrim unfurled his wings. "Funny, after the Vadram, this doesn't seem so bad."

Seventhirtyfour turned to me. "Okay, Grey. What's our play?"

I grinned.

I was exactly where I should be.

After all, I wanted to be a space alien superhero.

AFTERWORD

Thanks to everybody, my wife Marjo first and always. Fellow writers Stephen, Brent, Ricardo, Jess and Matthew for encouragement. Sally and Matt as my early alpha readers who thought the first draft was good enough to develop. Julian, Nyssa, Claire, Erin and EM as my beta readers who kept me straight.

This finished product owes a lot to Geoff from Shadow Dragon Press, and two artists who worked on the cover, Ed for some early character design work and Ian for the rather marvellous finished cover. I know I drove all three of them mad at various stages with my fussiness.

My family, both British and Finnish, and the guys at Imperial College, who let me take the time off, so I could finish this novel. Sorry, I'm not coming back now!

Thanks also to you for reading!

By the way, if you're wondering why Dez keeps suggesting Captain Crepuscular as an alias for Pilvi, you should look up Crepuscular Rays, and it might help to know that Pilvi is Finnish for 'cloud'.

Follow me on twitter as @storycastrob and visit my website www.storycastrob.co.uk if you want to hear more of my stories, in podcast form.

Oh... and if superhero movies can do after-credit scenes... why not novels?

Rob

AFTER CREDITS

Oh! Kayda. You're quite right, I'd almost forgotten about her. I guess this story isn't complete without a little Kayda coda. Now I wasn't here for this, but I gather, it goes something like this:

# # #

Kayda Buchanan's fingers twisted in the scientist's hair. She slammed his face into the floor. "This isn't really your fault, I know," she said. "But it's not mine either. I was just coming to collect this little box for my Mirabor, thank you so much for lending it to us, and then your silly news program had to go spoil our fun with its lies." She slammed his head to the floor plate again. She had to focus, take a breath, slow down. The console updated so slowly; if she wanted to check what she'd seen, she had to slow to a crawl.

There it went again, the impossible headline: "Mirabor Gravane: Tech Heir Arrested"

Kayda uncurled her fingers, let the dead scientist's head fall to the floor. Absently she patted it. "There, there. Not your fault. It's the fault of that imitator. That fake. Grey. I told Mirabor he should have let me kill him at the beach. Or let me stay on Nymanteles. He wouldn't have beaten me." She giggled.

"You there! Put your hands behind your head and lie down on the floor!"

Kayda looked over her shoulder at the three security guards covering her with stun pistols. All of them human.

"Hi guys, sorry, I quite forgot where I was."

"Put your hands behind your head and lie on the floor, we will not warn you again"

Kayda grinned. "Did you know, that the average reaction time for a human is about 0.2 seconds?"

There was a blur. A line of micro-explosions flowed towards the guards, then back again. The three guards were flat out unconscious.

"It means that I'm bored for 0.18 seconds of our fight," Kayda concluded. She stared at the unconscious men and giggled. She hadn't meant to. It seemed that since she'd Ascended she was laughing at things that she wouldn't have found funny before.

"The plan has changed," she told them, suppressing another laugh. "Mirabor will still want this thing, I'm sure. But first, I'll need to get him out of prison. I have a great idea who can help with that. 'Grey' and his little friends want to be 'space alien superheroes'?

"Time for them to meet some supervillains."